THE FOUNDATION

JACK EMERY 1

STEVE P. VINCENT

First published by Momentum in 2014

This edition published in 2017 by Steve P. Vincent

The moral right of the author has been asserted.

A CIP record for this book is available at the National Library of Australia

The Foundation

Cover design by XOU Creative

Edited by Kylie Mason

Proofread by Hayley Crandell

For anyone that likes to daydream, imagine and ask "what if...?"
Keep it up.

PROLOGUE

Chen Shubian cursed under his breath at the old Hewlett Packard as it whirred to life. He was seated at the rear of a little internet café on the outskirts of Taipei, watching the light in the middle of the case occasionally flash with activity. He was losing patience and about to force a restart when the Microsoft logo appeared.

Chen shook his head. "Vista."

He dug a small envelope from his pocket and tore it open. Inside was a piece of paper with an alphanumeric code, meaningless to most people. It was Chen's key to the private server set up by his employers. They'd found him on the Darknet, a refugee searching for his vengeance, and brought him to their community. Now, the private server allowed them to conduct business outside the view of the authorities.

The code wasn't all that was required to access the server. He plugged his Hello Kitty USB into the front slot of the computer and tapped his fingers on the desk as the ancient machine whirred some more. He typed the code into the black command box that appeared on the screen and hit enter. The black box was replaced by an ordinary-looking web browser.

Chen clicked the only bookmark on the browser, which took him to a message board where likeminded people connected to chat about politics, sport and blowing up international infrastructure. A message at the top of the screen reminded users to ensure the security of the network, lest they end up in residence at Guantanamo Bay.

Chen searched his pockets again and found a small photo. He put it below the computer screen and stared at it for a few moments. His mother and father stared back at him, standing on either side of a slender fifteen-year-old boy with straight, shiny, black hair. The photo had been taken the last time Chen and his parents were all together.

Chen's life had changed forever when his father—an employee of a large American investment bank—had been arrested on a routine business trip from Taiwan to China. He had been charged with espionage and executed after a show trial. In grief, Chen's mother had taken her own life soon after the death of her husband.

Chen blamed China, but he also blamed the American bank that had left his father to rot. They'd obviously determined that their business interests in China were more important and had done nothing to help his father. The thirst for vengeance against China had guided Chen's life ever since: from school, to university, to the Taiwanese Army and then its Special Operations Command. It had honed his anger and his skills.

Though the attack he planned would rock China, his employers assured him that the act would also cause great heartache for the United States. It was a happy coincidence.

He smiled with pride as he browsed the thread, which connected him with others slighted by China and united them all under one cause. He left a message for those who would help him undertake the attack, confirming the final details. He typed another to his employers in the endeavor, noting that their funding had been received and confirming the details of their meeting in a few days' time.

When he was finished, he ejected the USB and all signs of the message board vanished from the screen. Chen left the internet café as anonymously as he'd entered, satisfied that everything was in place for the attack. He had no expectation that he'd bring down the Chinese Government, though he did believe that a heavy enough blow could cause a fracture in the monolith. He felt a small degree of guilt for the innocents who'd die, but their lives were the price of vengeance.

Men of decisive action changed the world, and if it had been good enough for Mao, who'd driven Chen's ancestors from mainland China to Taiwan, then it was certainly good enough for him.

ACT I

1

In London today, Ernest McDowell, Managing Director of
EMCorp, fronted the British Parliamentary inquiry into the phone
hacking of UK politicians, sports stars and celebrities. During his
testimony, Mr McDowell denied all prior knowledge of the crimes,
but also noted that the company's head of UK operations had been
fired and the London Telegraph had been closed. Despite these
moves, and Mr McDowell's assurances that he'd stamp out any
remaining rogue behavior in his company, the inquiry chairman
seemed unimpressed. Mr McDowell will not enjoy any breathing
room when he arrives home in the US, with a similar investigation
about to get underway in the United States Senate and mounting
pressure from his board to step down.

Jarvis Green, BBC World News, August 31

J ack Emery woke with a groan, face down in a pool of
vomit. The sickly soup had matted his hair and dried
on his face. He dry retched, one more protest from a
body familiar with this type of abuse. He had the worst
hangover of all time, or at least this side of the crucifixion. He
rolled out of the puddle and onto his back. As he moved, his

head felt like it was a tumble dryer. Once he was still, he took a minute to do a physical stocktake. He moved his fingers and toes, then his limbs, pleased that everything seemed to be in working order—more or less.

"That's a start." His voice was raspy, and he considered calling for a crime scene unit to stencil some chalk around him, haul him off and call it even.

He opened his eyes and looked around, glad that he'd found his way back to his hotel. He stood, walked unsteadily to the window and opened the curtains. Despite the frost on the window and his aching body, the sight of New York City made him smile. The skyscrapers and the bustle. It was chaotic, but somehow it all worked. He turned to the bed, mad at himself for lacking the sense to pass out onto it rather than the floor. At least he didn't have to make it every day. It was the only advantage of being forced to stay at the Wellington Hotel for the past month.

He sighed and decided to bury that particular set of thoughts for the time being. None of it was going away in a hurry, so there was no sense adding mental anguish to his physical trauma. He needed a shower, a shave and breakfast. He staggered to the bathroom and started the shower.

As Jack waited for the stream of water to become warm, then scalding, he stole a look at himself in the mirror. It wasn't pretty. His hair was greasy, his skin dry; he was showing every second of his thirty-five years. He stepped into the shower and successfully washed away the stink of stale beer and vomit.

Once out, he toweled off and then tore at his stubble using the terrible complimentary razor. He felt a bit fresher, and left the bathroom to do his best to find some clean clothes among the piles of dirty laundry that littered the room. He dressed and slipped on the same shoes from the night before, complete with speckles of vomit. He gathered his keys, office security pass, cell phone and wallet, then made his way to the first-floor diner. He pushed open the double doors and took in the scene with distaste. No matter how many times he ate here, it never looked welcoming. He sat.

It didn't take long for a waitress to shuffle over. "What can I get you?"

Then his phone beeped. He fumbled around for it and looked at the message. He absentmindedly waved the waitress away. As he stared at the text, bile rose in his throat

Not attending this morning? I didn't think you'd sabotage your career to avoid me.

Erin. Tall, blond, beautiful. Good colleague and great shag. Unfaithful wife.

Jack looked at his watch and realized he should have been at the morning *New York Standard* staff meeting, being handed the assignment of a lifetime. Instead, he was in a diner. His life was a mess.

"Bitch."

Thoughts of breakfast forgotten, he went outside and hailed a cab. He jumped in and gave the driver the address. As the cab drove downtown, Jack's head never left his hands. He'd wanted the job for months, but had probably lost it because of his self-annihilation.

The cab pulled to a stop and the driver turned his head. "Eight seventy, pal."

"Thanks, mate." Jack gave a ten-dollar note to the driver. "Keep the change."

"Thanks, pal. You Australian?" The driver gave a toothless smile. "See you 'round."

Jack rushed into the *New York Standard* building, through the security gates and into the elevator. He tapped his foot impatiently as the elevator climbed to the eightieth floor, and as soon as the doors opened he burst into a run past the reception desk. Every additional second he was late reduced the chance of him getting the China gig.

He slowed as he reached the large wooden door and placed his hand on the knob. He took a second to compose himself, but knew he looked like shit: out of breath and sweaty. He sighed, opened the door and stepped inside. Two dozen pairs of eyes bored into him like lasers.

The booming voice he didn't want to hear came from the head of the table. "Nice of you to join us, Jack."

"Thought I'd let the rest of you get some work done." Jack kept his eyes down.

Nobody spoke while Jack found his way to his usual seat. Coffee cups and all manner of food covered much of the table. At its head in a high-backed leather chair sat the paper's managing editor, Josefa Tokaloka, a Pacific Islander turned American citizen who'd been with EMCorp for decades. Everyone else sat on far more modest chairs.

Jack found his seat and looked up to see Tokaloka's eyes on him. They held the stare for an awkward few seconds. Eventually, Tokaloka nodded so slightly that Jack thought he might be the only one who noticed, and that was it. He knew there would be no chewing out, the point had been made.

Tokaloka looked back down at his papers. "As I was saying, this stuff from Britain is killing us. We've done nothing wrong, but we're one of the few brands in the company that can say that. Keep yourselves clean. If you're in doubt, don't do it. I don't want anyone deciding they don't have to play by the rules."

Jack looked around and saw plenty of nods. The troubles at the *London Telegraph* office—the hacking, the denials—had led to a decision by Ernest McDowell to close the whole paper. A century-and-a-half-old institution gone overnight, with hundreds of colleagues out the door. There had been issues elsewhere, as well, including the US.

"Anyway, only one more thing to cover. China." Tokaloka paused. "Erin, it's yours."

Jack's head moved so fast he risked whiplash. The World Trade Organization Conference in Shanghai was supposed to be his gig, the career boost he needed to get over his current malaise. Tokaloka had obviously decided otherwise and abandoned him. He'd had a hunch he would lose the gig when he was late, but not to her.

Jack slammed his hands on the table and stood. "Hold on one bloody minute, Jo. That job was mine!"

Tokaloka stared at him. "You're too flaky at the moment. You walk in here late and looking like shit. It's not good enough. You're benched until you get it together."

Jack was about to argue, but decided against it. Making a scene would just dig him into a deeper hole with the boss. He bit his tongue and sat.

Tokaloka turned to Erin. "I want you on the ground in two days. You're going to be as busy as hell, but you'll have Celeste along to help."

Erin flashed the smile Jack had fallen in love with. "Happy to help, Jo. Thanks for the opportunity."

Tokaloka nodded. "Right, we're done."

Jack stayed where he was as the room exploded with conversation and staff rose to go to their desks. He was still in shock. He'd spent weeks doing the prep work on the WTO conference. While he knew his mind had been off-track for a few months, he could still do the job. Tokaloka taking it away wounded him. They were friends, after all.

Jack waited for the bustle to clear and for the sting of losing the China assignment to ease. When he looked up, he was confronted by Erin, Celeste Adams alongside her. He was trapped, and couldn't escape without looking like a fool. He hated to admit it, but Erin looked great. He knew that if she offered, he'd take her to the nearest secluded place, undress her and mess up that blond hair. That would never happen, though, because she'd continued to shine while he'd spiraled down into a dark mire.

"Got a minute, Jack?" Her voice was soft.

"Fuck off, Erin."

"Suit yourself, just remember it's me trying to heal this, at least a little." She shook her head as she turned and strode away.

"Heal yourself! We might've had a chance if you had." Jack's words were wasted, because Erin was already out of earshot.

Celeste smiled. "That had nothing to do with me. I'm just shadowing whatever she does, which apparently includes relationship destruction." She was younger and different to his wife in every way: average height, where Erin was tall; preferred dresses to the hard, boxy pant suits that Erin wore; and had a mane of fiery red hair that flowed across her shoulders.

Jack snorted and changed the topic. "You're one of the refugees from London, right? Your accent is as strong as mine used to be."

"Yeah." She laughed. "I started at the *Telegraph* a few weeks before they shut up shop. I hadn't done anything wrong, so I managed to get a job here. I'm trying to adjust."

"Listen to Erin. She'll be your ticket to bigger things."

"Got it. I'll see you around."

As Celeste left him, Jack's cell phone beeped. It was a message from Jo.

You're letting me down, Jack. I need more of the Pulitzer Prize winner and less of the current version. It's time to bite the bullet on your divorce, my friend. I want you to meet me for a beer later in the week.

Jack sighed and started to type his reply.

No hard feelings, but did it have to be her? Meeting the lawyer tomorrow.

ERNEST McDOWELL—MOGUL, *visionary, ruthless bastard.*

Ernest stared at the magazine for a long while. His deeply lined face stared back at him from under gray hair. He sighed, picked up the magazine and threw it at the small table. It fluttered the short distance and landed cover up alongside a few papers and other weekly news magazines, though none of the others had his face on them.

"Never should have rejected that buyout, right Peter?"

His assistant didn't take the bait, even though Ernest was sure that, deep down, Peter Weston was feeling vindicated. A few years ago, Ernest had declined an opportunity to buy the same magazine that now plagued him, despite Peter's advice to the contrary. Ernest had rarely gone against his advice since then.

Peter smiled from the seat opposite. "Don't worry about it."

"Easy for you to say." Ernest sighed. "It's not every day you get subjected to a dozen-page hatchet job in the largest weekly news magazine in the United States."

"It's poorly researched and full of errors. It won't do any damage." Peter waved his hand. "There are bigger things to worry about."

Ernest laughed. "You mean the British Parliament going for my jugular or the US Senate going for my balls?"

Peter laughed. "Quite a dilemma, I suppose."

Ernest massaged his temples with the tips of his forefingers, trying to see off his headache. He wasn't sure if it was caused by the sound of the aircraft engines, which droned in his ears like a fleet of mosquitoes, or the million or so conflicting ideas ricocheting around inside his head.

He sank deeper into the brown leather seats of the Gulfstream IV. He hated these trans-Atlantic flights, even if he did get to ride on a private jet. He was looking forward to getting home after a few days in London, which had cost Ernest his head of UK operations and the *Telegraph*.

"Want a drink?" Peter held up his hand to get the attention of the flight attendant. "I think you need one."

Ernest looked up as the woman swayed down the aisle with a bottle of Laphroaig and a pair of glasses. She knew their poison.

"I'll take it neat, thanks, Clara." Peter flashed her a grin.

She nodded at him and smiled at Ernest. "One for you, Mr McDowell?"

"Not now."

Peter laughed. "Normally you'd be all for a little recreational drinking on such a long flight."

Ernest frowned. "Not now."

He watched absentmindedly as Clara poured Peter's drink. Ernest knew that he was being difficult, mad at himself because he hadn't yet found a way to control the situation. He'd work it out eventually, but for now he was content to feel sorry for himself. Once Clara had finished, she left them.

"I want to know how I managed to build this company, see off three wives, raise a daughter, stare down takeover attempts and get us through the global economic meltdown, only to be undone by an ambitious jerk hacking the phone of a former British prime minister!"

Peter was silent for a few moments as he sipped his drink. Ernest didn't mind. He'd learned to appreciate Peter's careful, considered advice. "It was more than just one cowboy, Ernest. It was a systematic regime of criminal activity. We were right to shut it down, but despite that, we'll take our hits."

Ernest took a deep breath and exhaled slowly. "We already have. They want more."

"The UK issues will dissipate. We're through your testimony and you've cut away most of the cancer. The problems we have there were an appetizer."

Peter was right. The evidence of EMCorp wrongdoing had first emerged in the UK and it was limited to the activity of one overly ambitious newspaper. It had burned hot for a few months, and led to the Parliamentary inquiry, but Ernest's contrition and swift action had cooled things down a bit. A much larger fight was looming at home.

He closed his eyes. "The British are used to this sort of thing from Fleet Street. But trying to get the Senate and Patrick Mahoney to back off is a larger challenge."

Peter said nothing as he took another sip of his drink and leaned back in his seat.

"I really do hate the fat bastard, Peter."

Peter laughed. "Well, given the fat bastard chairs the Senate Judiciary Subcommittee on Privacy, Technology and the Law, which is on you like a fly on shit, he's a problem."

Ernest snorted. "Usually it'd be easy, but we can't even threaten to disrupt his re-election in a few months' time. He's retiring."

"Wouldn't be easy even if he wasn't." Peter shrugged. "We've got nothing. He's clean."

"Hate it when that happens."

They sat in silence for several minutes. Ernest stared into space while Peter occasionally sipped his whisky. He wondered how it had come to this, after all this time. He'd built EMCorp—the largest media company in the world—from the ground up. He'd thought it was impregnable, but now it was beset on all sides. He felt old.

Ernest's reverie was broken by the buzz of the plane intercom. The sound pierced to the very heart of his bad mood and made him want to strangle the pilot with the phone cord. Peter placed his drink on the table and rose to answer the phone.

Peter spoke in a series of pauses. "What is it? Sandra? What's wrong?"

Ernest's interest was immediately piqued when his wife's name was mentioned.

"Ohio?" Peter frowned. "Why was she there? An attack? Be sure that she is."

Ernest's heart pounded as Peter hung up. "What is it?"

"It's your wife." Peter paused. "She's been admitted to hospital in Ohio."

"Which one?"

"Sandra."

Ernest glared. "Not which wife, Peter. Don't be an idiot. Which hospital?"

"It's in Columbus. She's alright, but she's had another severe panic attack. She's insisting on seeing you."

"We should go." Ernest sighed. "Why the hell was she in Ohio?"

"Charity gig. We can't for a few days, Ernest. We're meeting Mahoney in Washington tomorrow. Once that's done, we'll go and see her."

Ernest stood and his back staged a protest in the form of sharp pain. He paced as he processed this new information. He'd hated these last few weeks most of all because, just when he had things figured out, the game would change again. Sandra would have to wait.

"Doesn't she fucking understand what we're dealing with here? The last thing I need is her going off the deep end again."

"The tabloids will get a hold of it and have a field day. But at the least we can keep it quiet in Ohio and give Sandra some peace."

"Owning the only major paper there helps." Ernest scratched his chin. "Okay, let her cool her heels. But I want to be out of Washington as soon as possible."

"I'll make sure we're fueled and ready to leave Dulles tomorrow night, as soon as we're done with the senator."

~

MICHELLE DOMINIQUE'S guilty pleasure was the ten-minute casual snooze she took after silencing her wailing alarm clock. She liked that the simple press of a button granted time to reflect on the day ahead, safe in the cocoon of self-denial that although the day was close, it hadn't quite arrived.

Today was different. She'd slept in and the day was well and truly here. Michelle watched the clock with one eye open, the rest of her body coiled under the covers. She dared it to grind the last painful minute to 11am, and when the alarm started she pounded the snooze button several times. Ten more minutes. On most mornings she'd wake much earlier, but she'd had a very interesting night.

She sighed as the bed's other occupant started to stir and she felt a hardness press against her back. For him, seemingly, the ten-minute snooze was an excuse for mischief. She searched her memory for his name, but it abandoned her, probably in response to the tequila the night before. He pressed in closer.

"Good morning, gorgeous." His hand cupped her breast, too hard. "Was hoping you wouldn't be working today and we could get to know each other."

She closed her eyes. This was the part Michelle hated. While she was happy to indulge in what her grandmother called the physical trappings of Satan, she hated the next morning. She just wished the split could be as free and easy as their efforts the night before. She had work to do.

"Why? I've got to get moving."

His hand started moving south. "Come on, babe, there's always time for a quickie."

"I thought that's what last night was supposed to be." Her voice had all the innocence of a former St Augustine's choir girl's.

His hand froze and he gave little more than a grunt in response.

"You can call a cab, or there's a bus stop out the front."

Not wanting to entertain his advances any longer, Michelle stretched her legs out and committed the crime of rising before the second alarm. She stood and walked to the shower, earning a sigh of acceptance from the man. Yet again, she promised herself that, one day, she'd pick a man based on him being something more than an attractive Neanderthal. One day.

It was just easier this way, she'd decided long ago. Michelle Dominique. Single. Hates cats and children. Her job was demanding and she had planned a future that was more demanding still. She was in no hurry to settle down and have it all end in the horrible drudgery of suburbia.

She closed the bathroom door and untied the mess that was her post-sex hairstyle. Her reflection worried her. Too thin. She'd been working too much lately and had probably lost a bit too much weight. Her face looked hollow with stress and lack of sleep. She vowed to look after herself better.

"Just a few more months."

She showered and completed her morning routine. Once out of the bathroom, she was pleased to discover that her companion had gracefully exited. Careful not to dislodge the towel holding her wet hair in place, she dressed in a black dress and blood-red pumps, then looked in the mirror again and nodded. Good enough.

Michelle walked to the kitchen and opened her fridge. Though she had a nice enough apartment, the food situation was bleak. Some beer, a bottle of milk and a jar of pickles. She was just not home enough to make stocking it worthwhile. She sighed, grabbed the milk and some muesli from the pantry and combined them to make a dismal breakfast.

As she ate, she checked the news on her iPad. It was the usual leftist rubbish and propaganda, though the stories from the right of politics depressed her as well. She flicked through it all very quickly, getting across the major items. She was about to close the browser window when a small item caught her attention.

"Oh Ernest, Ernest, Ernest." A small dribble of milk escaped her mouth and ran down her chin. She swiped at it. "You're in a bad spot."

She knew that Ernest McDowell was in trouble in the UK, but the scandals engulfing him at home in the United States were about to get much worse. She closed the browser and opened up Skype. She dialed the first name in the contact list:

Anton. It took a while to connect, and she smiled at the thought she might have woken him.

Her smile grew when he answered the call wearing nothing but a towel. "Hello, Anton, sorry to disturb you."

He frowned, and the light above him reflected off his shaved head. "An email wouldn't have sufficed? And wipe that smile, or I'm going to think you planned this."

"Seen the news?" She lifted another spoonful of muesli into her mouth.

He raised an eyebrow. "What in particular?"

She swallowed and gave a wide smile. "McDowell will be fronting the US Senate next month. Told you so. Democrats want a piece. Republicans aren't any better, either."

He seemed to consider the news for a second or two. While they were in broad agreement about most things to do with the Foundation for a New America, the topic of Ernest McDowell had divided them in recent months. She wanted him on the hook, Anton didn't see the point. Maybe this would convince him.

"So?" Anton was clearly unimpressed. "He'll just take his lumps."

"He could be an asset if we handle him correctly."

"I remember the last time you said that. Cost us four lives." He shook his head. "No. You need to focus on China and your Congressional campaign."

Michelle grimaced internally, but did her best to keep the expression on her face even. He was right to point out that she'd compromised an entire cell in Houston on what, in hindsight, had been a hunch. But that was the risk in the high-stakes game they played. The fallout had been contained and the organization had moved on. But she conceded the point —for now.

"China is under control. My flight is booked and the assets are in place. Don't worry about that. My Congressional campaign is going fine, as well."

Anton smiled. "Now you're talking. Relax, though, while your campaign is on track, we need to think about the others who are running. McDowell is a distraction."

She wasn't going to win this, but tried one more time. "He'd make it easier. Having the influence of his company under our belt would all but ensure success. Every candidate we put up would stroll across the line."

He started to say something, but seemed to reconsider. He frowned, and enough lines formed on his forehead to tell her she'd broken through and he was considering her point. "I'm not convinced, but let's talk about it more in Shanghai. He could be handy, but he's also the sort who'd out us and take the flak, just for fun."

"Okay, fair enough." Michelle was happy enough that McDowell was back on the agenda. "I've got to get ready for my flight. I'll see you in Shanghai."

2

Celebrity Weekly can report exclusively that Sandra Cheng, socialite wife of Ernest McDowell, has been admitted to hospital in Ohio after a breakdown at a charity function. The latest admission is her third in as many months. A source close to the McDowell family has expressed doubts about her mental health and revealed that Ms Cheng is distressed about events involving her husband's company. Ms Cheng, a high-profile lawyer prior to her marriage, gave up her private practice upon marrying Mr McDowell. It appears that despite impressive public achievements in her own right, Ms Cheng is struggling to cope with the increased scrutiny of recent months.

Cherry Adams, Celebrity Weekly, *September 1*

"I can have my assistant work up the forms and courier them to your office. You'll have them by the end of the day, and then it's up to you to sign them." Winston Clay raised an eyebrow. "As long as you're sure, Jack?"

Jack wasn't, but he nodded anyway. He'd decided at some point during the meeting that he really didn't like Clay, who was one of the better divorce lawyers in New York. Though he needed him, he was tempted to tip over the coffee table and storm out of the room. Instead he continued to sit and listen to advice he didn't want to hear, which also cost him a fortune.

Clay stood and extended his hand across the coffee table. Jack stayed put, sinking further into the leather armchair that probably cost more than he—a minted Pulitzer Prize winner— earned in a month. After a few seconds, Clay dropped his hand and retook his seat. Jack reached up, scratched his nose and stared out the window behind the lawyer.

Clay sighed. "If you still have doubts, Jack, there are options that fall well short of divorce. Not that I'm trying to put myself out of business, you understand, but could counseling work? Time apart?"

Jack leaned forward and took hold of the glass of scotch on the coffee table. He threw back the remains with a flick of his wrist, then put the glass back. Morning drinking was for losers, but he didn't care much right now. He'd replayed the events of that terrible night a million times in his head, and it made less sense with each pass.

He'd thought Erin would be fast asleep by the time he got home. Instead, he'd found her upright in bed, surrounded by a hundred tissues and an empty bottle of red. Blind drunk on wine and antidepressants, she'd told him everything. How she'd slept with the neighbor, many times, but was now laden with guilt.

The next day, with sunlight flooding their room and a clearer head, she'd recanted. Jack had tried to speak to her about it, but after her denials he'd given up and left the house a shattered man. While he'd first spoken to Clay a while ago, having to stay for so long at the Wellington Hotel and losing the China gig had convinced him to proceed.

Jack shifted his gaze down slightly, and looked straight at Clay. "I'm sure, Winston. She slept with my neighbor, got drunk, admitted to it, got sober and then denied it all again.

She hasn't given me any reason to think there's any hope, or that she even gives a damn."

Clay shrugged. "Your call. I just want you to be across your range of options before you pull the trigger. You need to think about your finances, handling the fallout..."

"Give her half. I just want it over with. It's done." To say those words broke Jack's heart again."

"That's quite unusual, Jack." Clay's eyes narrowed. "You need to protect your interests and—"

"I understand." Jack sighed. "You've done your job, now do what I ask."

He'd built a life with Erin. They'd pursued careers, supported each other, consoled each other and loved each other. Now he simply wanted to be done with it. With her. He wanted to retreat into a dark hole with a bottle of nice scotch, and wake up only after the decade or so it would take to stop hurting.

Clay nodded and stood for the second time, hand outstretched. "Okay, Jack."

Jack stood and shook his hand. "Thanks."

"And Jack, on a personal note, some advice free of charge. Clean yourself up, get a massage. You look like shit."

Jack gave a thumbs up to Clay and walked to the door. He deliberately didn't look around at the oak bookshelves or the six-figure artwork in the office. He'd made that mistake last time and felt enraged when the bill had come. It was all paid for by sad men and women who'd had their lives together guillotined, with Clay the executioner.

ERNEST WONDERED how many of his tax dollars were paying for the office of Senator Patrick Mahoney, Democrat for Massachusetts. The office looked as if it had been painted by a drunk spinning around on a chair and then furnished by a child. It hurt Ernest's sense of good taste. He and Peter sat opposite the senator, a bullfrog of a man who spilled over the sides of his chair. Between them was a hardwood desk, which had apparently belonged to a Kennedy. Or so Mahoney said.

Ernest took a deep breath and leaned forward. "So what you're telling me, Senator, is that the US Senate is ready to destroy my company?"

Mahoney smiled. "That's about the sum of it. Your enterprise has become a little too big, a little too powerful, and now you've trampled on the civil rights of Americans."

Ernest bit his lip, but couldn't resist. "Unlike drone attacks, indefinite detention without charge or all-pervasive electronic signals interception and intelligence?"

"All perfectly legal, Ernest." Mahoney smiled like a shark. "The conduct of your company, on the other hand, was not. That necessitates a reaction."

The allegations against EMCorp in the US were as serious as those in the United Kingdom, if Ernest was being honest. Though, to the best of his knowledge, the company had dealt with and disclosed all misconduct, it was an almighty assumption. It was also a gamble, given the looming inquiry. If more illegal activity emerged, he'd be scuttled. Ernest wondered if the company had just become too big for him to control, even as he did his best to fight Mahoney and his ilk.

Ernest felt his face flush. "I'll concede that we're in a bit of trouble, Senator. But I didn't think you and your colleagues were quite so stupid."

Mahoney frowned. "I don't follow."

"I suspect you don't. You're probably daft enough to think that it's policy and good governance that gets representatives re-elected, Senator."

Mahoney leaned back in his chair and Ernest felt his anger grow. He hoped that the other man would tip back just far enough to fall over and maybe snap his neck on the way down.

No such luck—Mahoney continued to stare straight at him and started to tap his finger on the armrest.

"I know the public like their bread and circuses, Ernest. Who manufactures them is largely irrelevant. Though it's currently your company, you're not indispensable."

"You're wrong. Who manufactures the content, and with it the message, is very important. While I respect the right of our duly elected representatives to destroy one of the greatest bastions of freedom that the American people have, they should know that I have an almighty bark, Senator, and quite a substantial bite."

Mahoney smiled. "I'm retiring from public life at the coming election. Given it's only a few months away, I'm not sure which is more underwhelming, your sense of self-importance or your threats. Both are at odds with reality."

"I don't agree, Senator. It's entirely plausible that you're done with public life, but I'm yet to meet a thirty-year veteran of the hill who doesn't care about his legacy."

Mahoney raised an eyebrow. "I'm listening."

"The key to securing your achievements is sitting in front of you, and you're doing a pretty good job of pissing him off. I'm also doing all I can to fix the issues that EMCorp has had and I can assure you there won't be a repeat." Ernest knew this was his chance. He let his words sink in before he continued. "Back off, remove the noose from around my neck, and you'll have friendly smoke blown up your ass for the next century."

Mahoney seemed to consider his offer for a moment, then shook his head. "Not good enough, Ernest. I get more out of destroying you than working with you. I'll be a hero."

Ernest looked to Peter for support.

Peter sat forward. "Need we remind you, Senator, of the generous donations that came your way following the *Boston Chronicle* endorsement at the last election?"

"The support surely was appreciated, son, but I've got the public baying for blood."

Ernest sighed. It was time to cut to the chase. "What're you proposing?"

"An understanding. If you dig your heels in, it will end in sanctions against your company, including its dismantling, and destruction of your own wealth and influence. But all I really want is a scalp to hang on my wall."

Ernest said nothing; he knew where this was going.

"Instead, I propose that you come before the committee and announce you're stepping down as head of the company. Whoever takes over—I don't care who it is—promises to fix the problems. You lose the power, but your company is intact and I get my scalp."

Ernest was in awe of Mahoney's gall. He'd tried reason, he'd tried bribery; he had one option left. He looked at Peter and gave him a slight nod. He watched as Peter searched for a single piece of paper from among his notes and day planner. Once he found it, he calmly placed it face down on the desk.

"I'm afraid I can't accept your proposal. I didn't really want to bring this up, Senator. But we've uncovered some... anomalies in your past." He knew exactly what was on the sheet of paper: nothing. Despite months of looking for something, anything, to bury Mahoney, he was clean. Ernest had nothing he could use against the senator except a blank sheet of paper and his reputation for smear.

Mahoney sat in silence and his face drained of color. Ernest was surprised, and wondered what it was that he and Peter hadn't managed to uncover.

He pushed home his advantage. "I've got the largest army of dirt diggers on the planet. They're very good at it. The ball is in your court, Senator."

Mahoney shook his head. "You can't prove anything. Besides, I can't just halt a committee hearing, son. There are other members you'd have to ride roughshod over."

Mahoney was right, but Ernest had planted a seed of doubt.

He laughed. "Oh, I don't want to stop it. I want to make a mockery of it and destroy its conveners."

Ernest only wished he was as confident as his bluster suggested.

~

MICHELLE SIPPED her coffee and grimaced as it assaulted her taste buds. She wondered why she kept faith with the company when she was disappointed every time. She'd walk in, order a grande from the overly cheery staff, and sit down in one of the comfortable chairs. Lulled into a false sense of hope, she'd take a sip, then curse.

Anton laughed. "I know how much you love Starbucks."

She sneered at him. "Yeah, like cancer."

Anton made a face, the small benign tumor he'd had cut out a few months ago apparently still a sore spot. "No need to get personal."

Michelle snorted and looked up at the entrance again, irritated. She was jet lagged from the eighteen-hour flight from New York to Shanghai, via Chicago, and was in no mood to wait. Once the meeting was done, she was going straight to her hotel room to get some sleep.

"Where is he?" She knew it was a pointless question, given they were situated in the back corner. If he had arrived they'd have seen it.

"How should I know? He's your man."

"No, Anton. He's not mine, or yours, or ours. That's the point."

He rolled his eyes. "Relax, I didn't mean it literally."

She was about to take further issue when the door chime sounded. She looked up and saw an Asian man in full business attire. He stood in the doorway and as he scanned the tables he looked ordinary in every way. Most importantly, he wore a red and black striped tie. Michelle raised her hand and gave him a small wave.

"He's here."

The Chinese man saw her, gave a small nod and moved to the counter to order. Michelle and Anton waited in silence. Michelle used the time to gather her thoughts and Anton wore a poker face. The meeting was mainly to reassure Anton about the man she'd selected to complete the operation. The next few minutes needed to go well.

Michelle stood and held out her hand as the man joined them with a cup of tea in hand. "I appreciate you joining us, Chen. This is my colleague, Anton."

Chen shook her hand. "Good afternoon, Michelle and Anton. It's a pleasure to finally meet the enablers of my vengeance."

Michelle smiled again, and after the two men shook hands she gestured Chen toward the vacant chair and sat in her own. She glanced at Anton, who now sat with his elbows resting on his knees and his chin cupped in his hand. She knew this look. She'd seen it dozens of times. He was going to pounce.

"Are you prepared to die?" Anton's tone was casual, as if he was asking how the tea tasted or what the weather was going to be like.

Chen showed no expression. "I am trained to do the job, and I will live up to my commitments. That's all you need to know."

"I beg to differ. Great piles of my organization's money and effort have been poured into this mission, which is key to our broader agenda. I'll ask whatever I please."

Michelle didn't speak, but watched Chen lift his tea and sip it. A lot of her influence within the Foundation had been staked on the selection of Chen Shubian for the operation. She'd found him on the Darknet, carefully cultivated his fury, then connected him to the Foundation's server. Since then, she'd worked painstakingly with Chen to plan the operation, including the selection of others to assist him.

While her position as number two to Anton gave her a lot of power within the Foundation, he didn't suffer fools or mistakes. Since she'd joined a decade prior, she'd seen how ruthless he could be to friends as well as foes. If, at the end of the meeting, Anton had any doubts about Chen's commitment, a Foundation for a New America wet squad would make the Taiwanese man disappear. Better that than a messy operation.

Anton continued. "You were chosen by my associate because you have the skills and commitment to achieve our objectives. I don't care about your motivation and you shouldn't care about ours. We're a happy alliance of convenience that will result in thousands dead, vengeance done and a world changed. But I still insist on excellence."

Chen laughed softly, and the sound chilled Michelle. "I have planned wisely. My equipment is excellent, my companions sound and my preparations meticulous."

"I'm glad to hear it, but I still have some concerns about your willingness to see this through."

"Sitting here together is proof that we've already won." Chen looked around. "If the secret police had any clue that I was a threat, we'd be rotting in prison."

Anton smiled. "Glad you're on board. You have my blessings and the green light. I wish you well."

Michelle waited impassively as Anton stood, and had started to stand when he gestured for them to remain seated. "You two finish your drinks. I want to get some shopping in before we unleash your handiwork, Chen."

Chen smiled, but said nothing.

Michelle waited until Anton was out of earshot. "Nicely done, he can be quite difficult. You handled it well."

He shrugged. "The last matter I need confirmed is that my identity will remain anonymous. I have a family that needs to be protected."

Michelle nodded. "The only way a soul will know is if you fuck it up, and that's entirely up to you."

"That won't happen."

"Well, here's to you, then." She raised her coffee in salute and took a long sip, then grimaced again, having forgotten how poor it was.

Chen smiled slightly as he stood to leave. "Make sure you have a good view, I will make the night as bright as day."

3

"The first day of the WTO Conference is in the books, Garth, and traffic disruption to date has been horrendous. But I'm sure what is most concerning the Chinese Government are the large protests taking place across Shanghai. While the authorities have kept things in order for the most part, the audacity of the protests must frustrate them, given China's reputation for strong-arm tactics. The few protesters I spoke to this morning linked the protests to separatist campaigns in Tibet and Xinjiang, rather than opposition to the WTO. In particular, the Tibetan and Uyghur protestors said the conference offered a unique opportunity to air their concerns while the eyes of the world are on Shanghai."

Erin Emery, News Tonight, *September 3*

C hen had eagerly anticipated another ride on the Shanghai Maglev. When he'd arrived three days ago, he'd ridden the wondrous train from the airport to the city. Man's ability to create something so remarkable—a transit system where the train rode above the track, without needing to touch the rail—amazed him. He didn't understand the science, but was amazed nonetheless.

With his business in Shanghai nearly concluded, he arrived at the Longyang Road metro station for the Maglev that would take him to Pudong International Airport. The station was amazing, wrapped in a large curved roof that made Chen feel like he was in a spaceship. He waited on the platform with a mix of tired-looking businessmen and tourists.

After a few minutes, the train pulled into the station. The doors on the other side of the carriage opened and the passengers disembarked. Once the carriage was empty, the doors on Chen's side opened and he stepped onto the train, took a seat near the door and put his backpack on the seat beside him. The train wasn't scheduled to depart for a few minutes, so he clasped his hands and waited.

An old woman stepped onto the carriage just as the intercom beeped, warning that the doors were about to close. She was hunched over heavily on her cane. Chen moved his bag off the seat beside him and gestured for her to sit. The old woman smiled at him warmly and sat with an audible sigh of relief. The doors of the carriage closed and the wondrous machine began to move.

As the train gathered speed and he settled in for the seven-minute journey, Chen pulled his cell phone from his pocket and sent a quick message. It would set in motion the synchronized attacks he'd planned for Shanghai—several large bombs, a few targeted killings and a wave of cyberterrorist strikes. Half the incidents targeted the arteries that made Shanghai move, the other half aimed to disrupt the World Trade Organization conference. All were designed to inflict the maximum amount of damage.

He smiled at the perfection of his timing, knowing he'd be out of the country before the Shanghai authorities knew the full extent of what had hit them. He'd leave a horrible, destructive wake that would have ramifications for the entire region and rock China to its very foundations. His vengeance would be complete.

His thoughts were interrupted by an announcement that the Maglev was arriving at the airport. He checked his watch, pleased that he had a bit of time to get a snack and a drink before his flight. He moved closer to the doors and looked outside as the train slowed and the platform came up alongside. The train stopped and the doors opened.

He was about to step off when the old woman waved at him, before coughing several times. "Your bag! Young man! Your bag!"

Chen felt a degree of panic as he waved at the woman. "The bag isn't mine. I'll inform the stationmaster that somebody has left it unattended."

The woman smiled and placed the bag back down on the seat. Chen moved out of the way as passengers bustled past him, including the kind old woman. As he waited, he made sure that nobody removed the bag. At the last possible moment he stepped off the carriage, relieved that the bag was still in place and the train was ready to go.

He raised his cell phone, entered a number and then waited. As the train pulled out of the station and built up speed, he marveled again at the science that made it work. Once it was out of sight he hit the green call button. He waited ten seconds to be sure and then hung up.

He couldn't help smiling when he heard the explosion in the distance, a muffled boom that shook the glass windows of the station. Within seconds, a plume of dark, greasy, brown smoke rose into the sky, confirmation that his strike had been successful. Without further delay, he turned around and walked to the platform exit. He opened the back of the cheap phone and took out the SIM card. He threw the phone into one trash bin and snapped the SIM card in half before dropping it into another.

His next decision was what to eat in the terminal once he'd passed through security. He really felt like pizza.

~

"A TOAST to my soon to be ex-wife!" Jack raised his glass.

The patrons closest to him joined his salute to Erin as Jack laughed and drained half of the double whisky in one motion. The news break had shown the replay of a report by Erin from Shanghai. It was bad enough that she'd received the gig for the *Standard*, but she was also apparently a darling with the TV guys. Thankfully, the news break was over and the network had crossed back to the baseball.

He was just glad he hadn't been able to hear her voice over the noise in the bar. While Clay's staff had delivered the papers to Erin's lawyers the day before, the news had apparently not reached her, or else she was unconcerned. She looked as fresh, happy and gorgeous as ever. He hated that, but most of all, he hated the fact that he still cared. It was another kick in the balls.

For his part, Jack had made a formidable effort to forget the whole thing, enlisting the help of Josefa and Shane Solomon. He'd worked with Josefa for a decade, and known Shane for just as long. Jack followed the whisky with a long pull from his beer. He slumped back into his seat and looked around the table. The others stared back at him, concern evident on their faces.

"I knew you were struggling, Jack, but this is something else." Josefa reached out and pulled Jack's beer away from him. "Maybe this wasn't my best idea."

Shane laughed. "I bet Jack thinks it was."

Jack flared. "Fuck off, Shane. You left your wife to marry your secretary. I left mine because she was fucking the neighbor."

With his beer now out of reach, he considered ordering another from the big-breasted waitress. She was the one highlight of the bar, which was the lowest of low. The tables were scuffed by the love and care of thousands of drinkers and the carpet was stained in some places, sticky in others. He ignored the rest of the conversation at the table and turned his attention to the game. Though he wasn't much of a baseball fan and had never watched it at home in Australia, it would do.

He was just about to find that waitress when jeers sounded out across the bar as the game feed was cut. Jack snorted as one fan threw a beer bottle at the screen, but missed. A razor sharp news anchor appeared, doing his best to get the public up to speed on some momentous event. He looked anxious, though Jack couldn't hear what he was saying. It was the news ticker across the bottom of the screen that told him everything: thousands dead, a city attacked and a country in chaos.

It spoke of Shanghai.

"Hey, shut up, fellas." Josefa stood and pointed to the screen. "Turn the sound up!"

As Jack stood and swayed, nearly losing his feet, the barman turned up the volume and the sound of the broadcast flooded the bar. "*...it appears as if the attacks, which began just minutes ago, have struck at the heart of the Shanghai summit. The hotel housing the world's media has been severely damaged, and it appears that other parts of Shanghai are also under attack, including the Bund.*"

"Erin's there." Jack tried to clear the cobwebs from his head as he looked between Josefa and Shane. "That's where she's staying."

"Stay calm, Jack." Josefa placed a hand on his shoulder. "I'm sure she's fine. Shanghai is a big place."

"No!" Jack cried out in distress. "Her report was from outside of that hotel, Jo!"

Josefa nodded as Jack continued to watch, unable to peel his eyes away from the screen. The bar was silent. The vision shifted to shaky footage of a large building, racked with fire. Whoever was filming ran toward the building. The shot panned down to a woman, huddled in the fetal position, bloody and frantic.

"That's Celeste." Josefa pulled his cell phone from his pocket. "I need to make a call. Shane, keep an eye on Jack."

Jack watched as closely as he could for any sign of Erin, but the vision cut back to the presenter in the studio.

"*That was footage from what appears to be the focal point of the attacks, the Grand Hyatt Shanghai, where international media are staying during the WTO conference.*"

Jack slammed his fist on the table, knocking two drinks over in the process. He remained standing, frozen in place, not knowing what to do or where to go but needing to do something. The thought of Erin, wounded and alone in Shanghai, felt too much for him to process.

He also knew how this sort of disaster was reported—drip-fed information, half-truths and speculation by reporters. Added to that would be interviews with subject experts usually starved for relevance, who took the opportunity to pitch sensational theories. Good for the viewer, but not necessarily for someone with a missing loved one.

He strode toward the exit, though he had to push past patrons who were chatting loudly about the attacks. Once outside, he tripped and landed roughly on the sidewalk. He was breathing heavily and felt like vomiting. Nothing came except sobs. He felt two people move closer, and turned to see Josefa and Shane standing over him.

Shane crouched down. "I think she'll be alright. Jo's on it, I'm sure she'll be fine."

Jack nodded and tried to regain his feet, but failed spectacularly. He landed on his right wrist and a shot of pain lanced up his arm. He cried out, and Shane placed a hand on his shoulder, no doubt to reassure him but also probably to prevent him from doing further injury.

Josefa was in the middle of another call, obviously having tried Erin with no luck. "We've got people over there, Ernest, we need to help them."

While it reassured Jack that Erin was about to have the

resources of the company looking out for her, it wasn't enough. Despite how much she'd hurt him, he still felt a connection to her that went as deep as his marrow. He needed to act. He pulled out his cell phone and held it out to Shane.

"I need to get over there, Shane." He paused. "I need to find her."

Shane nodded. "I'll get you on the next flight."

MICHELLE FELT like a god as she surveyed Shanghai from one of the top-floor rooms of the Marriott Courtyard Shanghai. She'd chosen the room carefully to ensure a view of the Shanghai New International Expo Centre, the site of the WTO conference. She was relieved that the attacks had gone well, at least if judged by the amount of smoke that billowed from a dozen different places across the city. In front of her was the evidence that she had the ability to achieve anything. Yet it was more than that: it felt like the final cremation of her past, a signal that her rebirth was complete.

Though she'd had a rough family life, which explained her slightly obsessive interest in guns, she'd made it to Yale and studied law and political science. While her grades had been outstanding for two years, that had changed after an internship with a senator during spring break. They'd slept together and she'd thought it was a relationship, but later found out that she'd been the latest in a long line of wide-eyed interns. Her grades had plummeted and all thoughts of her future had changed. From that moment onwards she'd hated the Washington establishment to her core.

But years later, as a graduate, Anton had spotted her potential and recruited her, then spent the next few years slowly introducing her to the truth behind the Foundation for a New America. Her career since had been fighting for the

American rebirth and for the Foundation's power. Now they were on the verge of success.

She shook her head and focused on the scene in front of her. There would be time to reflect once she was back in the States, but until then she needed to be alert and careful. Martial law had been declared since the attacks and the airport and other major facilities were closed. Hungry for updates, she'd been forced to rely on state television and what she could see from her hotel window. She'd smiled at the grainy picture on TV of the burnt-out remains of the Shanghai Maglev, derailed and embedded in the side of a building. She couldn't have asked for a better visual from a Hollywood studio.

Chen had done well. Michelle knew that no matter how quickly the fires were put out, and how swiftly the wounded healed, it would take China years to get over this. They could fix the Maglev and rebuild the other targets, but it would take far longer to soothe the anger. She was counting on it. The Foundation was counting on it.

She turned away from the window and smiled when she saw Anton asleep, naked, on top of the bed covers. Once the attacks were underway, she'd taken him to bed. The sex had been furious and energetic—an outlet for the pent-up stress and emotion of the previous few days. It seemed a fitting climax to this part of their plan. She crossed the room and sat on the edge of the bed, next to where Anton was asleep. She put a hand on his shoulder and gave it a squeeze. He was awake in seconds, staring up at her. He looked satiated, but she still saw the deep intelligence and cunning in his eyes.

He lifted himself up onto one elbow. "What is it?"

"It's time to go. We've done what we needed. I don't want to push our luck."

He smiled. Michelle didn't feel it was friendly. "Not quite everything."

"What do you mean?" She stared at him. "What've you done?"

He stared straight into her eyes. "Leaving Chen alive is too risky. I've sent a team."

Michelle was dumbstruck. This was the first time she'd felt disconnected from him. The attacks had been designed to help preserve the correct world order—and America's place in it—by pointing the Chinese at Taiwan. They'd painstakingly linked the evidence trail back to the island and its government, leaving little doubt who was responsible and what the Chinese reaction would be.

More importantly, with China focused on the island rather than its greater strategic interests, America would have the opportunity to flex its muscle and pull itself off the mat after the financial crisis. It would also signal the beginning of the next part of their plan: for the Foundation—and Michelle—to get a significant presence in the US Congress. Enough of a presence to exert more control.

A minute ago, she'd felt closer to him than ever. Now, Anton was playing a new game. There had been no talk of outing Chen. She'd been his handler. She'd helped him to plan the attacks. Most importantly, she'd given him access to their secure network. He'd repaid her efforts beyond her wildest imagination. The thought of terminating him such success was an anathema to her.

"Are you insane? We gave our word. The man has a family."

"They'll be taken care of as well." Anton laughed. "Bit late for sanctimony. We just killed thousands of innocent people from thousands of families."

"This is different. He's our man."

"He's a loose end that needs tying up. Once he's dead, nothing can be linked back to the Foundation." He sighed. "Look, Michelle, you've still got a lot to learn. I'll get us some room service and we'll talk about it some more, okay?"

She ground her teeth. "I don't want room service. I agreed with the plan, Anton, and I still agree with our purpose. But I don't like being in the dark one bit, and I don't like selling out our people either. There's nothing to be gained by killing Chen."

But he'd made up his mind, and she knew he wouldn't change it. In making this decision, Anton was revealing a part of himself she hadn't seen before. He'd always been ruthless, but until now she'd never considered that he'd so ruthlessly deal with someone who'd done a good job. She had to wonder if she'd suffer the same fate one day.

She lay down next to Anton, who was now on his back with his head resting in his hands. She didn't say anything, but rolled over and feigned sleep to consider her options. It felt like everything had changed. She was a woman of her word. She'd promised Chen that his family would be safe.

A few hours passed. When she was sure Anton was asleep again, she climbed carefully out of bed, grabbed her cell phone and walked to the bathroom. She locked the door and dialed a number from the address book. It rang for what seemed like an eternity until the call was picked up.

"This is Rodriguez."

She exhaled with relief. "This is Dominique. Are you still in Taipei?"

"Sure am. At the embassy."

"Okay. A Taiwanese family need to be looked after. I'll text you their details. I want them taken to the States. Set them up with a house and some cash. This is urgent."

"Okay, shouldn't be a problem, but I'll need Anton's green light. This will blow my cover at the embassy."

She paused. She'd anticipated this. "Anton is indisposed. You can consider this from the top, though."

"Your call." Rodriguez sounded unconvinced. "I'll take care of it."

4

China's Foreign Minister has expressed outrage at the attacks on *Shanghai and blamed Taiwan, describing it as the single most destructive act against the Chinese mainland since the Japanese atrocities of the Second World War. It's hard to argue, with a death toll in excess of ten thousand, French colonial buildings along the Bund damaged, the Maglev train derailed and dozens of other buildings damaged or destroyed. In response to the attacks, China has announced that military readiness has been stepped up and military assets and missiles in the south-east of the country prepared to strike Taiwan if necessary.*

Garth Angell, Foreign Correspondent, *September 4*

"I just need to get to Shanghai!" Jack leaned in closer to the small Japanese woman behind the Air China ticket counter. "My wife is missing and I need to reach her!"

The woman nodded sadly. Though he was enraged, Jack could see that she was unsure about how to proceed with the shouting *gaijin* in front of her.

"*Sumimasen*, sir. I am sorry. I'm unable to get you on a flight to Shanghai. Many airlines have stopped flying, and the remainder are full. There are no available seats aboard Air China or any of our partner airlines. Have you tried Japan Airlines?"

Jack stared at her for a long few moments, then took a deep breath and ran a hand through his hair. "Yeah, and everyone else. Look, money is no object. I'll buy you a Ferrari. I just need a seat." Technically it was true, with Ernest McDowell footing the bill.

Despite this, the woman shook her head and looked behind him. Jack turned to see two Japanese police officers standing rigidly, batons in one hand and radios in the other. They nodded at him, and gestured with their white-gloved hands for him to step away from the counter and over to the side.

Jack exhaled deeply. "Sorry, guys. I know it's not her fault. I just need to get over there. This is important, you know?"

The policemen looked at each other. They clearly didn't know, but just wanted Jack to stop harassing the desk staff. His shoulders sagged. They'd probably seen the same thing a hundred times in recent days, and stood with him while he calmed down. After a few minutes one of them patted him on the shoulder and they moved on.

Jack didn't push his luck. While he was glad he hadn't been arrested, he was clearly no longer welcome at the Air China counter. It had been his last port of call for the day—he'd tried every other airline that was still flying from Tokyo to Shanghai. He'd have to renew his attempts to beg, bully or bribe a ticket tomorrow.

He sighed and walked away from the ticketing area, resigned to the fact that he was probably not going to reach Erin any time soon. He made his way to the bar that had become his second home since arriving at Narita, in between irregular sleep on plastic chairs and abuse of airline staff. The bar was empty, apart from a few people killing time. It frustrated him that even though he couldn't get where he wanted to go, others could. In one corner sat a Japanese man with a briefcase at his side, laptop out. In one of the booths, a couple faced each other and talked with passionate eyes and expressive faces, their relationship not yet weighed down by the baggage of time.

He nodded at the bartender and pointed at the nearest beer tap. "Kirin, please."

The bartender smiled and Jack watched as he slowly filled the glass. He found himself hypnotized by the slow swirl of froth through the amber liquid. He longed for the numbness that the beer would induce, once he'd had enough of it. He craved it. He needed it.

The bartender placed the beer in front of him. "Four-hundred and twenty yen."

"Airport prices." Jack fished around in his pocket for a 500-yen coin, which he handed to the bartender. "Thanks. Keep the change."

As the bartender walked away, Jack's cell phone rang. He fumbled around in his pocket and dug it out. He didn't recognize the number. "Hello?"

"Jack? Oh, Jack, thank God. It's Celeste." The relief in her voice was clear.

The beer shook in Jack's hands, so much that he placed it on the bar. Celeste was calling. Erin might be alive. Or might not be. Celeste was calling. Not Erin. It was too soon to know for sure, or so the US Embassy had told him. Celeste seemed relieved, so it might be good news. Or might not be. He wanted answers. But didn't.

He felt empty. "Hi, Celeste."

"Jack? The line isn't great. I'm calling from Beijing Airport. They evacuated me out of Shanghai for some minor medical treatment, but I'm fine. It took me a while to find a phone and get sorted, but I spoke to Jo. I'm flying to Tokyo."

"Why?"

"I'm sorry, Jack." Her voice started to break and he heard a sob. "Erin is gone. She was standing near me when the bomb went off."

Jack sagged. "How? I saw you on the TV..."

Another pause. "It was a large piece of shrapnel. I'm so sorry. I waited with her as long as I could. She was gone by the time they forced me into an ambulance."

Jack felt dizzy. He leaned toward the bar to catch himself, but failed. He slipped off the stool and hit his head on the bar on the way down. The phone clattered down next to him. He reached up and touched his head, then looked at his hand. Blood. He'd split his head open. He closed his eyes and tried to compose himself.

Celeste's words had kicked in the doors of his preparation, and he felt the grief rushing in. He'd thought himself mentally fortified for Erin's death, though he'd hoped she was still alive. The reality of it was unbearable. The woman he'd loved, despite their recent issues, was gone. He picked up the phone.

"Jack?" Celeste's voice dripped with concern. "Jack? Jack, are you okay?"

He just wanted to be alone. "Thanks for telling me."

He hung up and stood. He righted the stool, sat again and a single tear streaked down his cheek. It was all over. His wife was dead. Deep down, ever since he'd left the bar in New York, he'd known it was likely Erin was dead. The life they'd built together was in ruins. The events of the last few months seemed trivial now.

He took a mouthful of his beer and considered what he'd see if he was outside of his body. He'd see a wreck of a man, mourning the death of his wife and the wasteland of his life. He'd see a man with a beer and little else. He'd pity him. For a while he thought of nothing, just tried to clear his head of the noise, the mess and the despair.

Soon, the sobs came, long and drawn out. Each one felt like it penetrated him to his core. He was as alone in the airport as he was in the world.

~

ERNEST CONCEDED that the hospital was quite nice, with a sloped driveway and an impressive garden that gave way to a four-story white building at the center of it all. It was far better than the rest of Ohio, at least. He was frustrated that it had taken him nearly a week to visit his wife after the meeting with Mahoney, because of issues with the US and UK governments, crazies blowing up half of Shanghai and leaving several of his journalists dead or missing.

"You know, Peter, this place is a pain in my ass to get to. Are you sure there's no way we can get her moved to another facility? In New York, perhaps?"

Peter shook his head. "I'm afraid the doctors were insistent. She's to stay at this facility in this fine state. They say that to move her will be detrimental to her wellbeing."

Ernest sighed as the car came to a halt. He opened the door and climbed out of the black sedan with a groan; his back was giving him hell. At least the driver had parked in the spot closest to the hospital front door, ignoring the "CEO" sign. They entered a cavernous lobby so white it hurt his eyes through the double automatic doors.

A large security guard was seated behind a desk with his feet up and his stomach protruding, the buttons on his blue shirt threatening to burst from the strain. Ernest could barely mask his contempt for Sandra's gatekeeper. He approached the desk and the guard pointed at the guest book on the counter. Ernest stared for several seconds, before scrawling his name and the time on the page without a word. Peter did likewise.

The guard took his feet off the desk, rummaged around in a drawer on the reception desk and held out a meaty hand clenching two identity tags. "You'll need to put these on your jackets, gentlemen."

Ernest looked at the tags, then down at his suit jacket, appalled at the idea of a pinhole in his five-thousand-dollar suit. He raised an eyebrow at the guard, who didn't seem to recognize that he was talking to Forbes' fifteenth richest man.

"No tag, no entry, sir." The guard shrugged. "I don't make the rules."

"Fucking hell. Peter, give me your jacket."

Peter frowned.

Ernest slid off his jacket. "I saw that look, stop whining, I'll buy you a new one."

In most circles Peter would be considered well dressed, but their suits couldn't be compared and Ernest was in no mood to haggle. After a short pause, Peter undid the button on his jacket and gave it to Ernest. Ernest slid the jacket over his shoulders and clipped on the security pass. The jacket fit well enough and he handed his own to Peter.

"Wait here."

The guard waved Ernest through and after a short walk down the hall, he found Sandra's room. He peered in through the small circular window on the door before he entered. She was seated near the room's largest window, which gave a good view into the garden. He opened the door as quietly as he could to avoid disturbing her, but as usual it didn't work.

"Good morning, Ernest." Her voice was cool. "Nice of you to fit me into your schedule. I haven't seen this little of you since our honeymoon."

He leaned down to kiss her on the cheek, but backed off when she pulled away. "Sorry, it's been a frantic week."

She shrugged. "It doesn't matter. Though when you didn't visit right away the staff were a bit worried I might get sad and end myself. I couldn't stop laughing."

The couple of days in hospital had clearly ticked her off. She still looked beautiful though, even in her pajamas. Peter had done some digging about her incident. Sandra had harassed a couple at a charity function, but the couple had laughed it off as stress. Though no harm was done, it was a concern. Ernest felt guilty that it had taken so long to get here, but he had other responsibilities. She knew that.

He gestured for her to move over on the sofa and sat next to her. He placed a hand on her leg and she placed her hand on top of his. They sat in silence for a few minutes. Ernest exhaled deeply and tried to relax. It felt like the first moment he'd been off the clock in weeks. He closed his eyes, and she cuddled in to him. It was as close to perfect as he could remember.

He thought about their marriage. He'd courted her, briefly, but in reality Ernest was sure that Sandra had targeted him. He didn't mind, he loved her and she was an impressive woman in her own right. When Sandra had arrived on the scene, she'd been an enigma. An intelligent Chinese beauty who was completely opposite to his previous wives. This fact hadn't stopped the two of them being regulars in the trash magazine society pages, and Sandra had found herself compelled to quit her legal career because of the publicity. He'd considered trying to have a child with her, to add to the adult daughter he already had, but at his age he'd decided against it.

"I'm glad you're here." She lay down in his lap. He struggled to think of a more serene moment they'd spent together in the past few months.

"Sandra? What can I do to help?"

"Short of staying here with me?" She laughed sadly. "I want all of it to go away. The hacking, the inquiries, the attacks in Shanghai. I can't handle it all."

He smiled down at her, though she couldn't see his face. "I'm working on the first two. The hacking has stopped and I'm doing my best with the inquiries. It's bleak."

"Okay."

"As for the terrorist attacks, I can't do much about them, Sandra. I lost some people over there, and a few more are injured."

He felt her tense up. "I'm worried, Ernest. Please be fair in reporting it. We don't need your usual henchmen stoking the flames of war."

Ernest frowned. She knew his business and what made it profitable as much as he did. "What happens next is up to the Chinese, Sandra."

~

MICHELLE SIGHED as the car sped along the quiet road. She was seated in the passenger seat next to her driver, Mr Liu, on the way to a small private airport in the middle of nowhere. They'd left Shanghai in the afternoon. Now, hours into the drive, Michelle just wanted to get on the plane and close her eyes. That was still a few hours away though.

She was mad at Anton for his betrayal of Chen, but madder yet at his ability to get out of the country from a normal airport —he'd managed to get a commercial flight, but it was Foundation procedure not to have two leaders on the one plane. By the time her flight had come around, it had been canceled. Now she had to fly out of a dustbowl airport. The only consolation was that Chen's family should have been extracted by now, though it would anger Anton and probably cause her problems down the track.

Mr Liu, who'd been silent for the whole drive, suddenly cursed under his breath in Mandarin. She knew enough of the language to recognize he'd said something about sons of whores. The car headlights picked out a drab sedan parked across the road and blocking it. She feared that this surprise was not a good one. As their car drew closer, she could see two men in Chinese military uniforms leaning against the sedan. While they seemed casual, talking and smoking, she felt threatened.

"Want me to turn around?" Liu spoke calmly in English.

Michelle swallowed hard. "I don't think that'd be the stealthy way to handle this."

He shrugged and kept driving. Spotting the car, one of the soldiers stood up straight and sauntered into the middle of the road. He held up his hand with the palm facing outward and blew a small whistle. Liu stopped the car a few yards away from the impromptu checkpoint. He killed the engine but left the headlights on. Liu was experienced in dealing with Chinese authorities, including in less than official ways, so she could do little except hope that he was worth what the Foundation was paying him.

The man who'd stopped their car seemed fresh-faced. He was probably newly minted from the recruit factory. She felt her heart beat faster as the young soldier approached the car on the driver's side. Behind him, the older soldier unbuckled the holster on the belt under his paunch. She regretted not having a weapon of her own, but it was too much of a risk to carry a firearm in the circumstances. Her cover wouldn't hold up under too much scrutiny.

The younger soldier tapped on the window and Liu wound it down. Michelle sat, powerless as they exchanged pleasantries in Mandarin. She knew it would take a few moments of skirting the issue before the two Chinese men reached the point. She followed along with parts of the conversation. The soldier eventually said something about the regional airport being closed, and having to search the car. Liu scoffed and threatened to involve the Party if the soldier didn't move immediately.

Without warning, the man pushed his head inside the car and started shouting. Michelle had been the beneficiary of enough combat and survival training to know the signs of danger. She unbuckled her belt as carefully as she could as the soldier started pointing at her, to which Liu shouted back and slapped his hand away. Michelle lost the thread of the exchange as the two men shouted too quickly for her to follow.

With no gun and no other weapon, flight was looking like her only option. She reached for the door handle as the soldier shouted at Liu to freeze. As the first gunshot cannoned in her ear, she pulled on the handle and leaped from the car. She ran as fast as she could toward the darkness. She had no idea where she was, or where she was going, but she had to get away from the car and the soldiers.

Liu was probably dead and she had no way to protect herself. She had to keep moving. She ran into the scrub on the side of the road, but there was nowhere obvious to hide. Distance and darkness were her only friends, but after another few steps she stumbled and fell, hitting her head on the ground. Before she could rise, a fierce blow to her midsection drove the air out of her.

"Don't move." A voice said in broken English. It was different to the young soldier's. It had to be the older one. "This does not need to be painful."

Michelle closed her eyes as a pistol barrel was pressed against the back of her head. This was it. After all that she had achieved, it was going to end on the roadside in the dark in the middle of the Chinese countryside. Nobody would know about her death, or mourn her. She didn't know what to do, but she wouldn't beg. There was no point. This was an orchestrated hit —Liu was already dead, and she was about to be.

She did not look at him. "Get it over with, you fuck!"

He laughed, then the world exploded with a bang as loud as two asteroids colliding.

She lifted her hands to her ringing ears and felt something wet on her left cheek. Blood. And something that felt like marshmallow—a small piece of the soldier's brain.

She opened her eyes and turned around, confused. Liu was standing over her and the body of the old Chinese soldier, a flashlight in one hand and a pistol in the other. He crouched down and wrapped one arm awkwardly around her.

"How?" Her voice wavered only slightly. "How did you survive?"

Liu shrugged, barely visible in the torchlight. He lifted his shirt and she saw Kevlar.

"Well, thanks. Are you okay?"

"A few ribs will be broken, but nothing too bad."

Michelle shivered and huddled into him. "Why would they attack us?"

"Money. The young one said he'd let us live if we gave him more than he had been given to kill us. I gave him a bullet."

Michelle's eyes widened. "It was a hit? Ordered by who?"

Liu said nothing. His silence was damning. He knew as well as she did that there was only one other person in China who knew who she was and the significance of the Foundation. Only one who'd known where she would be. Liu had foiled that plan, because of his paranoia and a Kevlar vest. She stumbled to her feet and they walked back to the car in silence.

She didn't say anything as he started the car and resumed their drive to the airport. Only then did Michelle dare to breathe evenly, despite both of them being covered in blood and the car smelling like gun smoke. She'd survived. It made her more determined to get back to the States. Anton had betrayed Chen and now he'd betrayed her. He was tying up all loose ends.

There was only one thing that could be done.

She had to kill Anton.

5

Taiwan has rejected allegations by China that it is responsible for the terrorist attacks on Shanghai, despite evidence produced by China that suggests Taiwan is linked to the attacks. The crisis appears no closer to cooling down, with reports of dangerous maneuvers of military aircraft by both nations. As China continues its forceful rhetoric, Taiwan has called for international condemnation to pressure China to stop any further aggressive military posturing. As tensions in the region grow, the US Secretary of State has called for calm, a plea mirrored by Japan, South Korea and other regional powers.

Kelly Vacaro, Al Jazeera, *September 5*

As the Narita Express pulled into Tokyo Central Station, Jack's head hurt so badly from the hangover that he could barely remember the code to the luggage lock. He entered the combination and was relieved when it opened with a small click. He wrestled with his case—a small Samsonite that contained his hastily packed clothes and personal items—and got ready to disembark.

Since Celeste's phone call informing him of Erin's death,

he'd given up on his attempts to get a flight to China. He'd made some calls, and the Chinese weren't going to release her body until the investigations concerning the attack were completed. He'd also spent some time getting to the bottom of a few bottles of liquor, which he was now paying the price for.

He'd faced a choice: return to the States right away, or home to Australia, but he liked the idea of a few days' rest in Tokyo. The train came to a stop and the doors opened, and he stepped off the train, inhaling deeply. Given the hour, he was surprised at the large number of people milling about, getting on and off. If this was Tokyo before dawn, he didn't look forward to the peak-hour rush.

He stood on the platform. He knew the name of his hotel and where it was on a map, but that was no help. The walls were covered in arrows and Japanese characters. Helpfully, these were accompanied by English translations underneath, though they may as well have been written in Latin—none of the locations sounded right. With no help in sight, Jack picked a direction and walked. Eventually he found a booth with a big blue I and went inside. Behind the desk sat a friendly looking Japan Rail staff member.

Jack tried his patchy Japanese on for size. "*Konichi wa.*"

The Japan Rail employee smiled. "*Konichi wa*, sir, good morning."

"Ah. You speak English?" Jack wrestled his case alongside him and placed his satchel on the counter.

"A little, sir. Can I help?"

Jack smoothed the crumpled map out onto the counter. "I'm looking for the Mercure Hotel in Ginza, but I can't find the right exit."

"First time in Japan, sir?" The man looked down at Jack's map.

"Sure is."

After a few seconds he looked up and pointed in the

direction Jack had just come. "That way. Head outside and find *Chuo-dori*. Then it's straight ahead."

Jack was dubious, but felt too embarrassed to ask for more assistance. He expressed his thanks, gathered his things and left the little booth. Once he'd emerged from the station, he looked up and saw the street sign he needed. Smiling with relief, he started walking. He'd traveled less than a block when his cell phone rang. Jack stopped and fumbled around his pockets to find it. He looked down at the display and saw it was Josefa Tokaloka calling. He hurried to answer before Jo hung up.

"Hi, Jo."

"Hi, Jack." Jo paused. "I'm sorry again about Erin."

Jack sighed. "Thanks."

"No luck getting to Shanghai?"

"No. And there's no point now anyway, if they're not releasing her body until the investigations are complete. I've decided to rest a few days in Tokyo then head home."

"I'm here for you, Jack. Whatever you need."

Jack knew that Jo was genuine. He was one of the few people who'd stuck by him, more or less, in the last few months, when most had obviously considered it too hard. Erin's death just made it all the worse. For some reason, he found himself thinking of Afghanistan. Things had been simpler then. Embedded with a unit in the Green Zone for two years, he'd met some great people and seen plenty. Hell, the worst thing he'd seen had won him a Pulitzer, though he'd agonized for weeks about filing that story.

"I want to get back to work, Jo." Jack was surprised that he'd blurted it out before he'd had a chance to think about it. "Is there anything I can do? It's either that or drink."

"No, Jack." Jo's voice was firm. "You only found out about Erin yesterday, work is the last thing you need. You need time to heal."

"That's not what I want. I've had too much time to myself in the last few months. It's part of the reason things are so shitty at the moment. I want to work. Give me anything."

Jo paused again and then sighed. "Well, you being in Japan is opportune."

"Name it."

"It's against my better judgment, but if you're determined to get back to work, the Navy is deploying the USS *George Washington* battle group out of Yokosuka late tomorrow. They want a few embeds and you're my most experienced option. It's yours if you want it, but I'd prefer you didn't."

Jack smiled. It sounded perfect. Onboard the carrier, he'd travel where he was told, sleep where he was told, eat when and what he was told, and focus on work. Better, given the ship was sailing into a potential conflict zone, there was half a chance it could be a dry environment. He'd have a much easier time staying off the booze.

"They're sending a carrier to China? That's a real bright idea."

Josefa laughed. "Just flying the flag, I guess. Warn China off being stupid."

"That sounds pretty stupid to me, but I'm on it."

"Okay. I should let you know, though, Celeste is in Japan and she'll be joining you."

Jack paused for a second, unsure what to say. His recent history with Celeste hadn't exactly been great. "I'd rather do it alone. I'm surprised she's even up to it."

"You can talk." Jo paused. "She's okay. The doctors have cleared her and she's refusing to come back to the States. She wants to keep busy. There are worse places she could be than next to you. Honestly, I think she feels a bit guilty about Erin, so tread carefully."

"You're not going to let me work if I don't agree?"

"Nope."

Jack sighed. "I'll call you from the train."

He ended the call. While he was glad he didn't have to

navigate his way to the hotel, he now had to find his way back in to the station, find the ticket counter and get to Yokosuka. Still, the job gave him something to keep him occupied, which was the main thing.

And if it got him a little bit closer to Shanghai, so much the better.

~

As usual, Ernest had arrived for the meeting of the EMCorp board earlier than necessary; he liked to have time to get into his groove, sip his coffee and wait. As others entered the room, he'd size them up from a position of strength, considering any advantages or disadvantages. He would plot.

Not today.

Today the room closed in around him, suffocating. He felt exhausted and vulnerable, tired and beaten. This was usually his arena, where he fought his greatest foes. More often than not he'd subjugate them and emerge victorious. Today though, he felt like a Roman slave, given a sword and told to go fight a lion.

He turned to face Peter, who was sitting in the usual position to his left, ready to take the minutes. "They're going to get me this time, Peter."

Peter looked up from his paperwork. "Don't count on it. They're all bluff and bluster. They've had you on the ropes before and never managed to bring you down."

"This might be the day. Too much baggage. Too much politics. Too many ex-wives diluting my stock holding, waiting for their turn to help stick the knife in one last time."

Peter sighed. "You might be okay. Hit them hard from the outset, draw your line in the sand and force them to cross it. It's the only chance."

Ernest nodded and turned back to the table. He arranged his papers as the boardroom door opened and the rest of the board filed in, escorted by Ernest's secretary. He kept his face blank and didn't say anything. His few allies on the board would know how dire things were and he saw no need to give his enemies an advantage.

"Thanks, everyone." Peter paused as the others settled. "I confirm that we have a quorum and that the board meeting is open."

Ernest looked around the room absentmindedly as Peter recalled the minutes from the previous meeting. He knew that a challenge would come today. He could feel it. But he didn't know who'd have the balls to do it. This situation was as fluid as it was professionally deadly. He had a list of suspects, but only time would tell.

The two most senior and most obvious candidates were Steve Wilson, who'd sat on the board for a decade, and Dan Grattan, the Chief Operating Officer. Neither liked him much, but they didn't feel right. Ernest was certain that the challenge would come from one of the lesser lights, preordained by the others. He readied himself.

"So, if there are no objections to the minutes, we'll endorse them and move on."

"Okay, thanks, Peter. I just want to note that we've got some people missing or deceased." Ernest cleared his throat. "Now, the first order of business is—"

"Sorry for interrupting, Ernest." Al Preston leaned forward. "I've got an extraordinary motion burning a hole in my pocket."

Ernest waved a hand. "Let's hear it then."

Preston seemed slightly taken aback. "Well, thing is, a few of us believe the time might have come for you to stand aside, Ernest. Voluntarily, if possible."

Ernest laughed boisterously for several long seconds. "A half-assed appeal to my better judgment, Al? Fuck your beliefs, you'll need to do better than that."

Preston looked shocked, and momentarily lost his composure. "Ernest, please, it doesn't need to be like—"

"Sure, it does. I gave your father his place on this board, rest his soul, and I did the same for you. I'll drop dead before I step down for you. Now shut up."

Ernest sat back and grinned as murmurs and sideways glances were shared by the other eighteen board members. They obviously hadn't expected him to be so belligerent, and he thought for a second that Preston's plea might be it. Peter's advice to hit them hard and early might have worked.

He noticed movement to his left. He looked and felt his confidence and bluster vanish in a second as Duncan McColl, the EMCorp Chief Financial Officer—and one of Ernest's closest friends—stood. He had a somber expression on his face and wouldn't look at Ernest.

"Of all people, Duncan, I thought you'd be solid."

"I'm sorry, Ernest." McColl started to pace. "I've been here nearly as long as you. And I've always been silent on the issues you've walked us into, but it's time."

Ernest said nothing as McColl walked behind each board member. It was a tactic Ernest liked to employ himself from time to time, because it put people off guard, and now McColl was copying it. He'd have laughed at the absurdity of it all if the situation wasn't so dire.

"We can't have it, Ernest. The newspaper arm of the company is dying, the United Kingdom is a mess, there are new scandals by the day and our share price is bleeding. We could handle all that, we really could, but now there's to be a US Senate inquiry as well? You've put the United States operations at risk. It's over. We ask again—"

"Judas!" Ernest shouted.

"I'm sorry?"

"I was ready for an attack by any of these other plebeians, Duncan, and just about ready to turn my back and let them sink the knife in. But you?"

"I don't do this lightly, Ernest. But given the troubles we're sailing into, it's with the greatest respect and sincerity that—"

"Oh, fuck your sincerity!" Ernest slammed the table with both fists, causing his coffee to spill over his papers. He turned to Peter. "What's my total shareholding?"

Peter was matter of fact. "Between your personal holdings and the trust for your daughter, about thirty-seven percent. Add in your wife and it jumps to forty."

"Well, there you have it. In short, gentlemen, I've got you all by the short and curly hairs." He looked to the only female board member. "Sorry, Janice."

McColl was unrepentant, but seemed slightly crestfallen. "Ernest, be reasonable. Think of what's best for the company."

"I've been doing that for the past thirty-five years, Duncan, and I've survived longer than many of the doomsayers who've sat in these very chairs, telling me how wrong I was. If you're so fucking confident, then call a spill, and let's see who the shareholders back. Here's the rub, though: I've got a fair head start."

McColl shook his head. "Are you so confident that you're right again? That you're not going to annihilate this company with your little tantrum?"

Ernest laughed. "Not in the slightest, but I've earned the right to find out. We're going to stay the course, stare down these inquiries, and emerge on the other side."

McColl looked up and down the table, clearly seeking the support of his co-conspirators to carry the argument further. When none materialized, he sat down. Ernest could tell his CFO was crushed. Despite his anger, he felt regret at what was to come.

"I thank you all for the faith placed in me." His voice was cold. "I'd like to adjourn for five minutes, given the drama. But before we do, Duncan, your services as CFO will no longer be required, and I'd ask that you step down from the board as well."

McColl's head shot up and he looked around the table. When nobody defended him, his nostrils flared. "This is an

China make a proper job of attacking the Taiwanese, we're in the game anyway. We're not trying to provoke the Chinese. Hell, this sort of thing has often worked in the past to help keep the peace."

Jack laughed as he walked alongside McCulloch. "Keep the peace? By sailing a fleet past their front door?"

"Sounds crazy, and I understand the skepticism, but the balance of power in this region is fragile." McCulloch turned down a hallway. "China, Taiwan, South Korea and Japan all have legitimate fears and grievances at the best of times."

"Nothing so bad as half of Shanghai being blown up, I'd think."

"You'd be surprised, son. The folk in this region don't forget easily. They still hold grudges from centuries ago. It's our job to mediate and be the counterweight to too much ambition on any one side. The policy has worked for half a century."

"Surely the Chinese understand it's not Taiwan's fault. Despite the bit of evidence that has trickled out, it seems capital-S stupid."

"Speculation isn't my business." McCulloch shrugged. "Who knows? But the State Department thinks that things are different now. China and Taiwan have been cautiously friendly for the last few years, but that's gone—Shanghai changed everything. China blames the island, and they're going to keep flexing some muscle. That's why we just need to cool everyone down."

Jack wasn't sure he believed the premise that more guns equaled less likelihood of conflict. "Guess we'll have to see."

"Damn right."

They walked in silence through the maze of long corridors, Jack doubted he'd be able to find his way back to the deck. As they went deeper into the ship, junior sailors stood to the side and saluted.

Eventually they reached a door and McCulloch paused in

front of it. "Here we are, Mr Emery. If you'll excuse me, I've got a fleet to get moving."

"Of course, Admiral, appreciate the chat."

"Welcome aboard the *George Washington*. We'll catch up once we're underway and you're settled in a bit." McCulloch turned and walked away.

Jack opened the heavy steel door and stepped inside his quarters. He was immediately taken aback by the sight of Celeste Adams seated on the bed. While he'd known that she'd be here, he was shocked at how she looked. Her face was covered in grazes and scratches, and her left arm was in a sling. She smiled at him.

He put his bag down in the doorway and approached her. "Looks like you've seen better days."

"Hi, Jack." She stood and held her one good arm out. He was surprised when she put the arm around him. "Thought you could use a friendly face once you got aboard."

He recoiled instinctively from the contact, but she persisted. He gave in and put his arms around her as well. He held her loosely, awkwardly, not sure what was expected. In truth, he wished it was Erin he was holding, despite their issues. He wondered for the first time if agreeing to work on board the carrier was a mistake.

Eventually, after she pulled away and looked at him, he fumbled for words before the moment became awkward. "I'm glad you're alive."

"You're glad I'm alive?" Celeste's laughter broke the tension. "Erin told me you were strange at times, Jack, but come on."

"You know what I mean." Jack smiled at the memory of Erin, who'd used to say that a lot. "Too many good people died over there."

"Yeah." Her voice trailed off. "You've got a nice room. Bigger than mine, anyway."

Jack looked around. The cabin was not spacious, but he was certain it was better than most of the men and women on board enjoyed. A single bed ran the length of one wall, and there was a small table with two chairs against the opposite wall. There was also a small door that probably led to the bathroom.

She sat back down on the bed and punched the pillow. "Feels okay."

"Yeah, it'll do."

They sat in silence, before Jack turned to her and blurted out what he'd been thinking for several minutes. "How did it happen, Celeste? How did she die?"

She continued to stare straight ahead and didn't look at him as she spoke. "We were both outside the hotel. Erin had just filed and we were going to get a drink when it went off. I felt the shockwave. It knocked me over and stunned me. But once my head cleared, I realized what had happened. The front of the hotel was just gone. The rest was on fire."

Jack felt empty. He wanted more. "That's it? She didn't say anything? Do anything?"

"Most of the rest is a blur. Erin was still alive, barely. I did some first aid, but there was a lot of blood and she didn't last long. Then they bundled me into an ambulance."

Jack exhaled heavily. "I saw you on the news and hoped she might be okay. But when you called me in Tokyo..."

"I'm so sorry, Jack. I don't know what to say." She smiled sadly. "I was just lucky."

He felt his head cloud over, and he suddenly felt sick. He continued to stare at her, and finally she looked at him. They locked eyes, and Jack could see the strain etched on her face. "There's something else, Celeste. Something you're not telling me."

She smiled sadly, and a tear splashed down her cheek. "The last thing she said before she died was to tell you that she loved you and was sorry."

~

MICHELLE HELD her breath as she eased the door to her apartment open. The light from inside the apartment peeked out like a small, curious child as she crouched and probed her finger slowly inside the crack. When her finger grazed a thin steel wire, she exhaled with relief, reached inside and unhooked it.

She stood up, pushed the door open and hauled her case through, careful not to trip over the limp wire. It would be ironic to be blown up by her own trap, when she'd just organized to have a chunk of Shanghai destroyed, and she enjoyed a small chuckle as she closed the door behind her and locked it. She turned on the lights.

Evidently, nobody had disturbed her apartment. On the other hand, she also knew that while her defensive tripwires and a few other surprises would keep casual interest away, it wouldn't deter a pro. She'd half expected to return from China to a room full of gunmen, but things seemed safe, though it was ironic that the training she'd been provided by the Foundation was now being used to defend against its leader.

She shook her head as she wound up the wire and separated it from the grenade, but stopped short of putting the trap away. There was a fairly good chance she'd need to set it again soon. While Anton had clearly decided to end her, she'd escaped that situation and Chen and his family were safe. There was a chance Anton wouldn't try anything too ambitious on home soil, given she had her own support network within the Foundation.

But if he did decide to make a move, the clock was ticking. With the Congressional midterm elections drawing closer, if Anton had decided to remove her from play, he'd have a much harder time of it once she was elected. That put him on a timetable that was dangerous to her ongoing health.

She made her way to the kitchen, threw her keys on the kitchen counter and took a beer from the fridge. In the living room she found her pistol in a drawer and felt safer for it. After the close call in China, she'd vowed to never be so helpless again. She found her way to the couch, put the gun on the cushion beside her and took a long pull of the beer.

Anton wanted her out of the picture, but that knowledge meant nothing without proof. Her supporters would only move on him with proof or provocation. For now, she had no mechanism to bring the matter to a head. She opened her eyes and placed her beer on the coffee table. It was time to test a theory. She picked up her cell phone and dialed.

The call was answered in less than a second. "Foundation for a New America, you're speaking with Grace, how may I help you?"

"Hi Grace, it's Michelle." She paused for a moment and took a deep breath. "I'm back in the country and I need to speak to Anton."

There was a delay, which did not surprise Michelle one bit. "Just hold on for a moment, can you, Ms Dominique?"

Michelle tapped her foot as the hold music played. She knew exactly what was happening, but needed to be sure. Grace was asking her manager, who sat alongside her. The manager would buzz Anton on the intercom. Anton would refuse to take her call. The manager would tell Grace, who'd give her apologies to Michelle and suggest she try another time, or try his direct line.

The music stopped. "Ms Dominique? I'm afraid he's unable to take your call. He's also unavailable for the rest of the day. I suggest you call tomorrow or try his private line."

Michelle terminated the call. It was the first time that Anton had ever refused to speak to her. Thankfully, with Shanghai now sorted, she had more opportunity to focus on other matters. She was surer than ever that the way to shift momentum in her favor was through control of Ernest McDowell and EMCorp. She picked up the phone and dialed again.

"What?" Senator Patrick Mahoney had a level of aggression that surprised her.

Michelle laughed softly. "Senator, I trust you're well?"

"As usual, Ms Dominique, much better when I'm speaking to you."

Michelle didn't blame him for the sarcasm. Though the Foundation had their friends in the Capitol Building, most duly elected representatives were suspicious of her and the organization. Most of the conversations she had with them were a mixture of carrot and stick, and more than one congressman or senator had been whacked.

"I want a meeting. At your convenience, of course."

Mahoney snorted. "Of course. When and where, Ms Dominique?"

"Your office. I'll come tomorrow at noon. We need to discuss the EMCorp inquiry."

"Why? It's open and shut, really. Especially since he threatened me."

That was news to Michelle. "Don't be too cocky, Senator."

She hung up the phone. If all went to plan, the result of the inquiry would soon be a foregone conclusion. She hoped it would be clear to McDowell that he needed to take drastic action to save his company. He would be backed up against a cliff, with the ocean below. She intended to be the one to save him, or push him over.

It all depended on his attitude.

She picked up the beer again and finished it. While she thought about the situation further, she peeled the label and tore the damp paper into several smaller pieces. She thought of Ernest McDowell, of Anton, of the Foundation and its plan for an American rebirth and controlling the agenda from Congress. It was coming together.

Her goals weren't modest, but neither were her successes so far.

Shanghai was just the beginning.

~

ERNEST WALKED BRISKLY through the crowd of the charity function. He skirted around clusters of guests and dodged waiters with trays of drinks and canapés, protecting their precious cargo from potential disaster with practiced hands. A few looked his way in anger, then relented when they realized who'd nearly bowled them over.

He'd almost reached the safety of the bar when he felt a tap on his shoulder. He turned and feigned surprise. "Oh, hello, Catherine, how nice to see you."

She smiled coldly and handed him a glass of champagne. "Found you."

Ernest looked down at the champagne flute. The liquid inside bubbled away, and for a brief moment he considered how a slight flick of his wrist would fling the contents all over his ex-wife, enabling his escape. He thought better of it.

He waved toward the bar. "I was just enjoying a drink. What can I help you with?"

"What can you do for me?" A nasty snarl grew on her face. "You can give me what's mine. You can answer the fucking phone when I call."

Ernest sighed. While it had cost several million dollars to cut away the cancer that Catherine Salerno had been, the outcome had been positive. A watertight prenuptial agreement and a sympathetic judge who'd been considerate of her narcotics issues had seen him escape relatively unscathed. Daddy Salerno, a Supreme Court Justice, was still a danger, but if things stayed civil, he left Ernest alone.

"I owe you nothing, Catherine. Our relationship ended with the court ruling. You've got every dime you'll ever see out of me."

He stepped back as two large men approached from behind her. The larger of the two tapped Catherine on the shoulder and whispered something in her ear. A dark look came over her face. He knew it well: shock, mixed with anger and just a touch of indignation. Only Catherine's father could paint that particular picture. One of the suited men put a hand on her waist and led her away. The other came closer to Ernest, discretely apologized and said he'd find her a cab.

Ernest sighed with relief. "Thanks. She's unwell."

"We know. Justice Salerno sends his regards." The man turned and walked briskly after his colleague.

Ernest leaned on the bar. He put down his champagne and ordered a whisky, the barman pouring him a double without any hesitation. Ernest downed half of the drink in one gulp. While the burn of the whisky as it followed the path to his stomach satisfied him, he'd pay for it tomorrow. He was tired. In Washington for the Senate hearing, he'd been roped into a charity function at Sandra's behest. She was fresh out of hospital, despite his protests. The evening had been organized months ago, and he'd agreed to attend and do his best to drum up some money for the cause.

Fortunately, he hadn't had to do much. Sandra was a natural, and he just needed to keep out of her way and let her do her thing: raise large amounts of money with a smile and a few minutes of conversation. He searched for his wife and spotted her across the room, resplendent in a navy blue ball gown, complete with a scandalous split up the left side. She still took his breath away. She moved from group to group, not letting herself get bogged down but leaving each guest she spoke to with a smile on their face and fresh concern for cancer-stricken children.

Ernest downed the rest of his whisky and plucked another champagne flute from the tray of a passing waitress. He gave her a pained smile and received a wink for his troubles. He pushed himself away from the bar and stepped into the crowd, determined to at least stay through the speeches. He was quickly engaged in conversation with a rotund investment banker and his trophy wife. He took the path of least resistance, nodding at everything the man said while he considered what was bigger, the banker's account balance or his wife's cleavage. It would be a close call.

Ernest held up a hand as the banker continued to prattle on. "Hey, President is on, better listen up."

As the applause lifted the mood of the room, Ernest smiled at the sight of the President of the United States, Philip Kurzon, his friend since college.

Kurzon waited for the applause to die down. "Ladies and gentlemen, thank you all for coming tonight to support such a great cause. Ms Cheng and her fellow directors do a great job at events such as this one, helping the families of childhood cancer victims stay together while they're in treatment. Let's give them a round of applause."

Ernest joined the rest of the crowd in polite applause.

Kurzon frowned and glanced at the glass prompter, positioned slightly to his left. "I'd ask that you give generously to the fine cause we're here to support tonight. I was planning on saying more on that, but certain fast-moving international events have forced my hand and made this speech a little less intimate than I'd intended."

Kurzon gripped the lectern and leaned forward. "In recent days, the People's Republic of China has suffered great trauma at the hands of a well-organized group of terrorists. This is a pain the United States of America is familiar with, and we stand united in fury with China that this could happen again."

He paused briefly. "However, it appears that the PRC is using this attack as justification for aggression against its neighbors. Though some evidence appears to link Taiwan to these attacks, the United States does not consider it compelling. Nor do we consider it a legitimate basis for Chinese saber rattling.

"Yet earlier today, a missile was fired from the south of China over Taiwan. Though it splashed down in the ocean south of the island, it represents an escalation that's both worrying and unacceptable. It is quite disgusting that China would respond to acts of terror by terrorizing the civilians of Taiwan."

Kurzon lifted his hands, palms facing upward, the model of reassurance and calm. "I speak now to the government of the People's Republic of China. Stand your forces down. Work with the United States and the international community to secure justice for your dead."

Ernest's eyes widened. It was not often you saw the leader of the free world plead with the leaders of the oppressed world to stay in their own backyard. Not so bluntly, at any rate. He had a feeling that the speech would push his looming Senate testimony from the front pages, especially in the papers he didn't own.

Kurzon continued. "For our part, we will not be idle. To ensure ongoing peace in the region, I've ordered the USS *George Washington* carrier group to deploy from Yokosuka, Japan, to the South China Sea. There, the carrier and its aircraft will provide the world with eyes and ears into what's happening in that region.

"I've requested that members of our media travel with the carrier, to document this mission and ensure the world can see the truth. It's my hope that the nations of the region step back from the precipice of war, and recognize the prosperity and security we all gain from continued peace.

"But let me be clear. The United States is bound by an Act of Congress to defend Taiwan. With force, if it becomes necessary."

Ernest wasn't surprised by anything in the speech, having caught wind of it earlier in the day. Kurzon left the stage and Ernest decided to leave the party as conversation started to buzz with the ramifications of the announcement. He was certain that Sandra would understand his early departure. She knew he had a lot on his mind.

He nodded at the doormen when they opened the oak

doors of the convention center. As he started his walk down the marble stairs that led to the car park, a tall, black-haired woman pushed herself off one of the decorative pillars to intercept him. He was also aware of the two large, suited men standing nearby.

"Mr McDowell, can I have a minute of your time?"

He kept walking. "I'm sorry, miss. I've got a very busy day tomorrow. If you need to make an appointment, my assistant would be more than happy to take your enquiry."

"I'd really like you to hear me out!"

He didn't look back as she called after him.

7

"Carl, the President has given the strongest possible warning to the Chinese about where America stands. He expressed the sympathy of the American people and offered cooperation on an investigation, but on the other hand made it clear that China better not step an inch further towards a military confrontation with Taiwan."

"So what options are on the table here, Admiral?"

"Without a doubt, the decision to move a carrier group into the South China Sea is an escalation in the US response. It gives the Joint Chiefs the option to aggressively defend Taiwan by air and sea, to monitor developments and, if they choose, to strike at China."

Interview with retired Admiral Jay Calloway, Counterpoint, *September 7*

Michelle stood outside the door to one of the better suites at the Jefferson Hotel. She took a deep breath, then nodded at Andrei and Erik Shadd. The two hulking Czechs counted down from three in their native tongue and at zero, Erik gave the door a heavy kick. It gave little resistance to the strength of the six and a half foot–tall behemoth.

"What the fuck?" Michelle heard from inside.

She followed Andrei and Erik into the cavernous space, lit by the torch app on one of their phones. They moved through the sitting area and into the bedroom at the same time as the bedside lamp flicked on. She sat in an armchair near the window and made sure to keep the bulk of one of the Shadd brothers between her and the bed.

She watched from the comfort of the chair as Ernest McDowell, bleary-eyed and confused, looked from her to the two men and back again. She noticed his eyes drift down to the suit jackets the brothers wore. He must have spent enough time with bodyguards to spot the tell-tale bulge of a concealed handgun.

Tap...tap...tap...Michelle said nothing, simply tapping her pen on the side table.

"Will you be tapping that damn pen all day?" McDowell exploded eventually. "Or are you going to tell me what the hell you want?"

She laid the pen on the table, then leaned forward, rested her elbows on her knees and steepled her fingers. "Ernest McDowell. Eighty-two. Married to Sandra Cheng, prominent lawyer turned socialite. Fourth marriage. One child to a previous wife. Masters in journalism and...theology?"

McDowell shrugged. "Easy subject. Left me more time to chase skirts. I'd like to congratulate you for managing to find your way to my Wikipedia profile. Who're you?"

Michelle laughed. "Quite forward. I like it. Explains the four wives. My name is Michelle Dominique."

McDowell frowned. "Whatever you want, was it entirely necessary to break into my hotel room to achieve it?"

"I gave you the chance to talk last night. Your refusal forced more drastic action, including my friends here." Technically it was true. In more normal circumstances, Michelle would have spent additional time working her way into McDowell's life. As it was, with Anton gunning for her, events in China proceeding at breakneck pace and the election just a few months away, she needed to get a move on with EMCorp. Having the brothers with her—a protection against Anton's adventures—was just a happy coincidence on occasions such as this.

He looked to Andrei and Erik again. "Fine. So what do you want?"

She stood up and walked over to the drinks cabinet. She browsed the labels before settling on the Bombay Sapphire. She turned over two glasses and poured. "Are you aware of the danger America faces today, Ernest?"

He didn't reply.

She dropped a couple of ice cubes into each glass. "Of course you are. Your papers got good mileage out of hundreds of our boys coming home from Afghanistan in pieces last year."

She poured the tonic, then carried both glasses over and handed him one, which he put on his bedside table. "I'm here to help ensure the elimination of the greatest threat to America since the terrorists we've battled for the last decade: weakness and complacency. Congress is deadlocked by the two parties fighting to be the most petty. Our financial might is in ruins. Our military is weary. Our freedoms are curbed more each year. This complacency, this weakness will lead to our destruction."

McDowell snorted, his skepticism plain on his face. "Forgive me, but this is all sounding a little Tom Clancy to me. I just run newspapers."

"Don't be a fool, Ernest. The media in this country is the hinge that great change turns on. It decides whether a president is free to act in America's interests. It shapes opinions. It changes governments and fortunes. Companies like yours remodel the world."

"They sure do." McDowell yawned. "You should get one of your own."

Michelle smiled, but didn't rise to his bait. "Today the front lines are newspapers and blogs, Twitter feeds and Facebook posts, television stations and talk-back radio. And this space is populated by sheep, but led by only a few, including you. My organization seeks to harness these assets for a greater good: making America great again."

McDowell raised an eyebrow. "Nice theory. And who exactly do you work for?"

"The Foundation for a New America." Michelle left it at that. McDowell didn't need to know about her difficulties with Anton.

"Okay. And what're you trying to achieve with this little monologue?"

"Rebirth."

He snorted. "You could just get a good man, a good bottle of red, wait nine months and you'd have your birth, miss."

"Smart. Rebirth for America. Whenever it has grown stale, America has always rejuvenated itself through war: the War of Independence, and the birth of modern America; the Civil War, and the forging of an American social identity; the Spanish–American War, and the arrival of the United States on the world stage; World Wars One and Two, and America becoming a global power; the Cold War, and America becoming the Superpower."

McDowell seemed to consider her statement carefully. "Your thesis has problems. What about Nicaragua, Lebanon, Vietnam, Iraq, Afghanistan? Wars that the US has fought, and lost. Or at least not won."

He was done with batting away her statements with bluster and derision, and was now engaging in the contest of ideas. She knew she had his interest. "Tactical missteps. America has thrived from big conflict, from the contest of big nations and big ideas."

"So what exactly are you suggesting, Ms Dominique? What's your end game?"

This was her chance. If Michelle was going to enlist McDowell and his company to her cause, she had to hit him between the eyes. It was the key to shifting the balance against Anton and ultimately prying power from him, while still keeping the Foundation intact enough to make its—*her*— run for Congressional control.

"War between the United States and the People's Republic of China." She smiled sweetly. "Then, the rejuvenation of America through dozens of my colleagues and me in Congress, able to fix the problems."

"Ah." He laughed. "Republicans? Can't beat the Democrats fairly the last few times around, so you look for the wacky way to do it? Usually I sympathize with your side of politics, miss, but I am increasingly daunted by their level of crazy."

"No, we're not Republicans, though we do hide ourselves among them for now. They loathe our message, and are equally responsible for this mess. No, Congress requires a new force."

"You're nuts." He shook his head. "Isn't there a chance that America will lose this theoretical war of yours?"

Michelle shrugged. "Empires on the wrong side of great conflicts have fallen, but America has yet to fail. What's worse? To try and fail, or to never try and be overtaken?"

"Well, whatever. But keep me out of it."

"History is on my side, Ernest. Unfortunately, technology is on yours. While the reality of America's need for war hasn't changed, the means for fighting those wars has. I've already explained how the media fits in. I'm interested in how far you're willing to go to help stamp out these problems."

"Not an inch."

Michelle sighed and signaled to Erik, who drew an envelope out of his jacket pocket and walked over to hand it to McDowell. He looked at it in confusion. "What's this?"

"This is the means for you to destroy the good Senator Mahoney. The whole nasty business of the Senate committee will just go away. If you make the right choice, it's also the way to create a greater future for your family and all Americans. The right future. The future I decide."

"And the cost?"

She rolled the dice. "Print what we tell you to, just every now and then. It will help us to stoke the right flames, and to get my colleagues and me the public support we need. Things will be fine. It won't be difficult, given what the public expects of news. Surely that's a better option than letting them ruin you and dismantle your company."

She waited and continued to sip her drink as McDowell weighed up his options. The bait in front of him must be impossibly tempting—exactly as she'd designed. She knew that with McDowell and his organization on her side, the war was nearly guaranteed, her power base against Anton would expand and the Congressional run of Michelle and the other Foundation-aligned candidates was much more likely to succeed.

"I don't see the link?"

"We create an incident, you stoke the flames, war erupts, public dissatisfied with response of President Kurzon and both major parties and clamor for change." She sighed. "You're our ticket to the party, Ernest, and I'm your ticket to destroying your enemies and keeping your company. It really is the perfect scenario."

McDowell stared at her, then placed the unopened envelope on the bed. "I'm sorry to have wasted your time breaking into my suite. I don't like being at the mercy of anyone, but given the choice, I'll try my hand with the government. At least I can see them coming. Unlike you and your friends here."

Michelle shook her head and put her empty glass on the table. She'd known that this was a strong possibility, but had hoped he'd take the easy route. "How unfortunate. I hope you don't come to regret this decision, Ernest."

❧

ERNEST WAS SEATED at a table in the Senate inquiry hearing room. In front of him was the bench from where the eleven senators would judge his fate, while behind him, the public gallery was full to bursting. He'd been offended by their stares and glared back until the EMCorp Director of Legal Affairs, Saul Alweiss, had discreetly told him that stink-eyeing the public wouldn't look great on CSPAN.

As he tapped his foot and worked his way through the day's third coffee, Ernest hated to admit that Saul was right. The wrong look and his testimony would get wall-to-wall coverage on television and in print. He didn't relish the thought. Since Saul's quiet word he'd simply stared straight ahead, sipped his coffee and showed no emotion. He couldn't help the leg shake that he'd inherited from his father.

He thought back to the invasion of his hotel room earlier that morning. While he'd initially written Michelle Dominique off as a nut, he'd done some digging. There was more to her than met the eye, including a Congressional tilt in the coming midterm elections. She clearly had some crackpot theories, so even if she could get him out of his current mire, it wouldn't be worth the cost.

"Will they get on with it any time soon?"

Alweiss smiled and leaned forward. "Usually takes them a while to get going."

"It's ten am. Don't these bastards do any work?" Ernest kept his voice down. "I'm usually well into my day by now."

While Saul had handed the first part of the hearing, Ernest was glad his time to speak had arrived. The Senate Judiciary Subcommittee on Privacy, Technology and the Law had oversight of laws and policies governing collection of information by the private sector and enforcement of privacy laws. Because of the activities of EMCorp, Ernest was squarely in their sights. Part of him was terrified about what the hearings would bring.

Alweiss placed a hand on his knee. "Keep your cool, Ernest. Everything hinges on that."

Ernest laid his palms down flat on the wooden table as the senators walked in to the room. Last to enter was Senator Mahoney, Chairman of the Subcommittee, who took his seat on the middle of the bench. As the senators settled in, Mahoney stared straight at Ernest with a large, shit-eating grin on his face. Ernest was sad that he was too old to leap the table and stab the bastard with a pen.

After a few moments of quiet chatter between the senators, Mahoney cleared his throat. His microphone carried the sound across the room well enough that most people seemed to get the point. Chatter stopped and people readied themselves for the showdown. Ernest stopped shaking his foot, put down his coffee and sat up straight in his chair. He stared at Mahoney, who started to speak.

"Good morning, everybody. I call to order the third day of the inquiry into the conduct of EMCorp within the borders of the United States." Mahoney paused, apparently for dramatic effect. "Mr McDowell, thanks for joining us this morning."

"And a good afternoon to you, too." Ernest managed to draw a few short laughs from the gallery. "Glad to be of service to the duly elected representatives of our fine democracy."

Mahoney bristled, but continued. "As you know, EMCorp, the company you chair and have a large holding in, has been embroiled in significant controversy overseas, most notably the United Kingdom. The opening two days of this inquiry heard a catalog of allegations. Our role is to determine the extent of misconduct in the US."

Ernest waited until Mahoney was done, then lifted his coffee cup and drained the contents. He looked to each of the eleven members of the committee in turn then spoke. "Nice editorial, Senator. Give me a call once you're out of politics."

Mahoney laughed. "I'll take the first question, Mr McDowell. Quite simply, can you guarantee EMCorp hasn't engaged in illegal behavior of the kind that we've seen overseas inside the United States, beyond what has already been declared?"

Ernest looked to Alweiss, who took the question. "No corporate leader could offer such a guarantee, Senator. But we're confident that, beyond what we've already disclosed to the authorities and to the markets, no further activity along those lines has occurred in the United States. The company has performed a full audit."

Mahoney tapped his pen on the bench, seemingly annoyed that Alweiss had answered the question. "While I thank your lawyer for his response, Mr McDowell, it's apparent to many people, myself included, that the level of control that your company has over the political and economic direction of this nation is far too high—"

Ernest tried to interrupt. "Sorry, Senator."

Mahoney persisted. "I was speaking, Mr McDowell. I'd actually liken it to a man, even a large one, being crushed to death by a snake. The man is this country, your company is the snake. Though the man might be strong, he has nothing to compete with the constricting strength of the snake, ever tighter."

Ernest knew he was in trouble. This was about more than potential illegal activities—it was a power play. Mahoney was playing for keeps, and despite his looming retirement, he had the power base in Washington to have a chance in the game. This was going to be the biggest fight of his professional life.

With Mahoney finished, another senator leaned in to her microphone. "Mr McDowell, do you have anything to say from the outset?"

"Yes, I do, actually, miss." Ernest paused and looked at the senator's name plate. "Sorry, Senator Woodyatt. Yes, I do."

When the senator nodded for him to proceed, Ernest

looked at Alweiss, who shook his head only a fraction. Ernest ignored it. "I find substantial levels of media ownership to be wholly compatible with the entrepreneurial spirit of this country. I started this company and it's now a global enterprise employing thousands of Americans.

"Regardless of troubles elsewhere, I'd hoped that at home, at least, EMCorp would be welcome, yet here I sit. It's a sad day indeed when such a committee can begin a witch hunt in such a manner. So let's get on with it."

Ernest sat back in his chair. Alweiss had a blank look on his face and was probably considering the weaseling he'd have to do to reverse the damage of the statement. Mahoney had an even bigger grin on his face, but the other senators seemed unconcerned. The CSPAN cameras were on Ernest and several cameras flashed.

He knew that this was going to end badly and that the committee had the power to orchestrate sweeping changes to his company. He'd seen off the EMCorp board only to run headlong into this mess. He wondered again about Michelle Dominique and her offer, before shaking his head and readying himself for the next question.

MICHELLE'S BOOTS clicked on the red bricks as she walked to the dining hall at a brisk pace. She'd spent the afternoon doing one of her occasional lectures at Georgetown University, but a flurry of student questions had made her late for a coffee date. She hated being late. The lectures were just part of the façade of legitimacy that all of the senior staff at the Foundation had to have, but they also helped with her campaign.

She looked back over her shoulder and smiled at the sight of Andrei Shadd. Though he kept a respectable distance, she had no doubt that she was well protected. Given the likelihood of a second attempt on her life by Anton, she'd made a habit of having one of the Czech brothers in tow whenever she was out. The brothers were part of the dark work that the Foundation did. There was a cell in each major US state and some foreign countries, each responsible for agitation, low-level terrorism and whatever else needed doing. Beyond that, there was an investment branch that sponsored overseas subversives, and a wet squad of ex-special forces guys. The light side was a think tank, well funded and politically hyperactive. It was involved in everything from presidential campaigns to policy advocacy and research. It looked and acted every bit the legitimate organization. It also carried a lot of punch in Washington.

As she neared the door of the Leo J. O'Donovan Dining Hall, she rubbed her hands together, trying to coax some warmth back into them. She took out her cell phone, and fired off a quick text to Andrei. *I'll need some privacy, Andrei. No interruptions unless someone hits the big red button.* A glance was all it took to see he understood. She entered the hall.

The room was abuzz with the evening undergrad rush, each seeking a slice of pizza or equally dismal fare. The tables were full with groups of students eating or doing work on their laptops. There was very little spare space, and Michelle was worried that she'd missed her appointment. She paused and looked around, then nearly jumped into the air when someone placed a hand on her shoulder.

"Sorry." Sarah McDowell flashed her white teeth and held out a cup. The dimples on her cheeks were pronounced and she was pleased with herself. "Couldn't resist."

Michelle took the coffee from Sarah with a smile and leaned in to kiss her on the cheek. "Hey, Sarah, how's it going?"

Sarah turned and nodded back toward the door. "Alright. Thought I'd get us some takeaways. It's crazy in here."

Michelle nodded. "Hey, tough break for your dad today."

The younger woman frowned, and Michelle realized she'd need to be careful. Even though Sarah McDowell seemingly took very little interest in the professional affairs of her father and his business empire, she was still a loving and loyal daughter. Michelle risked poisoning the well of opportunity with misplaced words.

"They didn't give him a chance." Sarah pushed the door open and Michelle followed her outside. "He's going to get crucified."

Michelle glanced toward Andrei, who'd had the foresight to sit well away from the dining hall. "How many days of questioning does he have?"

Sarah brushed her blond hair behind her head. "At least a couple, his assistant tells me. Peter isn't usually wrong."

They walked together in silence for a few moments, past the law building and toward the center of the Georgetown campus. While parts of her plan were ticking along nicely, her efforts to recruit McDowell to her cause had been a massive failure. For now, at least. The inquiry had been hotter than she'd expected, so she retained some hope.

Sarah broke the silence. "How was your lecture?"

"It was alright. First time I've spoken on terrorism since my PhD, so I think I was a bit rusty. But they had an appetite for it, given everything that's happening in China."

Sarah nodded and frowned. "What was the gist of it?"

"Outrage about the attacks in China on one hand, the need for us to stand beside Taiwan and renew our focus on the threat of terrorism on the other. My political advisors thought it would be a good idea to get some talking points on the record."

"Dad lost some staff over there. You must have heard."

Michelle feigned surprise. Since meeting Sarah at a gallery opening, she'd gone to huge effort to avoid expressing much knowledge of EMCorp. Sarah knew only that she was a conservative, and involved in politics. Sarah was studying art, and they'd become decent enough friends.

"How's that guy you've been seeing?"

"No good." Sarah seemed content to leave it at that.

Michelle nodded and took a sip of her coffee. The effort to

divest Sarah of her infatuation with a transfer student from the Wharton Business School had been worth it. He'd had too much husband potential for Michelle to allow the relationship to flourish. It was a shame he'd refused to take a hint, and she'd had to destroy his reputation. His promising career was now in ruins. He'd also never marry Sarah and be in the box seat for control of EMCorp. Michelle didn't like surprises, and the boyfriend had been one of those. Her relationship with Sarah was insurance against McDowell making the wrong choices.

8

In scenes nearly as vocal as those playing out in the South China Sea, the United States Senate Judiciary Subcommittee on Privacy, Technology and the Law spent a seventh day grilling Ernest McDowell, Chief Executive Officer of EMCorp. Sources from inside the company told Business Daily that many company executives expect it to be broken up, or other significant measures to be taken, to reduce its dominance in the US and global media market. Mr McDowell, looking more distressed by the day, was angered when the Committee chairman, Senator Patrick Mahoney, asked what should be done with his company, replying, "Nothing."

Francis McKay, Business Daily, *September 14*

E rnest had waited for hours in the most modern office he'd ever seen. It had angular chairs, an odd lamp, a coffee table shaped like a lightning bolt and all manner of other visual dross. It was lucky for the manufacturers that people paid a fortune for such crap, because he figured that once the business community came to its senses, a whole lot of furniture makers would be out of a living.

He lifted his coffee, took a mouthful then placed the cup down carefully on the lightning bolt. He was tired and knew that she was deliberately making him wait, to get him off guard and angry. But he had no control, so there was no sense in a tantrum. All the delay did was give him time to reflect on the disaster the last week had been. Although the Committee clearly had an agenda and a giant axe to grind, the previous night he'd been dealt the killer blow: a call from a despondent Saul Alweiss. He hadn't beaten around the bush—Saul had found proof within EMCorp of fresh phone hacking in the United States; it was only a matter of time before the evidence was discovered by the Senate inquiry; and if he was a religious man, he should start praying for deliverance. It made Ernest's testimony and denials at the inquiry worthless.

Eventually the door to the office opened with a mechanical whir. Michelle Dominique walked through the door and feigned surprise. "Ernest, nice of you to visit."

He snorted and doubted very much she'd been oblivious to his presence, but he kept the thought to himself. He had to admit that she was dressed to kill. Her black hair flowed over her shoulders in a way that made him think of Medusa and her snakes. Her white blouse and black skirt took none of the attention away from her legs, which were bound by knee-high black leather boots.

He shook her outstretched hand. "If I didn't know any better, I'd think you spent the last hour dressing to distract me."

"Hardly, you're a married man. And I have no desire to be wife number, what is it—five?" She smirked and nodded her head in the direction of her office. "Let's go in here."

He said nothing as they crossed the waiting area and entered her office. Clearly she had different tastes in furniture to whoever was responsible for the waiting area, with hardwood the order of the day. He couldn't deny that her view of the Washington Mall was spectacular as well, as she sat in a brown leather lounge chair and he sat opposite.

Her eyes were locked on to his. "I must admit I don't have any idea why you're here. I thought we left things fairly concrete in your hotel."

"I've changed my mind about your proposal. I'm in. Limited editorial control as long as you can make my little problem go away, as you inferred."

She laughed at him and his heart sank. "Do you make a habit of trying to revive the dead, Ernest? Strange fetish, and to each their own, I suppose. But I'm afraid our business is concluded. Events and my plans have moved on without you."

Ernest had expected this. He'd declined her attempts to control him and his company prior to the Senate hearing, and things had only become worse since. He was now at her mercy, and would have to fight hard to secure whatever terms she deemed to give. In terms of the balance of power, he was the Japan to her United States, circa 1945, and a couple of his cities had just been nuked.

"There must be something I could do that would change your mind. I'm desperate."

She winked. "Oh Ernest! You flatter! I'm sure that plenty of bright, beautiful young things have asked similar of you in the past, and you've been all too happy to take them up on it. But I'm afraid I'm not interested in old men in that way, no matter how rich."

He ignored her jibe. "I'm prepared to offer more than you previously asked for in return for your support."

Michelle leaned back in her seat and looked up to the ceiling. "Well, that's a different story."

She didn't immediately decline, as he'd expected. Instead, she seemed to consider her next move carefully. He was anxious. The next few minutes and the direction of the conversation would change much in Ernest's life, one way or another.

She looked back at him. "I'm still going to decline. You

rejected me, put all your chips on black, and the big green zero has come up. I've moved on, I suggest you do the same."

He looked at her in desperation. "The committee is going to split up my company, Ms Dominique. They'll ruin me and tear it apart."

She shrugged and stood. "As I said they would. Not my problem, Ernest. You had your chance, blew it, and there's no hard feelings. But you can't really expect me to backtrack now things have become worse for you."

Ernest felt it all start to slip away. Decades of working to acquire, spread, fine tune and protect his media empire. Countless birthdays and anniversaries missed. Friends and relationships sacrificed. Billions of dollars of profit and loss. His empire, his life. Within days, it would be broken up and all but destroyed.

"I don't believe for a second you've given up on your efforts to control my company, Ms Dominique. Not after such a fine speech in my hotel room."

She laughed. "I was head of the debating team in college, Ernest, I say a lot of persuasive things. Having you on side would have helped, but we've moved past this."

"I want the deal."

He looked up at her and she stared back, a look of pity in her eyes. "Oh, very well. I'm prepared to offer you the same deal on my part. I will, in essence, save your behind."

"You won't regret it." He exhaled loudly. "You've lifted a weight off my shoulders."

"I'm not finished." She leaned forward. "My part of the bargain hasn't changed. Yours, however, will be very different— my price for your delay in accepting."

He'd expected something like this, but was glad she'd listened to his pleas. "Okay. Name it and it's yours."

He felt some of his confidence disappear when she grinned at him.

MICHELLE KNEW SHE HAD HIM. Sitting in front of her was a man at his most desperate. He was facing the crushing reality of the Senate inquiry going against him, and he'd do just about anything to save his company.

She needed to get him under control, but also reduce his ability to go against the agreement they were about to make. She could have asked for the beating heart of his daughter—his heir—and he might have given it up. Thankfully for Sarah McDowell, Ernest's daughter was already under control. Michelle had other targets in mind to further reduce his options. At the same time, she had to keep up the façade of negotiation. She leaned back in her seat. He was still in the same position, as if he feared that by moving, even an inch, he'd break the tenuous chance of a deal between them and be cast adrift into the maelstrom of uncertainty.

"The deal has changed, Ernest."

"What're your terms, then?"

Michelle readied herself. There was a small chance that he'd be so outraged that he'd simply walk out. She doubted it though. It was a bet on his love for his company over his love for his family. With Sarah McDowell in her camp, she now needed to deal with the stock holding of Sandra Cheng. It was time to test his resolve and tighten the screws.

"You divorce your wife."

His head shot up and his eyes flared in protest. "Divorce my wife? She's nothing to you, a non-practicing lawyer who's spent more time in hospital than by my side in recent months. That's ridiculous."

Michelle shrugged. "Those are my terms."

She watched as he processed her words. No doubt he felt her reasons were petty, designed merely to inflict pain for his initial recalcitrance. But that couldn't be further from the truth. Michelle never relied on others, not entirely, and as soon as she'd locked her sights on EMCorp, she'd developed plans to control it, with or without Ernest McDowell. That meant befriending Sarah McDowell, removing Sandra Cheng and the Foundation buying stock of its own at the right time.

"There must be something else." He leaned forward, desperation in his eyes. "You can't force me to destroy my family to save my company. I don't understand what you gain."

Michelle was enjoying his rambling, but she had had enough. She decided it was time to push. "There are no other conditions that I'm interested in considering, Ernest. You asked for this meeting, not me, and you're welcome to use the door over there. If you do, be sure to pass on my best to the senator and his colleagues. But if you are interested in the deal, you need to decide right now. My patience is at an end."

His bluster disappeared and he cradled his head in his hands. "Is that really what it's going to take?"

"Afraid so."

He seemed to consider her terms for a long few moments, then sighed. "You've got a deal. Get rid of the Senate inquiry. Once they're off my back, I'll do what you ask."

Michelle smiled. "I don't like the precedent of you dictating terms, but in this case they're fair enough. I'll get things in motion tonight, and the inquiry should be history in a day or two. But you best hold up your end when the time comes. I think you understand the extremes to which I'm able to project my displeasure."

"Indeed."

"You can start with having a front page editorial in the *Standard* tomorrow, calling for America to protect Taiwan, deploy assets, recognition—all that jazz. A sign of goodwill."

He grunted, stood and exited without another word. Now that she had him, Michelle would have to act swiftly to hold up her end of the bargain. It would have been much easier to make the Senate inquiry go away before it had convened, but now things were underway, far more drastic action was needed.

She knew that the conspiracy theorists would look back in decades to come and point at the events as an example of the power of corporate America. As usual, she mused darkly, they'd miss the point entirely. The deaths, the professional ruin, all would be orchestrated behind the scenes, with no possible link back to the Foundation.

Things were moving, and it was time for her to make her final push. Shanghai had been a success, EMCorp was in her pocket, war was looking likely and the election was soon.

There were only a few things left to do.

JACK STOOD on the observation platform high above the flight deck of the USS *George Washington*. This was one of several times in the past few days that he'd watched in awe as men and women in brightly colored vests moved without apparent pattern around the deck. Yet the more he watched, the more he saw the routine—the choreography of jets taking off and landing under careful instruction. It mesmerized him.

Jack was only now starting to appreciate the sheer force that the carrier, with all its planes and attendant ships, allowed the United States Navy to project. He felt as if this ship would be enough to stop one nation, injured and angry, from striking at another, frightened but defiant. It really was proof that weapons built for war could help to enforce peace between nations.

The clear night sky provided the perfect backdrop for his thoughts, complete with full moon and millions of stars. The observation platform had become his second home on board the ship whenever he wasn't working, a place where he could be alone and think. It was one of the few places on the ship where that was possible, home as it was to thousands of men and women.

Tonight, as he stared out into the night, he was grateful

that nobody else was nearby. Between the roar of the jets taking off or landing every few minutes, he thought of many things. He thought of Erin, of Shanghai, of work and of life. He was proud that he'd so far managed to avoid the bottle, but didn't like the introspection that sobriety forced. He wasn't quite ready for the decisions that came next in many parts of his life.

He leaned on the rail for a few more minutes while his mind wandered. Then he heard the screech of the bulkhead door behind him as someone pushed it open. He involuntarily tensed at the intrusion.

"Hi, Jack. You've been out here for hours. I think the admiral is going to send out a search party if you don't surface soon."

Jack continued to stare straight ahead. He sensed her move closer, nearly close enough to touch him. Celeste stopped and settled in a spot just behind him, slightly to his left. He was glad that the roar of another plane taking off conveniently overwhelmed the awkward silence.

"Impressive, isn't it?"

He shrugged. "Probably enough to conquer some countries."

"Mightn't be enough though. The Chinese seem pretty pissed."

Another pause. "Sorry, but is there something you wanted, Celeste?"

Her voice quivered slightly. "I'm sorry. I shouldn't have told you what she said."

Jack turned to face her. She was looking up at the sky. He exhaled loudly. "You've done nothing to be sorry for. I've been a dick."

"No, you haven't, Jack. You're allowed to feel and act any way you want right now. Your whole world has been thrown upside down."

He reached out and grabbed hold of her shoulders. When

she didn't look at him, he squeezed her shoulders slightly. Finally, she turned. "Celeste, I'm sorry."

She smiled weakly and pulled away a little. "I was just checking my emails. I had one from Jo. He's telling us to change slant on this one and ramp up the focus on Taiwanese nationalism and how important it is for the US to support it—to a ridiculous extent."

Jack laughed. "Welcome to the company. Not often we get told which way the wind blows, but Ernest can be pretty bloody convincing."

She frowned. "I don't believe Ernest is *that* explicit about his agenda. I mean, I've heard stories, but—"

"They're true." Jack shrugged. "He's a ruthless bastard and we write what he tells us to write whenever he's interested enough to tell us. It's worse than that, in this case. I spoke to Jo an hour ago on the sat phone."

"Oh?"

"He gave me the same message that you got in the email. They're running with a pretty explosive editorial tomorrow—a demand for pre-emptive US strikes to keep Chinese brinksmanship in check. He also told me it's straight from the top."

Celeste walked over to the rail of the observation deck. "Are they trying to start a war?"

Jack shrugged. "Don't worry too much. Even though there's a war brewing, it's being held in check by this very ship. I'll take the lead on the reports, you just help me with the background. I won't make you write the piece that sparks the powder keg."

"Thanks." She looked relieved.

Jack turned to go inside the carrier just as everything around him went bright and a shockwave hit him. As he stumbled and fell, he heard the explosion and Celeste cry out. He managed to brace, but he still landed hard on the deck. His ears started to ring with a high-pitched whine.

He felt the cold steel of the walkway on his cheek. He tried to move, but couldn't. He was not sure how long he lay there, stunned, but it was long enough for the whine in his ears to subside. Through the gap in the safety rail, he could see several fires burning on the far side of the flight deck. The flames combined with the dozens of flashing red LEDs to light the night sky in a hellish scene. Men and women screamed.

Jack lifted his head and looked at Celeste. She hadn't moved. He was about to try to get to his feet when everything went black.

ACT II

9

While it's unclear exactly what's taken place aboard the USS George Washington, to have a US carrier stranded in such a hot zone is a difficult situation. We've already seen the Chinese scramble aircraft, claiming that the carrier is in its territorial waters and demanding it leave or be towed to a Chinese port—two outcomes the US would fight hard to avoid. The situation with the carrier adds more kindling to an already heated situation with China and Taiwan.

Hiroshi Kawahara, Asashi Shinbun, *September 15*

J ack's shoes clanked on the steel floor of the long, straight corridor. It was as if with each step the carrier was groaning again at the punishment it had taken. His nostrils were filled with the heady mix of burning rubber, insulation and electrical wire. Though most of the fires were out, the stink remained.

He was taking things slowly. Although he'd been let out of the infirmary with a few stitches and some aspirin, his head still ached. He couldn't blame the doctors for being more concerned about the real casualties—those with burns and shrapnel—than with his cut lip and sore head. Celeste had likewise been released.

"Step aside!"

Jack moved to the wall and sank into it as much as the cold, hard steel would allow. He waited as a small team of men and women rushed past him without a glance in his direction. In the hours since the attack on the *Washington*, the same crew he'd watched maneuver jet planes had worked to put out fires or clean up debris.

Once the path was clear, he walked through a final bulkhead and up a small flight of stairs. He paused at the top and looked around at the banks of computers. Harried-looking men and women were crowded around several of the terminals. Above it all, on a raised platform, sat Admiral McCulloch. He looked like a man in control.

"Permission to come aboard, Admiral?" Jack spoke loudly enough that the man in the chair looked his way.

"Ah, Mr Emery." McCulloch smiled. "Granted."

He stepped into the Combat Information Center, which felt strangely untouched by the attack. He walked to where McCulloch sat and wondered when the man had last slept. Nonetheless, McCulloch's aura of authority amazed Jack. He'd half expected chaos. Instead, all was calm, though the ship was listless and pathetic.

"Bad time, Admiral?"

McCulloch gestured for Jack to sit next to him in the executive officer's vacant seat. "As good a time as any. Glad you're okay, though. You had a fall?"

Jack shrugged. "Not too bad. Any idea what happened?"

McCulloch sighed. "Off the record? Chinese sub. A new one. Got right inside our guard, kicked us in the balls and got away again."

Jack's eyes widened. He knew a scoop when he heard one. "Anything for me on the record?"

McCulloch laughed. "You crazy? I'm not giving you your

next Pulitzer. If I say a word, and you print it, the nukes might start flying. I'm no coward, but I don't want to be stranded here if that happens. The Pentagon isn't saying shit. I think they might still be in shock. And if they're not talking, neither am I."

"Fair enough, Admiral. You should know, though, that the word from my superiors is to talk up Taiwanese independence, the outrageous actions of China, and so on."

McCulloch snorted. "That's going to do wonders for our health and wellbeing."

"Hopefully we won't be here to find out."

"I wouldn't count on it. We're sitting ducks. We've lost all propulsion and we're trying to patch a great big hole in the side of the ship. We're afloat but going nowhere soon."

Jack was staggered to think about the amount of damage required to bring such a large ship to a halt. If the explosion had been caused by a Chinese submarine attack, as McCulloch had suggested, it represented a massive increase in the stakes. It wouldn't take much more to trigger a war. Jack was surprised it hadn't already happened.

"Why are you telling me this, Admiral?"

"Posterity, son. I've seen too many of my contemporaries hang from the rafters after the fact. I want this documented, and I want history to remember we tried to avoid a war."

Jack smiled. "I can do that."

"Good. The Joint Chiefs have ordered the USS *John C Stennis* to make a beeline from the Persian Gulf, but it will take a while to get here. The USS *Nimitz* is halfway to Norfolk for its refit but has turned around. Nothing is close enough right now."

"So there's no help coming?"

"Oh, we've always got stuff in town. Some air power out of Japan and Guam. Some subs and surface boats. We've got enough to deny the Chinese sea control, if it comes to that, but we can't project power or do a lot of the things we usually take for granted."

"Who knew it would be this easy?"

"That's the problem with steaming full speed ahead into somebody else's war." McCulloch sighed. "Sometimes they don't like it when you appear on the horizon."

"At least we've got a mini-Air Force on board."

McCulloch stared at him blankly. "You haven't noticed the silence? The torpedo took out some pretty important widgets. My engineers are working on it, but all those jets are shiny paperweights unless we can get this tub fixed."

Jack's mouth went dry as he realized the implications—the carrier was static and had no air power umbrella. It didn't seem like a winning proposition. "Will the Chinese attack again?"

"I can't see why they would. They've proven their new nuke subs can get inside our defenses. There's no need to show off and spike the ball in the end zone."

One of the radio operators cut in. "Incoming transmission, sir. Chairman of the Joint Chiefs."

"Patch it through to my phone, Mr Jones." McCulloch turned to Jack. "You'll need to excuse me, son."

Jack nodded and stood. Clearly McCulloch was not going to start speaking to his boss until Jack had left the CIC, so he made his way out of the room as quickly as he could. McCulloch and his crew had been more than welcoming, and he didn't want to push his luck at a sensitive time.

He snaked his way back through the ship to his cabin. On the way, he saw more evidence of damage and the crews trying hard to fix it. Jack did his best to stay out of their way and at a respectful distance. He reached his cabin, kicked off his shoes and sprawled out on his narrow bed. He closed his eyes.

Jack's eyes shot open and he sat up in confusion when there was a knock on the door. He'd obviously fallen asleep. "Come in."

He rose to his feet as McCulloch entered and gestured for Jack to remain seated. "No need to get up."

"Admiral? What can I do for you?"

McCulloch sighed. "I need to get a few things on the record, for use if and when this little party gets kicking."

Jack frowned. "What do you mean?"

"My call was from the Chairman of the Joint Chiefs. The Chinese are insisting that we've drifted into their waters following the 'accident' and demanding we either abandon ship, allow them to rescue us or leave their waters."

Jack saw where this was heading. "I'm guessing there's a few problems with most of those options."

"You could say that. We're not moving without a tow truck, we're not letting them on board and we're certainly not abandoning a few billion dollars' worth of carrier that easily."

"So what can I do for you, Admiral?"

"I want it recorded that the Joint Chiefs have told us there's nothing close enough to defend us, but that our orders are to hold the airspace if at all possible. They've also expressly forbidden us from entertaining any options of surrender or compromise. I'm just starting to feel like we're the tripwire here. I'll need you to capture a few things."

Jack nodded. "I'll get my gear."

"*Good morning, New York, this is Dan Cuperino with your news on the hour.*"

Ernest opened his eyes with a groan. He resisted all temptation to throw the alarm clock across the room, or even to whack it a few times with his fist. Sandra stirred next to him and hugged in close, her head resting on his chest as he wrapped his arms around her. She was asleep again in a second despite the noise of the radio, an ability he never failed to marvel at.

"*First this morning, there is shock around the capital as news of the arrest of Democratic Senator Patrick Mahoney on fraud and perjury charges surfaces. Early reports indicate that the arrest stems from testimony the senator gave to the Supreme Court nearly a decade ago, which DC police are now saying they can prove was false. We'll have more on this as details come to hand."*

Ernest closed his eyes as his head spun. While he'd known that something like this was coming, he hadn't expected it to come so quickly. He was surprised that Dominique had held up her end of the bargain quite so boldly. Whatever her means, it was impossible to doubt her efficiency. Less than twenty-four hours after he'd agreed to her terms, she'd delivered.

Ernest turned the radio off and rolled onto his side. He scooped his wife closer into a hug, having not yet quite come to terms with the cost of saving his company. Mahoney was now the least of his concerns. He held Sandra tight, and she mumbled a little and stirred in his arms, but not enough to indicate any discomfort. He held her for several minutes, thoughts and options racing around his brain.

He knew Dominique would get everything she wanted: editorial control of his company whenever she desired and effective control over him. She'd have the means to influence, if not outright control, public opinion all over the world. It was a power Ernest had used at times, but soon it would be in her hands, not his.

The loss of his wife was a cost nearly too great to pay. But he knew, deep down, that it was no choice for him. His wives had come and gone, but the one constant in his life had been EMCorp. He had spent half a century building his empire, and it would be impossible for him to enter the last years of his life without it. It was his legacy. If given the choice, it was no choice at all.

She'd been a fine wife, the best of them all, by far. Intelligent, beautiful, resourceful and discreet, she'd been by his side during some of the more difficult years of his professional life. He wanted to hold her for days, weeks even, before delivering the news. She'd be shattered. Her whole life had been put on hold for their marriage. He'd compensate Sandra well.

He leaned over to check the time, and was surprised that a full hour had passed since the news. He hugged Sandra a little tighter and she snuggled in closer. He knew that this would be the last time he'd ever hold his wife, and possibly the last time he'd ever hold a woman, given his age. He'd never been the sort to procure sexual comfort through financial means, and he'd vowed years ago to never marry again.

He slid his feet into the slippers that waited on the floor like obedient pets. His back ached and his head hurt as he shuffled off to the shower. Sandra didn't even stir. She was used to his early starts and wouldn't rise for a few more hours yet, snoozing in blissful ignorance about the bomb he would be dropping on their relationship later in the day. He could have told her now, but whether from cowardice or altruism, he decided it would wait. When he closed the door to the ensuite, he felt like he was closing the door on part of his life. Whatever her motivation, Michelle Dominique had achieved what she wanted. Ernest had grave fears for the future of his company and the United States of America. The woman was now in charge of the greatest media company in the world, about to start a war and might even get a bunch of her people into Congress.

He ran the shower. When it was hot he stripped off his pajamas, stepped inside and closed the door. The hot water did nothing to wipe away the disgust he felt at himself, but he was resigned to his decision. Later in the day, he'd phone Sandra and tell her, then let Dominique know. In coming days, he'd organize a settlement, Sandra would move out with a lot of cash and he'd be free to get on with his life, minus his heart.

He was a man in control of his company again, or at least partially. Yet he felt nothing but dread.

~

MICHELLE WONDERED what it felt like to live in the White House and to work in the Oval Office—to sleep, eat and work within the four walls of one building, albeit an impressive one, leaving only under heavy guard for stage-managed occasions and the rare, discreet, family holiday.

While she knew that it was refurnished in line with each new president's tastes, there were also leftovers from past administrations, such as the original *Resolute* desk, a gift from Queen Victoria and made from the timbers of a nineteenth-century British frigate. The sense of duty and the burden of history must feel overwhelming to anyone who sat at that desk. From there, wars had been started, waged and finished. Economies had been changed at the stroke of a pen. Rights given or taken away. Great social achievements in education, health, taxation and social welfare made.

She didn't think that President Philip Kurzon was a garish man, or overly comfortable with the trappings of his wealth or power. She'd visited him in this office a few times during his first five years in office. Initially, he'd made minimal changes—a new rug, some curtains. But now into his second term, he'd redecorated.

Instead of opting for the less informal couches, she was surprised the President had elected to sit at his desk, with Michelle opposite. She was sure it was a bad precedent for him to lean back in his chair, feet resting on the century old desk, but he didn't seem to care.

"Ms Dominique, if I'm going to lead my country into its biggest war in eighty years—with a disgraced senator on my plate to boot—I'd ask you not to judge my posture."

It certainly looked like events were taking a toll on him. While the news about the USS *George Washington* had had half a day to sink in, it would still be a shock to the United States' political establishment for weeks to come.

"Of all the men in all of the offices in the world, you're the most entitled to have your feet on the desk, or anywhere you damn please, if you'll excuse me." It was late in the evening, and she was probably not his last appointment. When she'd called to ask to see him, she'd taken what she could get. Despite the power of the Foundation, and its tendrils that spread through all aspects of life in the capital, she was still sitting opposite the most powerful man in the world.

"I'm too used to snapping at my doctor and my wife." Kurzon smiled. "Now what is it I can do for you, Ms Dominique? I was surprised to see you in my diary."

Michelle had no doubt about that. Though she'd met him a few times on Foundation business, it had always been alongside Anton. That was precisely why she was here. Anton had refused to meet with her, and every other effort she'd made to get him out of his compound had been unsuccessful. Despite that setback, she had received some good news earlier—confirmation that McDowell had told his wife about the divorce.

"I wanted to meet with you personally, Mr President, to say the Foundation and all of its resources will be supporting the war effort."

He laughed. "All of your resources, Ms Dominique? I understand that Anton Clark is still the head honcho of your group of hatchet men."

Michelle didn't rise to the bait. "I'm working on that."

He exhaled deeply. "Besides, I'm not sure I need placards and megaphones right now, or an out-of-date sense of American exceptionalism."

She bristled. "You may not share our views, Mr President, but there's a lot of candidates in the upcoming midterms who do. You know that."

"Yourself included, if you win your seat?" He waved his hand, as though to shoo her retort away. "I don't listen to wingnuts like you. You're so far to the extreme right of the Republican Party that you aren't even really welcome on your side of the aisle. If they think you're nuts, Ms Dominique, why should I listen?"

"With respect, sir, all matters of ideology, policy and priorities must be put aside at times like this. You should know that you have the full support of the entire nation in what's to come. The attack on the *Washington* strikes to the core of America's place in Asia and the world."

"Noble sentiments, but not overly realistic, I'm afraid. We still don't know the motive for the attack on the carrier. I hope to avoid war."

"Now you're being fooli—"

"No. War isn't guaranteed. I wish everyone would stop acting like it is. The best result would be for the Chinese to back down and let a proper investigation take place. The evidence linking Taiwan to the attacks is tenuous, but there may even be a case for us just surrendering the field and letting them have Taiwan."

"War is guaranteed, Mr President. That is, if you want your country ascendant, your economy strong and your legacy secure."

He waved his hand. "At any rate, I've ordered other assets to the region, and the Air Force has deployed aircraft to Taiwan itself. I hope they won't be needed."

Michelle pursed her lips in thought. If Kurzon had forward deployed a significant number of troops onto the island, war was inevitable. China wouldn't take a backward step while US troops were in town, nor would the US concede, especially after the incident with the *Washington*.

She leaned forward in her seat. "They will be, Mr President. You simply cannot allow an attack on a United States Navy aircraft carrier to go unanswered."

As soon as he nodded, Michelle knew the tinderbox that would set the world on fire was waiting to be lit.

10

There's been significant fallout in Washington following the arrest of Senator Patrick Mahoney, chairman of the Senate Judiciary Subcommittee on Privacy, Technology and the Law inquiry into the activities of EMCorp. The newly appointed chairwoman of the inquiry, Senator Lyn Eddings, raised eyebrows this morning when she hinted that it may be abandoned outright.

"After our initial hearings, which included a substantial interview with Mr McDowell, we must consider whether there's sufficient evidence of misconduct to continue with an inquiry," Senator Eddings said. "Senator Mahoney had certain views on the viability of the inquiry, and it's true to say that some of my colleagues and I have a somewhat divergent view."

Frank Parzinkas, Your News Today, *September 16*

J ack continued to stare straight down the barrel of the small camcorder, which Celeste wielded with some difficulty, given her injured arm. "For all the latest from aboard the USS *George Washington*, join us on the *New York Standard* live video blog at twelve noon eastern for a Q&A session."

Celeste laughed as she lowered the camera. "One take. You'd think you'd done this before!"

"A few times. Blame the fusion of media." Jack scratched his nose, which had been itchy for the entire three-minute spot. "Used to be a newspaper was a newspaper."

"Delivered by horse and cart?" Celeste smirked.

Jack punched her arm gently. "Cute. Now we're a newspaper, with video, blogs, chatrooms and forums. And that doesn't even include the social media guys."

He started to walk back toward the heavy steel door that would lead them back inside the confines of the *Washington*. Celeste followed alongside, fiddling with the playback on the camera and watching his clip over again.

"Want to get a bite?" Celeste didn't look up from the camera. "Fish fingers tonight."

Jack smiled. "Sounds tempting, but no. I want to get some sleep."

The short video was just part of his day's work, the cherry on top of a two thousand–word feature he'd written for Josefa. Since the word had come down to push the Taiwan independence angle, Jack had been working up the piece, which would be on the front page of the *Standard*.

Jack was disturbed by the silence as they walked to the door. Though activity on the flight deck had slowly increased, the ship wasn't fully fighting fit, with bilge pumps working to clear away the water the carrier had taken on. The sight of the escorts on the horizon made him feel any better. The fleet was still well protected.

As Jack reached out to the door handle, klaxons started to wail and red LED lights flashed up and down the deck. "Bandits inbound! All hands to station."

Celeste cursed as she dropped the camera and grabbed his arm. "What the fuck now? Can't they just leave us alone?"

"We need to move!" Jack wrapped his arm around her and

hurried her away from the door. "We need to get to the chopper."

In his mind, Jack rehearsed the scenario that one of the carrier's junior officers had taken them through the previous day. McCulloch hadn't wanted to risk the two of them being aboard the carrier in the event of another attack, so Jack had been briefed about exactly what to do if the fireworks started again. He'd been told in no uncertain terms that flashing lights and alarms meant it was time to go.

They sprinted to the helipad as quickly as they could, careful to stay out of the path of the aircraft that were beginning to ramp up their engines. If the Chinese were inbound, McCulloch would want everything in the air, including the MH-60R Seahawk that would ferry the few non-essentials aboard the ship to safety.

"Just stick together and we'll be okay." Jack looked at Celeste, who nodded. "The group is designed to swat away any attack."

When they reached the squat gray Seahawk, it already had its rotors firing. The helicopter was surrounded with seamen loading the few passengers it was assigned to carry. As Jack and Celeste drew closer, the junior officer who'd briefed him on the process the day earlier waved him in. Jack pointed Celeste to the door of the helicopter and ran over to the lieutenant.

The lieutenant had to raise his voice to be heard. "We've got a whole load of Chinese bombers inbound, under heavy escort. We're sending you to the USS *Shiloh*. It's smaller than the carrier, so less likely to get painted by an anti-ship missile. It's also got more fireworks than a Chinese New Year to keep you safe. You'll be fine over there, sir."

"Thanks! Stay safe." He had to shout.

The other man smiled. "Been about seventy years since one of these tubs was sunk."

Jack nodded and ran for the helicopter. He reached the door and was pulled aboard by a crew member, who slid the door shut. Jack took a seat next to Celeste and looked over at her, but she didn't move and continued to stare straight ahead. He placed a hand on her knee and gave it a slight squeeze.

The crew member who'd helped Jack aboard walked over to them with a practiced ease, his hand held out. "Here, take these."

Jack took the two sets of large headphones. "What're they for?"

"Knowledge. You guys are reporters, right? So report. If shit goes bad here, the world is going to need to know. Just don't tell anyone I gave those to you."

Jack nodded as the wheels lifted off the deck. He placed the headset over his ears as the crew member returned to his seat. He held out the other headset for Celeste. She took it, but left them on her lap for the time being. The helicopter banked, and his ears were assaulted with radio reports from what could only be the fleet combat information center, its various ships and aircraft squadrons.

After a few minutes, he started to understand the gist of what was happening. It frightened him. He eased back into his seat and listened as the reports rolled in.

"One hundred and ninety-seven bandits at extreme range, and more every second."

"Squadrons, check in."

"Royal Maces, en route and on point."

"Diamondbacks, ready to engage."

"Eagles launching."

"Dambusters, awaiting takeoff."

Jack did the arithmetic in his head and felt trapped. No matter how mighty the carrier and its battle group, if they could only get a squadron or two in place before the Chinese started firing their missiles, he knew that bad things were going to follow. He looked out the window of the Seahawk and saw nothing but blue ocean. There was nowhere to run.

"All assets, this is Admiral McCulloch. You're about to get a little taste of how General Custer felt at Little Big Horn. Let's swat as many of these bastards as we can. Good luck."

Jack wondered how anyone could stay so calm in such a situation, with the safety of thousands resting on his shoulders. But the admiral's southern twang was somehow reassuring. In the minutes that followed, the radio chatter was mostly concerned with ships and aircraft getting into position for what was to come. As the number of Chinese aircraft inbound continued to rise, it was clear that the US forces were outgunned.

Jack turned to Celeste. "It's beginning." She looked over at him and nodded, placing her headset on as the helicopter banked again.

"Mr President." Jack recognized the call sign for the *Washington*. "This is Mace Prime, we've got what you could call a target-rich environment, over. Permission to engage?"

McCulloch's voice boomed in his headset. "Denied. Do not fire until fired upon or until they enter our threat box. Our rules of engagement are ironclad."

Jack wasn't sure about holding fire until you had a couple of hundred missiles coming your way, but nor was he a three-star admiral. He also understood McCulloch's reluctance to start World War Three unless absolutely necessary. Historians would be discussing McCulloch's actions for decades to come.

The minutes ticked away. Then McCulloch cut into the radio feed. "Right, they're in the threat box, put them down."

Jack heard acceptance of the order from both flight leaders and the fleet gunnery officers. Soon after, the radio was awash with confirmation of missiles being fired by both sides. Reports of aircraft running empty of missiles started to roll in, and other voices reported the fleet escorts were filling the air with defensive missiles. Still the Chinese missiles kept coming.

McCulloch spoke a second later. "All assets shift focus to the missiles. Disengage from the Chinese birds and protect the group."

Celeste grabbed Jack's hand as he closed his eyes and listened to the radio. He hadn't felt this helpless since Afghanistan, when he'd been in a convoy that had been attacked by insurgents. Surrounded, he'd had to wait in a Humvee while the Marines he was embedded with drove off the threat.

He opened his eyes and saw the deck of the cruiser USS *Shiloh* come into sight out of the window of the Seahawk. It seemed serene, stationary in the water as its two vertical missile launchers fired for the final time, then radioed that they were as dry at the rest of the fleet.

"Fire all close in defense!" McCulloch shouted over the radio, in a tone that made events sound pretty bleak. "Everything you've got, people."

There was a muffled boom in the distance. Nobody on the helicopter said a word, but many screamed or gritted their teeth. There was a second boom, closer, as the helicopter started to descend onto the deck of the *Shiloh*. Others followed. It was impossible to tell whether it was Chinese missiles being shot down, or US ships being hit.

"Attention all assets, this is Admiral McCulloch. The *Washington* has been hit twice and breached. We're abandoning ship. USS *Shiloh* has the command."

Jack began to wonder if he was living the last few moments of his life. He was reassured as the deck of the *Shiloh* came into view, a hundred feet below.

He turned to Celeste and smiled. "We'll be okay."

She smiled back.

The window outside the Seahawk lit up as the *Shiloh* exploded, and a huge ball of flame climbed into the air toward the Seahawk. Jack was driven back into his seat as the pilot banked and climbed again. He smelled smoke. He turned his head to find the Seahawk was aflame, a massive hole in the rear of the aircraft.

The helicopter lost altitude in seconds. Jack could do

nothing but squeeze Celeste's knee as the Seahawk ploughed into the South China Sea.

~

ERNEST'S private office in the penthouse of the *New York Standard* building was unique. From this office, decisions had been made that had changed the world. He'd helped governments to rise and to fall, influenced public opinion, and moderated the trends and fashions of whole generations. While Ernest's tastes in furniture and decor were modest, the office had been redecorated several times, most recently at the behest of Sandra. She'd protested that since he spent eighteen hours a day here, or so it seemed, it should have some nice things in it. After he'd agreed, it had taken mere days for the room to transform, from new chairs and paintings, to small touches like the books on display. At first, he was glad his wife had persisted, since the office felt more welcoming. Now he hated it. It was a stark reminder of what he'd lost in order to save the company.

He shook his head and returned to the present. He chewed on a bagel and savored the cream cheese, listening while Peter gave a rundown of the day's news. It was a key part of his day, their morning ritual, and one that required Peter to be up earlier than Ernest—no small feat.

"Plenty about the Senate inquiry. Looks like the consensus is that Mahoney was the inquisitor and without him it will blow over."

Ernest pursed his lips. He hadn't told Peter about his deal with Dominique and saw no reason to now. "I'm certainly glad that's gone away, but I'm annoyed that we never managed to find the dirt on him. We'll need to do better next time."

Peter laughed. "Don't be so dark. It will be fine. The senator has been dealt with and the committee will go away."

Ernest wasn't so sure. He resented having to be a patsy to

that woman and her organization. Already she'd started to call to make small demands. They'd been subtle: massages of the truth here or an omitted fact there; mostly harmless. But Ernest knew that with each passing day she'd try to extract more from their relationship.

On the other hand, he had to admit that Dominique had proven ruthlessly effective in the prosecution of their agreement. Within days, Mahoney had been disgraced, the Senate inquiry was a memory and the political mire that had dragged down his company for months was starting to relent.

"What sort of coverage is the divorce announcement getting? Am I the worst husband and father on the planet?"

"Close enough. Let me show you." Peter put a separate folder on the desk and opened it. It was piled high with articles.

"Fan mail?"

Peter nodded. "Basically all along the lines of: what's he thinking; how could he be so cruel; she has a mental illness; it must be some slut breaking them up; is anyone surprised, given it's wife number four; so on, so forth."

"Could be worse, then?"

"Probably not. Are you sure your divorce is absolutely necessary?"

Ernest closed his eyes. It probably wasn't. He could have weathered the storm, faced the Senate head on and likely seen a dismantling of his lifetime's work. But he had made a decision and followed through. After Sandra's initial pleading, she hadn't said a word to him. All of their contact since had been through lawyers and the paperwork was nearly complete. The pre-nuptial agreement would leave her a rich woman.

While the loss cut him deeply, he kept his feelings and his reasons to himself. "It was necessary and there's no point revisiting it. Leave it at that."

Peter looked a bit confused, but nodded his acceptance. There was a knock on the door and it was flung open before Ernest had a chance to summon whoever was on the other side.

One of his junior assistants looked flustered as he rushed across the room and placed a piece of paper in Peter's hand. The man nodded at them and left the room without a word.

Peter read the document and went white. "Shit, looks like China has gone and made the rest of the day's news irrelevant."

"What do you mean?"

"That stranded carrier, they've sunk it."

"When?"

"A few hours ago. We've got people aboard."

Ernest's head spun with the political and economic ramifications of the news, even before Peter had stopped talking. He was not prepared for his phone to ring, and even less prepared for who it was. He stared at the caller ID and willed the phone to stop ringing. He gestured for Peter to leave, and waited until he was alone before he finally answered.

"Took you long enough." Michelle Dominique spoke before he'd had a chance to say hello. "The point of giving me your direct line was not making me wait."

"Sorry, but I've just seen the news—with the world about to go to hell and all, what do a few extra seconds matter?"

"Whatever. I want it spun. Pro-Taiwanese independence. Moral outrage that our good boys and girls would get blown up like this. China evil. Taiwan good."

Ernest sighed. Since their agreement, he'd ordered his editors to start slanting things in that direction. The *New York Standard* had a strong front-page feature about it, and other EMCorp papers and television affiliates had run it to death. He'd done all he could, within reason, short of an outright declaration of support for a preemptive US strike.

He resisted the urge to fight her on this. "So you want us to further stoke the flames of war. Are you sure that's the best move at this point?"

"I don't want your advice, Ernest. I want results." There was a pause. "I also want criticism of the Kurzon administration's handling of the crisis. You need to stoke public dissatisfaction and pave the way for my people to be elected in November."

He heard a click and the phone went dead. He sighed and closed his eyes. He knew he'd better get used to it—getting calls from her like his editors were used to getting from him—but he still didn't like it. For someone who'd run his own operation with an iron fist for decades, it was a culture shock he'd continued to struggle with.

For now, he had work to do. Ernest kept the phone in his hand and dialed the number of one of his best friends in the world. When the secretary of the President of the United States answered, he explained that he needed to speak with the President urgently and was put right through.

"How's the wife, Ernest?" President Phillip Kurzon offered in greeting.

'Which one?"

It was their standard opening banter, but when friends got as old as the two of them, routine jokes could still bring a degree of comfort and amusement, even with a war breaking out. They'd been college roommates. Philip Kurzon had gone on to marry his sweetheart and lived happily with her since. Ernest had quite a different story.

"Ernest, that's a nasty business with Sandra. Are you sure it can't be salvaged?"

"I'm sure. The divorce will be finalized soon. As for the others, I haven't heard from Elle or Edith and Catherine is as unpredictable as ever. That's all of them. How's yours?"

"The usual. Incredible woman, my wife. I think she has a harder job than I do. Grandson made quarterback, you know?"

"Pass on my congratulations." Ernest paused. "Anyway, I do have some business to discuss with you, and I'm sure you're busy."

'Thanks, I know why you're calling. What've you got?"

"Not very much, just wanted to let you know we're running

hard for Taiwan on this one. I know that puts you in a bind, but I really don't have a choice."

While Ernest, a Republican supporter, and Kurzon, a Democratic president, disagreed on politics, it had never affected their friendship. No president reached the Oval Office without a patron in the media, and Ernest had thrown all of the support he could behind his first campaign. In return, he'd gained a powerful friend.

"I'm not surprised, but the last thing I need is more fuel on this particular fire."

"They sunk a carrier, Phil."

"And besides nuke them, what exactly would you have me do? The Joint Chiefs tell me I've got few conventional options with the *Washington* gone. I've got a meeting with Frank Maas in an hour, that'll tell me if the Agency has any ideas."

Ernest massaged his temples with his fingers. "Is the military situation that bad?"

"Normally, no. But they sank one carrier, the next nearest are in the Gulf and somewhere near San Francisco, and anything I send from the East Coast will take far too long to get there. We're going to war, but it's with one hand tied behind our back."

"Recognition for Taiwan?" Ernest pushed his luck.

The phone was silent for a few long moments. "It's really a formality after they hit the carrier. State is already working it through. The Euros aren't getting involved for now, but the Japanese, Koreans and Australians are howling. This is all off the record."

"Of course."

"Anyway, Ern, thanks for letting me know. Nice to know you'll be calling on me to beat the drums of war as hard as I can. I've got work to do. Call my office next week and we'll organize a round next time you're in DC, it's been too long since we caught up."

"You got it. Thanks, Phil. Bye."

Ernest sighed. While the President knew war was now inevitable, he clearly hoped to keep the engagement limited. Yet Dominique was using EMCorp and its public influence to corner the President of the United States with public opinion.

Ernest, and his company, had become a strategic asset.

JACK FELT VERY ALONE as he looked around the deck of the Chinese rescue boat, which he shared with a dozen or so armed soldiers and a large number of survivors. The sailors who'd been saved from drowning stared into the darkness or at the deck, and didn't engage each other in conversation or protest their captivity.

Their captors, on the other hand, barked orders through translators and weren't averse to using the butt of a rifle to make their point. They shared around bottled water and some meager food rations happily enough, but any dissent—real or imagined—was quickly dealt with.

Jack shivered. Though he had no injuries, he'd been unable to get warm since his plunge into the South China Sea, despite having three blankets draped over him. The dampness combined with the seasonal chill to make warmth impossible. He didn't mind so much. At least he knew he was alive.

The Seahawk had plunged into the ocean seconds after the USS *Shiloh* had exploded. He'd had no time to react before the helicopter was upside down and completely submerged. It had been hard enough to get out of his seatbelt, let alone outside the chopper. If not for the gaping hole in the fuselage, he'd have drowned. Several others had.

Celeste had been alive when he'd lost her. He'd helped her to unbuckle and they'd both reached the surface, but in the confusion of fire and terror that followed, they'd lost each other. He thought she was alive, but it was equally possible that she'd drowned before the arrival of the Chinese rescue boats, a mix of naval and civilian ships that made for a strange flotilla. He'd been lucky to get aboard one of the first few.

Best he could tell, most or all of the carrier group's warships were gone.

Besides the *Shiloh*, he'd been able to see one of the escorting destroyers crippled and continue to burn long after being abandoned. Beyond that, Jack had no idea what had happened to the rest of fleet, its escort submarine or the *Washington* air wing that had been aloft when their carrier started to go under. He hoped they'd had enough fuel to get to Taiwan or somewhere else.

He had been witness to the end of American naval dominance in the Pacific Ocean. Though the Chinese had no doubt taken significant losses as well, the result of their attack had been the loss of a ship thought impregnable and the death of sailors who'd paid the price for that hubris. No doubt the attack would have other ramifications as well.

Jack's face suddenly stung, his reverie broken by the cold hand of a Chinese naval officer. The slap was firm but not brutal. The officer spoke to Jack in Mandarin, his tone professional. Jack relied on the English translator next to the officer to make sense of what was being said.

"My comrade said you should pay attention." The translator's tone was entirely civil. "You aren't a navy man, so he wishes to know your name, occupation and role."

Jack rubbed his cheek, trying to will away the pain of the slap. He shook his head. "I'm Jack Emery. I had no role aboard the ship. I'm a journalist for the *New York Standard*."

He watched as the two men exchanged words. As they spoke, Jack looked around the small boat. This vessel had only a few dozen of the rescued, compared to the hundreds picked up by some of the larger ships. He looked back to the pair discussing his fate. As the translator spoke, the officer's expression grew darker. Jack was fairly sure that the officer didn't relish having foreign media on his vessel. Then, as if a dark cloud had lifted, the officer smiled at the translator and then at Jack. It didn't feel like a happy one.

The translator spoke. "Are you sure that's your answer?"

Jack stared at him. "Yes, of course. I need to get to Japan or the US. I also had a colleague on the helicopter that was shot down. She might be among the rescued."

"That will take some time, I'm afraid. We believe you may be a spy. You'll be under the guard of the People's Liberation Army Navy until we can confirm or disprove this."

Jack's mind raced. While China didn't have the most sterling human rights record, they were generally hands off with members of the foreign press. "That's crazy."

"That's fact."

"And suppose I jump overboard?"

The translator stiffened. "The troops on this vessel have orders to shoot if necessary."

Jack's shoulders slumped and he sighed. "So what next, then?"

The translator smiled. "There are procedures in place. I'm sure you understand."

Jack didn't, but he didn't get any further chance to contest the point as the translator nodded, turned and walked away.

He ground his teeth, resigned to the fact that he was in the custody of the Chinese for however long they pleased. Whatever happened on the trip between the rescue site and the mainland, Jack knew that nothing good was waiting for him. He simply hoped that Celeste had survived.

11

Following the sinking of the USS George Washington, the United States has delivered a declaration of war to the Chinese Ambassador to the United States. As the US continues to deploy additional assets to the area, the Air Force has launched wide-ranging air and cruise missile strikes against the Chinese mainland. While details are sketchy, it appears the US strikes were aimed at major Chinese airfields and port facilities. We'll bring you more information as it comes to hand. Meanwhile, the United States has formally recognized Taiwan as an independent state. Though there's been no reaction by the Chinese, it's unlikely that this move will do anything to calm tensions in the region, already white hot following the attack on the carrier and the retaliation by the US Air Force.

Kate Winston, Reuters, *September 18*

In an attempt to get his mind off the pain that throbbed around his body with every beat of his heart, Jack thought of happier times with Erin. He'd expected his treatment at the hands of the Chinese to be rudimentary, but had never considered the possibility of the brutality he'd been subjected to. The darkness bothered him nearly as much as the odor that seemed to permeate every inch of the prison, a combination of sweat, human filth and the putrid, slightly sweet smell of charred flesh. The smell added to the continual, dull moan of human misery—a cacophony of wails, high and low. Occasionally, he heard a sharp cry of pain or terror.

It was all testimony to the work being done around the clock to extract information, real or imagined, from those unlucky enough to be here. He'd had a taste of such treatment on his first night, when a pair of uniformed men had visited and kicked him around. One of them had welcomed him in patchy English, before laughing at his attempt to cower away from the pain. They'd left Jack in darkness, and he'd been on the floor since. His only comfort was a metal pail for his bodily functions, which he suspected was more for the convenience of his jailers than their prisoner. Blood, piss and spittle could be hosed away, Jack figured, but shit would probably block the drains.

He dozed off. Some time later, he woke and gave an involuntary whimper as the lock on the steel cell door gave a loud click. The heavy door swung open on poorly oiled hinges. He looked up, and there was enough light in the passageway for him to see a small, bespectacled Chinese man with a toolbox in his hand.

Jack wasn't sure what to expect. The man said something in Mandarin, and Jack was instantly blinded by harsh overhead lighting. He shielded his eyes against the pain of the first real light he'd seen in days, listening to the footsteps of the man as he entered the room and the screech of the door closing behind him. He was not sure how much time had passed between the first beating and now, but as Jack regained his sight, he saw it had been long enough for some of the blood he'd lost to dry in irregular streaks on the cell floor. The gruesome display wouldn't be out of place in a gallery of modern art.

The new arrival dropped to his knees beside Jack and put

his toolbox on the ground. He opened it and removed his tools. They were terrible instruments: some sharp, some blunt, some Jack had no idea about. But one message was loud and clear: this man could inflict pain. Jack backed into the corner, away from him.

The man spoke softly. "I'm here to hear your confession."

Jack closed his eyes as he felt a tear streak down his cheek. "I have nothing for you."

"Start with your name."

"Jack Emery."

"You're a spy, posing as a journalist. You were on board the US Navy aircraft carrier that was inside Chinese territorial waters."

Jack was slightly taken aback. He'd spent lots of time since his capture puzzled by his treatment. While China wasn't usually averse to impinging on the rights of the international media, they usually kept the heat to a low simmer. He wasn't sure why he was getting the special treatment, but suspected it was the pro-Taiwanese coverage.

He opened his eyes and stared at the man. "A spy? I'm a reporter. A pretty bloody famous one, too. Google me and you'll work out that I'm no spy."

The man laughed. "That's one of the more fanciful stories I've heard."

Jack felt his heartbeat quicken, and his mouth went dry. He had no doubts about what was in store should he remain here much longer. His heart pleaded with him to say something to the man, to convince him of the futility of what was to come, but his head knew it was pointless.

"Mr Emery, if you give me what I need, you'll remained imprisoned here but otherwise unharmed for however long the conflict lasts. Once it's over, you'll be free to join your lady friend back in the United States."

"Celeste? You have Celeste?"

"Of course. She's another valued guest. Now, if you don't

give me what I need, things become more complicated. You'll be deprived of sleep, comfort, food and any relief. You'll also experience pain unimagined, until your very nerves are screaming at you."

Jack closed his eyes. The beating he'd already taken would be nothing compared with any of that. He also felt a deeper fear, knowing they had Celeste. He'd thought she might be dead, which in many ways would be preferable to the Chinese hospitality. The man had clearly told him she was alive because she could be used against Jack.

"Close your eyes, Mr Emery, but don't think that the darkness behind your eyelids protects you. You do have a real choice, but only one is correct."

Jack felt hopeless. "Why are you doing this? All of this?"

The man laughed. "I'll indulge you. My leaders have decided the time has come to reckon with Taiwan. Given that the American bulldog stands in the way, it was necessary to smack it on the nose with a newspaper."

"You sank a carrier to send a message?" Jack shook his head. "Look, I don't even care. You know I'm no spy. There's no point in torturing me. I just want to go home."

"I do know that the company you work for has become a strategic element in this war. If my government can't control it, we can render it inert." He shrugged "Just business."

Jack's heart sank. If he'd had hopes of being released, or at least having an easier time of it, they'd now vanished. Suddenly Josefa's instructions to cover the conflict in favor of Taiwan made sense. For whatever reason, Ernest McDowell had cast his lot in the war. It meant Jack was in for a nasty time.

The other man slapped him lightly. "Now, I expect the same candor from you, Mr Emery. Concede that your coverage on board the American carrier was flawed. Admit that the ship was in Chinese territorial waters, and I will inform my superiors that they are mistaken about your espionage. It's inevitable, so we may as well get it over with."

Jack said nothing for several moments. He cowered in the corner as the other man waited for him to offer something to stay the threat of torture. Then, clearly tired of waiting, the man cocked a fist back. Jack tried to lift his arm to defend against the blow, but was too slow.

The fist slammed into his face. He wailed in pain as his nose gave a sickening crunch and the back of his head slammed into the blood-smeared concrete. He groaned but remained conscious, his head on fire. He continued to groan as the other man moved his head close enough that Jack could smell the cigarettes on his breath.

"I've seen some of the Falun Gong fanatics hold out until death, as well as some enemy spies, trained for such interrogation. But you're a journalist. Why do you fight?"

Jack coughed several times, and spat blood onto the floor. "Because I don't know what you want me to tell you."

"Aren't you afraid of me, Mr Emery?"

"I've been in the White House press corps." Jack coughed again. "This is little league in comparison, and you're the cheerleader that the entire offensive line is banging."

The other man chuckled and then moved back on the floor slightly. Jack was pretty sure he'd caught the drift. Despite his bravado, Jack suddenly wished that he hadn't insulted his captor. It would just mean more pain. As if on cue, he heard the scrape of metal against a whetstone.

"It is men like you who make my job a pleasure, Mr Emery. The ones who break immediately are no fun, they make my job feel like sweeping the floor. But every now and then, someone like you comes along, who gives me joy in my profession. You'll break, though. Everyone does. Some just break quicker than others."

ERNEST MOUTHED his thanks as the waiter laid a napkin across his lap. He considered the wine list for only a moment before settling on a bottle of the 1997 Penfolds Grange. The waiter nodded, thanked the two of them and backed away, leaving Ernest and Peter alone. Ernest sighed.

"While we're here there's a thousand or so corpses floating in the South China Sea, boys in Chinese custody, and pilots risking their lives over hostile territory."

Peter nodded. "Not to mention a country coming to terms with the destruction of American exceptionalism."

"You don't say." They'd spent the morning digesting the blanket coverage of the war and putting a particular slant on things. Ernest didn't tell him it was Dominique's slant.

He reached for a bread roll from the basket in the middle of the table. He tore it open, taking out some of his pent-up anger on the unfortunate sourdough. In addition to all the other carnage, he had reporters missing. Ernest had lost people before—like any proprietor who'd been in the game long enough—but never this many.

"Any word from our people?"

Peter buttered his own roll. "It's coming in slowly, but Fran O'Rourke from the *Independent* is still with what's left of the fleet on their way back to Yokosuka. Christian Malley has been picked up by the Chinese, but there has been no word on Jack Emery, or the other *Standard* reporter, Celeste Adams. They were on board the *Washington*."

"So they're dead or captured." Ernest assaulted the bread with a thick layer of butter.

"Yeah." Peter's voice trailed off. "Watch your cholesterol."

"Not now, Peter."

They sat in silence as the waiter returned with the wine and poured a glass for both of them. Ernest half expected a comment from Peter about watching his liver, but none came. In truth, Ernest was sure Peter felt as bad as he did about having so many people—EMCorp people—missing or dead.

Ernest picked up his glass and took a mouthful of the wine. It was as good as he remembered. He was about to have another when an Asian man approached the table from the side and came to a stop a respectful few feet away. Ernest sighed. This was the last thing he wanted to deal with right now.

"Ambassador." Ernest turned to look at him.

The Chinese Ambassador to the United States, Du Xiaoming, gave a small cough. "Excuse me, gentlemen, I noticed you were dining and wanted to pay my respects."

Peter stood and Ernest was glad that he took the cue.

"Just off to the gents. Please excuse me, Ambassador."

Du nodded at Peter and took the newly occupied seat. Ernest said nothing as Peter walked away, but signaled the waiter to bring another glass. It gave him time to think. He'd had some minor dealings with the ambassador in the past, mainly about EMCorp expansion into China, and knew that this was a business meeting. Ernest just didn't know the type of business they'd be discussing.

"What can I do for you, Ambassador?"

Du smiled again. "This is just a neighborly visit, as you Americans like to call it. A courtesy, since your dogs have strayed into our yard."

Ernest felt his face flush, but any potential outburst was stayed when the waiter placed a glass in front of the ambassador and filled it.

"May I take your order, gentlemen?"

"Steak, James, just the usual." Ernest gestured toward the ambassador. "And..."

Du kept his face even. "Two please."

"Certainly." The waiter took their menus then left them.

Ernest leaned forward to avoid any chance of prying ears. "You're talking about the three embeds? You know they're a part of the business."

Du shrugged. "Your people, your risk. I'm afraid my

government is seeing things quite a bit differently, though. All three are in custody and facing espionage charges."

Ernest sat back in his chair, lifted his glass and took a sip of wine. He never took his eyes off Du, who sat impassively. Ernest knew he was now neck deep in negotiation for the lives and welfare of his staff.

He put the glass down and inched forward again. "They're reporters, Ambassador. They were reporting events as they unfolded. They're not spies. I want them released."

Du held his gaze for a few moments, then nodded slightly. "Your company's reporting of the developing situation concerns my government. Now they've trespassed, their return will require adjustments in their owner's priorities."

It took all of Ernest's self-control not to scream in frustration. The deal with Dominique was to blame for this meeting, and for the fact that his people were probably being roughed up. He'd dug himself out of one hole only to land right in another. He had no doubt that the Chinese would release Emery, Adams and Malley tomorrow, for the right price. But it would be steep.

"Their reporting was fair and balanced. I don't know what more you want."

Du took a sip of wine. "That's the thing about neighborly disputes, isn't it? One side has a view, the other side has a view, but who knows who's right?"

"Maybe. But sooner or later it must be resolved."

"Yes, but unfortunately for you, we have your dogs. And their condition worsens with each passing day because of the grief they feel at not being at home with their owner."

Ernest flared. "If you've hurt them, it will be on your head."

Du held up a hand. "I haven't harmed anyone. But dogs must be trained."

There was a long pause. Neither of them spoke as they stared at each other across the table. Unfortunately for Ernest, the ambassador was right. It was EMCorp staff in danger, primarily because of his deal with Michelle Dominique. He had nothing to bargain with that he hadn't already promised to her. He forced his temper to subside.

Ernest sighed. "Where to from here, Ambassador?"

"We agree to disagree, and we part ways as friends, I'd suggest."

"Alright." Ernest wasn't satisfied, but there was nothing to be gained by more pushing.

"But one last friendly observation." Du spoke softly. "The world is changing and the great tectonic plates are shifting. The time has come for everyone to pick sides. As the plates grind against each other, only a stupid man would place himself or his company in between. Please, heed my words if you value the health and wellbeing of your dogs."

MICHELLE KEPT her gaze locked on Anton as he continued to shout, his spittle washing over her like rain. He'd been at it for a good ten seconds. She didn't break eye contact with him as she removed her glasses, wiped them clean on her cardigan and placed them back on.

"Are you done?" She stared at him from across the desk. "This is quite annoying."

"You cut off my funds, corner me, kill my security detail. And all for nothing." He pounded the table with his fist. "Don't you have anything to say for yourself?"

"I'm probably going to need a shower, whenever you decide you're done."

He huffed and sat down, giving her a small victory. Anton had been holed up in his compound, running the Foundation remotely since his return from China. They'd had an uneasy peace while Michelle put things in place for her takeover, until this morning. She'd cut off his funds and sent an email to the organization informing everyone that she was stepping up to take charge, while Anton was indisposed. It was a total lie, but combined with her recent efforts to ensnare McDowell and meet with the President, he'd had no choice but to react. He'd agreed to meet at a neutral office building. Things had probably seemed like they were going well for him, until the Shadd brothers had killed his security detail and left the two of them alone in the small office.

She was certain that he could recognize the balance of power shifting. She had control of the Foundation in her hand.

"I'm going to need more than that from you, Michelle. I'm currently weighing up the merits of continuing to allow you to breathe."

She laughed. "You don't frighten me, Anton. Nor do you recognize that you've lost all control. It's all slipping away."

He apparently didn't hear what she'd said. "This is the most shocking betrayal of me and our cause I could imagine."

Michelle made no attempt to hide her anger. "Is that so? I'd consider you trying to kill me to be worse."

He froze, unsure for the first time. "What're you talking about?"

"China."

"You're being ridiculous, Michelle. If I wanted you dead, you'd be dead."

She knew it was time to strike. She grabbed a metal paperweight off the desk and, before he could react, threw it at him as hard as she could. The paperweight hit his skull and gave a satisfying crack. She vaulted the desk in one bound as he screeched in agony, reaching up toward his head. She advanced on him with a bloody, single-minded focus as he staggered backward. He looked up and seemed to recognize her intent. As she closed in, she ducked under his hastily thrown roundhouse. She threw a quick jab at his stomach, which caused him to double over.

"I didn't mind when you kept me in the dark, because we were both motivated to make America great again."

She lifted her knee and connected with his nose, which caused his head to jerk back. He slumped to the floor.

"I didn't mind when you changed the plan, took credit and denied me mine, even though I did most of the heavy lifting."

She reached down to the floor and picked up a pen that had been knocked over in the scuffle, as he rose back to his full height with his hands over his nose.

"I didn't even mind when you arranged the death of Chen and his family, despite your promises, because I managed to save them."

She was surprised when he threw another punch. This one connected square with her jaw. Her vision exploded with color and she staggered to one knee. She winced as Anton followed up with a brutal kick to her midriff. She tasted blood in her mouth, but knew that if she didn't get up quickly, he was a more than capable foe.

She pushed herself off the floor, rushed toward him and tackled him around the waist. They fell in a sprawling heap. She climbed on top of him and swung several punches at his head, which he defended as best he could. She growled in frustration and punched him one last time. He held his hands up in surrender.

"I did mind when you tried to have me killed, and didn't have the good grace to do it properly or fuck off when you failed."

His eyes widened in apparent fear, then horror, as she raised the pen. "What're you doing?"

She brought the pen down, hard. The tip penetrated his eye socket and she pushed until the shaft would go no deeper. After a second or two he stopped flailing. She screamed as loudly as she could and felt the fury rush out of her. She leaned back on his stomach, and could smell the putrid scent of his bowels as they evacuated.

"What needs to be done." She climbed up off the lifeless body.

She'd been prepared to achieve the Foundation's goals together, but Anton had been too paranoid for that. That paranoia had cost him his life. She was now the nominal leader of the Foundation. She had people counting on her, plans that depended on her. She also knew that there were others, trusted lieutenants of Anton, who'd attempt to unseat her if they found out the method of his death. She'd need help tying up loose ends. The Shadd brothers would make his body disappear.

Once she had total control of the Foundation, America was next.

12

As the United States and China continue to trade blows, there appears to be little hope of halting the escalation of the conflict. This has potentially grave ramifications for the families of captured US servicemen and women, many of whom have shared with the New York Standard their fears about possible mistreatment or torture of their loved ones. In response to questions from this publication, the Chinese Ambassador to the United States stated that all detained personnel were being treated in line with China's international obligations. This publication—like the rest of the EMCorp family—continues to advocate peace and calls for China to halt its campaign of aggression and allow Taiwan to peacefully join the community of nations.

Editorial, New York Standard, *September 21*

"Turn it off, Peter." Ernest placed his head in his hands. "For heaven's sake, turn it off."

Peter reached over to the laptop and pressed a button to stop the audio recording of Jack Emery and Christian Malley being tortured. The screams of Ernest's staff were visceral and spoke of a deep pain. He'd heard them curse their torturer and cry out for their mothers, for God and for anyone else to help them. To Ernest, it felt as if they called out to him.

They sat in silence, but the recordings he'd heard burned Ernest to his core. Worse still, he knew it was decisions that he'd made that had placed his people in danger. Usually Ernest liked to distance himself from the people under his direction, and he had made decisions before that had ended livelihoods and changed life trajectories. This was different.

He looked up at Peter, who appeared as stunned as Ernest felt. "We have to get them out of there. They're not soldiers or spies. They'll be dead in a couple of weeks under this sort of treatment."

Peter looked down at the floor. "I put in a call to Dan Whelan at Princeton. In his opinion, under such stress, if the Chinese don't relent a little they'll be suffering immense psychological stress. They might not last that long."

Ernest's head was aching. How was he to navigate the release of his people while having to honor agreement he'd made to Dominique and the Foundation? He regretted not telling Peter about the deal, but it was too late to share now. The Chinese, via the ambassador, had made it clear that the way to ensure his people stayed alive was to alter the tone of EMCorp's reporting of the war. He was trapped in a pincer. The only option he liked was the idea of making it somebody else's problem.

"We need to take it to the authorities. Give them the files and whatever support they need. It's the only way to get them out of there."

Peter shrugged. "Who's going to care, with everything else that's going on?"

"We need to do something to help them! I'll call the President."

"You're being irrational. The US Government has more on its mind at the moment."

"We could try the Pentagon? Surely some of their people

are being held at the same prison. Get them out, and our people. Two birds with one stone and all that."

"Tried that. Yes, they have people there, but no, they're not going in. With thousands of their own dead, wounded or captured, a few journos don't top their list."

Ernest exhaled loudly. "So we're on our own."

"Everyone is frightened. The hawks want the nukes to come out."

Ernest had considered the chances of government intervention to be slim. His next consideration had been a private operation—mercenaries, who'd blast in, extract his people and get out. But he'd been told that nobody would run a private op in the PRC. He'd even privately asked Dominique to help, to no avail except her howling with laughter.

He sighed and leaned back in his chair. He had to comply with the Chinese request if he wanted his people back. But maybe there was one other way. He knew that every second he delayed meant more pain for his people, so if he danced the right dance, he could secure their return to the United States. Once that was achieved, he could deal with the consequences of what he was about to do.

He looked at Peter. "Okay, thanks. You've given me a bit to think about."

Peter took the cue to leave the room and started to gather his papers. As he departed, Ernest flicked through his business card holder, picked up his phone and dialed. When the phone was answered, he asked for the ambassador and waited for a couple of minutes with the sound of a local radio station his only company.

Eventually, the music stopped. "This is Ambassador Du."

"It's Ernest McDowell."

"Ah." Ernest could nearly feel Du's grin. "I've been expecting your call, Mr McDowell."

"I'll bet. You sent me the files, after all. I need to speak with your premier."

"I don't know what files you're talking about, but you may speak to me. In this matter, I speak with all the authority you'll need." Du paused. "Off the record, of course."

"If necessary to free my reporters, absolutely."

"I'll keep it short, since time is of the essence. As I mentioned at lunch the other day, your company has become a strategic asset in this conflict. This is of grave concern, made worse by the sheer scale of anti-China coverage in recent days."

Ernest was taken aback by the ambassador's blunt accusation. While his agreement with Dominique had indeed made him pick a side, he hadn't intended for it to manifest itself in quite this way. The coverage of the conflict by EMCorp's stable of media assets had all slanted in a particular direction, in line with Dominique's wishes, but she'd ordered it ramped up hugely. The Chinese had clearly noticed.

"I'll simply say that there were matters beyond my control that amended my attitude on this conflict. I won't apologize, but I'm willing to compromise."

"It was Mao who said, as communists, we gain control with the power of the gun, and maintain control with the power of the pen."

"How can I help with that?"

"We require immediate cessation of your pro-Taiwanese coverage, and a complete reversal of your editorial direction."

"I've been told that a lot in the last few weeks." Ernest laughed. "Do I have any choice?"

"No, not particularly."

"Then your terms are acceptable. Release my people."

"It will be done within twenty-four hours. I've been permitted to authorize travel of your private jet to China pick them up. I'll be in touch."

Du hung up and Ernest exhaled deeply. He'd promised the impossible. But he didn't have a choice, he'd done what was necessary to get his people back, and kicked the problem further down the road. He'd bought time, but his only chance, long term, was to try rework the deal with Dominique. He'd placed the noose tighter around his own neck.

~

A SINGLE SHAFT of light from underneath the door penetrated the darkness of the cell.

For several days now, Jack had mentally clung to it as if it was the final lifeboat on the *Titanic*. The abuse of his body had been nothing compared with the desolation of his mind. He was just glad he could recognize what was happening. But he knew that with each passing second his old life slipped a little farther away. With each beating, each threat to his life, each breakdown, he became more desperate. More despondent.

The door screeched open, and he flinched involuntarily; while he loved the small sliver of light, he feared its growth into a bright inferno. When it did, more abuse was imminent. He pushed himself weakly along the floor of his cell, hoping he might be able to hide.

The guards spoke in Mandarin as they entered the cell. He was surprised when they didn't immediately kick him or hurl insults. Instead, they picked him up off the floor. Each grabbed one of his arms and dragged him from the cell. They handled him firmly, but not too roughly. The possibilities assaulted his brain. More torture? Freedom? Or some other vile option he hadn't considered? Whatever was in store, for at least a minute or two, he'd been spared. What replaced it really didn't matter. While Jack might hope for his freedom, he'd be content with a little sunlight or a day free of pain.

He clearly wasn't to be kept waiting. They reached a steel door and the guard on his left side opened it. Sunlight flared in, stinging his eyes but warming his spirit. He was marched outside and before his eyes could adjust he felt the sharp pain of gravel underneath his bare feet. It crunched under the boots of the guards as they walked, but cut into his skin. Jack kept silent, knowing that any dissent or complaint would be met with brutality. His concerns about small, loose stones were chased away a moment later by the booming sounds of gunshots followed by shouts in Mandarin.

Jack's heart raced. As his eyes adjusted, he could see his fate. A rank of uniformed soldiers stood at attention and in a straight line across the gravel courtyard. Opposite them, a man was heaped, dead, in front of a stone wall. The wall was pockmarked with bullet holes and streaked with blood.

Another man was marched to the wall by a pair of guards. The doomed man didn't fight back, despite being tall and stout enough to try. He stood against the wall. It looked like he'd been beaten half to death, and his face was bloodied and bruised purple. Jack watched in silent horror, determined to cry out in defense of the man but kept in check by his fear. Jack's bladder released as the Chinese officer in charge of the firing squad ordered his men to the ready. His shame, fear and embarrassment trickled down his leg as the order was given. Shots barked out and the man slumped to the ground, a small spray of his blood adding to the grotesque mix on the wall behind.

Jack's shoulders slumped and the guards took up the slack to support his weight. They carried him toward the wall, slowly but with purpose. He did his best to resist, but their grip was strong and his body was weak. The grim procession stopped briefly when a third guard stood in front of Jack and handcuffed his hands to an iron ring in the wall. The guards moved away, chatting to one another.

Despite his best efforts, there was no beating them. He closed his eyes and steeled himself. Many seconds passed, and Jack wondered if he'd passed into blackness already. He was pretty sure he hadn't, however, when a radio crackled and a voice blared out. When the guards nearby laughed with each other, his hunch was confirmed. He heard the footsteps of a guard.

"Not for you today, my friend."

Jack started to sob as they grabbed him again and marched him back inside, relieved that he had been spared, but fearing what was going to replace it. He walked for several minutes, toward whatever fresh abuse was in store for him. He turned or stopped whenever they demanded, and eventually he was facing a steel door. It was not his normal cell. He was kicked inside.

"Jack?" He heard her voice over the slam of the door. "What have they done to you?"

He said nothing as Celeste approached him. He didn't resist as she took his head in her hands and inspected his face like a mother might a recalcitrant, dirty-faced child. He looked at her without word and as she completed her inspection, he did one of his own. She had bruises and injuries too, and looking down, he saw that her clothing was largely torn into useless rags. She was barely covered, and her body had other wounds.

"Eyes up here, mister." She smiled sadly. "I'm glad you're alive, Jack. Though it looks like you've seen better days."

Jack returned his eyes to her, ashamed that his gaze had lingered a little too long on her body. "I thought they'd done the same to you."

"Not quite." She wrapped her arms around him gently, so his wounds wouldn't scream. "They raped me, Jack."

Jack was speechless. He should have expected that, but it didn't make the news any easier to grasp. If they were single-minded in their efforts to break the reporters so that Ernest would agree to their terms, then physical brutality was just one of the available weapons. He pulled back from her embrace and saw she was crying.

He hugged her back. "I'm sorry, Celeste." He didn't know what else to say.

"What was all this for? What does it all mean? We're reporters, for fuck's sake!" She exhaled loudly. "What stopped them?"

"Orders. The torturer made it clear that this was all about getting to Ernest. I think it might have worked."

"Well, whatever the reason, I'm glad to have the company."

They said nothing for a while. He felt human for the first time in days, as safe in her arms as a newborn in its mother's embrace. He felt a mix of relief at being spared Malley's fate and fear of what was still to come, but whatever the next move was going to be, at least he wasn't alone. He hugged her and laughed.

She drew back from him slightly. "What's so funny?"

"I'm in here with you. I could just as easily be slumped outside with a bullet in me."

She nodded and sat on the concrete floor, gesturing for him to sit too. He didn't resist when she gently moved his head to her lap; it felt like a pillow after so many days without sleep. He enjoyed her strokes on his cheeks, and realized it was the first time he'd lay down in days without water, or light, or pain to break up his attempts to sleep.

She leaned in close and whispered in his ear. "Let's just stay sane until we're out."

He closed his eyes. "We might never be out."

~

CHEN SIGHED as he looked through the night-vision binoculars. He'd spent several hours on his stomach and now the front of his clothing was cold and damp. It was a less than glamorous way to spend an evening, but it was vital to getting in and out with his head still on his shoulders and with the information he needed.

The men guarding Anton Clark's house were in sight. The amount of security made Chen's job harder. More warm bodies moving about always did. The guards were all part of a small security detail that kept Anton's family and property free from threat, though it had done nothing to protect him from

Michelle Dominique sticking a pen in his eye. He knew they could outgun anything he had access to at such short notice. He couldn't worry too much about that, but he could stay hidden and hope his superior training would win out if he was seen. He was just glad that Dominique had managed to craft a story about Anton being overseas on business. The cover seemed to have held up.

He put the binoculars down and pulled himself up to his knees. He brushed his gloved hands over the front of him, removing the leaves and other natural detritus from his clothes. Within a few seconds he'd placed the binoculars in one of the many pockets on his combat vest and zipped it closed. Taking mental stock of his equipment, Chen made sure nothing was loose and he hadn't dropped anything on the ground. His Heckler and Koch USP Tactical pistol was loaded in its holster on his right hip. On his other hip, he had a small combat knife. Most importantly, among all sorts of utility equipment that he might need in the vest pockets, he had a pair of USB drives.

Chen took a deep breath and started off. He drew his pistol and walked as quickly as he could through the scrub. It took ten minutes to reach the first difficult part—the road. He took another breath, looked both ways, crouched as low as he could and walked rapidly across. When he was just near the base of the wall, he heard a small scrape to his left. He turned with alarm at the sound, raised his handgun toward the noise and pressed his finger slightly on the trigger.

He released the trigger immediately when he saw a boy, probably about thirteen, in the very dim light, staring at him with wide eyes. Chen cursed that he hadn't seen the boy during his reconnaissance, but it didn't matter now. He lowered his pistol slightly and quickly approached the boy. He was frozen, so Chen reached out and put a gloved hand over his mouth. The boy tensed and no doubt feared the worst as Chen crouched down towards him.

He put his mouth close to the boy's ear. "You look old enough to realize what's at stake."

The boy nodded vigorously and gave a barely audible moan.

"I need you to keep calm. You'll be fine and home with your mother tonight if you do. But I need you to be quiet. Understand?"

The boy nodded again.

Chen slowly removed his hand from the boy's mouth, and to his relief the boy said nothing and didn't move an inch. He could use him. Chen dug in his pocket, pulled out a few hundred dollars and held the money up in front of the boy. Eyes wide with recognition, the boy's eyes flicked back and forth between the cash and Chen's face.

"You can have all of this if you listen very carefully. In a few minutes I want you to throw some coins I'll give you over the fence, right there." He pointed to the compound.

"Okay." The boy's voice was barely a whisper. He seemed to relax a little now that his life was not in immediate danger and there was the promise of a large amount of cash. Americans—always about the profit. He handed the boy the wad of cash and a few coins. He squeezed the boy's hand shut around the coins, lest he drop them.

"Count to one hundred and eighty, then throw the coins."

"Okay." The boy smiled. "Easy."

Chen hadn't planned on this, but he could use it to his advantage. Anton's guards had a timed routine that took them around the property every thirteen minutes. Chen needed them to be as far from the house as possible and the coins would help delay them when they were.

"Once it's done you need to run straight home. Don't stay near here and don't tell anyone about me. You found the money."

The boy nodded and started to move to where Chen had pointed. Chen wasted no time, leaving the boy and creeping along the wall. He stopped just short of one of the gates. He hugged the wall and waited. He hoped that Dominique's hacker had taken out the cameras. He was alert to any sound, hopeful that the coins would land on the ground inside and distract the guards for an extra few seconds. The coast would be clear.

He looked at the watch on his wrist, which he'd synced with the watch given to the boy. Once the clock hit three minutes, he sprang into action. Chen hoped the boy had done his job and was long gone, but he didn't spare him another thought. He tried the gate latch with one hand. It was locked, but it took only a second for him to pick. He pushed the gate open.

He followed a preplanned route across the garden and to the house that should get him to the target of the entire expedition: the computer in Anton's study. He thought he might make it without incident until he rounded a corner and found two very surprised security guards.

As Chen's gun came up, the guards froze in place and started to draw their pistols. He knew it was the automatic response of most American law enforcement and security personnel, when they should have sought cover. It was their deadly mistake. His own pistol was on them before either hand reached a holster.

He fired two shots at the first guard; a sound akin to compressed air being released and the pattering of two spent bullet cases dancing across the hardwood were the only evidence. The guard didn't get the chance to make much more than a muffled gurgle as a bullet penetrated his throat, severing the carotid. The second bullet hit him in the chest.

The other guard continued to draw his weapon as Chen brought his own pistol onto target. The man's fate was sealed by his instinctive look to his left, where his colleague had just been. The man looked back to Chen, his eyes wide, before Chen put a bullet between them. The guard dropped limp, and his gun fell from his hands.

Chen moved quickly to the two men. One was clearly dead, while the other writhed on the expensive hardwood floor as his lifeblood escaped from his throat, forming a crimson pool next to him. Chen put a bullet in his head. He took both their weapons and threw them into the pot of a houseplant.

After a few more corners he reached the home office and pushed the door open. The room was empty. Chen closed the door behind him, moved to the computer and sat at the horribly modern glass desk. The laptop blinked on when he opened the lid. He clicked on Anton's username and entered the password. An hourglass appeared for a second and then a chime sounded. He was glad Dominique had been right about the password. He grabbed the two USB sticks from his pocket.

He inserted his own USB first and copied the documents folder from Anton's computer onto it. Chen turned and trained his pistol on the door, but nobody interrupted him for the minute or so it took the job to complete. Once the dump was complete, he pulled out the first USB and inserted the second. Automatically, an algorithm was activated and started the attack, just as Dominique had promised. When it had finished its work, he pulled it out of its slot and the computer went to sleep. Nobody would ever know he'd touched it.

He smiled at the wizardry of it all as he put the sticks in his pocket, then moved to the study door. Anton's computer had been savaged. Dominique would now have all the files she'd need to run the Foundation, along with any of Anton's secrets. A few pesky files that she'd wanted destroyed were gone, too, while others had been planted.

Chen had paid her back for extracting his family from Taiwan and now had all of Anton's documents as insurance.

Within five minutes he'd be back in the trees. He'd be home in Wisconsin in a day.

13

_____

CHINA LAUNCHES ALL OUT MISSILE AND AIR ATTACK ON
TAIWAN!

*After a week of high tension and tactical strikes, the island of
Taiwan woke this morning to the sound of jet engines and the heat
of explosions, as China launched the heaviest attacks yet in the
conflict. The United States Air Force and ground-based missile
defense units failed to halt the onslaught, leaving Taipei heavily
damaged. China has reportedly delivered a letter to the United
States Ambassador in Beijing. Reuters has learned that this letter
was a guarantee that China will not use nuclear weapons. Despite
this, it may only be a matter of time before China launches a full-
scale invasion.*

Correspondents, Reuters, *September 28*

Jack couldn't hear the explosion, but he could feel the
heat of it. He was unable to escape, surrounded by fire.
He looked around. Celeste was next to him, mouth
open in mute terror, no words able to escape. Others
were flailing their arms. One man, Jack didn't know him, had a
shard of steel through his stomach that he gripped and tried to

pull out, just as they plunged into the icy water of the South China Sea.

Jack's eyes shot open and he sat up on the air mattress. He winced in pain and rubbed his eyes, confused. A second ago he'd been on the Seahawk as it plunged into the ocean, but now he was in his hotel room. He exhaled deeply and lay down. Never before had the cobweb on the plain white ceiling that housekeeping never got around to cleaning been such a welcome sight. He was home.

"You awake?" Celeste stirred on the bed. "You okay?"

"Sorry."

She smiled. "It's alright. Anyone ever tell you you snore really loudly?"

"Every friend, roommate and girlfriend since puberty." He laughed. "Erin, too."

He felt a small measure of regret as her smile disappeared, replaced by a frown. "Which one this time? The Chinese cell?"

"Nope, the chopper just as the destroyer blew up. We hit the ocean and I wake up." Jack snorted. "I guess I don't like the cold even in my dreams."

Celeste laughed softly. "At least your mind gives you a bit of variety in the nightmares."

Jack was more glad than ever that Celeste had offered to stay at his hotel room once they'd arrived back in the States. Ostensibly it had been to look after him, but he did not doubt that she welcomed the company and support as well. Neither of them had family in America, and Celeste had sold him on the idea of sticking together. He'd agreed, on the condition that she took the better bed.

He turned his head to look up at her. "What were you treated with last night?"

"The rape." She didn't open her eyes. "Again."

"I'm sorry, Celeste."

"Wasn't you doing it."

That much was true. While Jack's nightmares ranged from

the helicopter going down, the variety of torture he'd received and others that didn't make much sense, Celeste had only one. The rape. He struggled up, his body screaming in pain the whole time, and sat on the edge of her bed. He placed a hand on her shoulder and she finally looked at him.

"I'm here if you want to talk about it."

She smiled weakly. "I don't want to add to your smorgasbord of head-fuckery."

He squeezed her shoulder. "Try me."

She stared at him for a long moment, seeming to size him up, then nodded slightly. "On the first night, three men entered and stripped me naked."

Jack immediately felt uncomfortable. "You don't have to talk about this if it's too hard."

She stared at the wall, not even acknowledging that she'd heard him. "They laughed at me and took my clothes. The next day, they returned and did it."

"Did what?"

"They held me down. They watched one another." Her bottom lip quivered slightly, and Jack placed his arm around her. "The third day was the worst. Objects..."

Jack closed his eyes. "I'm sorry, Celeste."

"Like I said, not your fault." Her voice trailed off. "They returned my clothes just before they threw you in with me. I knew then that something must have happened."

"Yeah. Ernest gave them whatever they were after."

She nodded, and closed her eyes again.

Jack still hadn't managed to speak with Ernest McDowell, despite his best efforts. From the prison, they'd been taken along with Christian Malley to a private airfield, placed aboard an EMCorp jet and flown home. They'd eaten, been looked over by a whole team of medical personnel and slept for hours on end. Once they'd landed, the two of them had been chauffeured to the hotel. But his calls to McDowell had been for naught.

He laid down on the bed beside Celeste, who was already asleep. He reached over to the side table and found his phone and earphones. He listened to the news, and felt a sense of hurt that the radio announcer who prattled away in his ear didn't interrupt the broadcast to curse the world on his behalf. Jack had learned that no matter how long you spent in bed, it took a great deal of time to heal when you had been abused.

At least this morning there was some fresh news—as depressing as it was—about the attacks on Taiwan. For the past week the US and Chinese airforces had danced with each other, but been unable to deliver a killing blow. That had apparently changed this morning—half of Taipei had been hit.

At some point he must have dozed off, because he woke up with a new program in his ears and a mouth as dry as the Sahara. He sighed, removed the earphones and did his best to sit upright. He reached for a glass of water, took a mouthful and placed it back. He let his head collapse onto the pillow and cursed under his breath at the spike of pain.

In the week spent at the hotel, he'd been able to gather his thoughts. It felt like he'd taken only a few breaths in the last month, given the incredible speed at which events had spiraled out of control. The divorce. The bombings. Erin's death. The sinking of the USS *George Washington*. His torture. The war between China and Taiwan. He felt like he was at the center of it all.

His phone rang. He picked it up off the side table. "Hello?"

"Hi, Jack? Peter Weston calling."

Jack frowned, unsure why Ernest McDowell's assistant was calling him. He switched the call to speaker. "Hi, Peter."

"How're you feeling?"

Jack laughed. "It's a regular party town over here. Come over if you like, but don't forget the scotch."

Peter laughed. "Maybe another time? Ernest wanted me to invite you and a guest to the company box at the Yankees playoff game. If you're feeling up to it by then."

Jack didn't even consider it for a moment. "Baseball tickets? Not for me. Stupid sport. But thanks anyway."

"You sure? They're expensive tickets." There was a note of incredulity in Peter's voice. "Ernest would appreciate it if you could make it."

Jack was about to decline for the second time when Celeste shoved him lightly. He looked at her and she gave him a thumbs up. He'd have hell to pay if he didn't accept. He reasoned that it would probably be worth it if it took her mind off her experiences, even for an afternoon.

"Alright, I'll be there. I'll be bringing along Celeste Adams." Jack looked at Celeste. Her eyes had grown wide and she nodded vigorously. He smiled at her.

"Great. Someone will email you the details. I'll give Celeste a call and invite her if you like."

Jack paused. "She accepts."

"I'm sure she will." Peter sounded confused. "But I'll still have to call."

"Celeste is here, she accepts."

Celeste leaned into the phone. "Hi, Peter."

Weston was silent for just a second too long. "Oh, well, you two have fun."

"Plan to. Speak later, Peter, thanks." Jack hung up.

"Plan to what?"

"Nothing. But he thinks we're fucking."

Celeste went beet red, then punched him in the arm again, lightly, before lying down with a sigh. "Thanks a lot. You've really done wonders for my career there, Jack."

"You'll just have to impress him at the game."

Jack rolled onto his back and closed his eyes. He was content to be warm and safe for the time being. He'd recuperate, mourn for Erin and then work out what came next. Hopefully it would include getting his life back on track. It wasn't much of a plan, but it was enough for now.

"I love baseball." Celeste rolled over. "It's going to be wonderful."

"It's going to be horrible."

~

ERNEST CLOSED the lid of his laptop with too much force. It slammed shut, causing the ice in the glass next to the computer to jingle a little. He let out a long sigh as he swung back in the leather chair, closed his eyes and massaged his temples. He'd been at his desk for fourteen hours, trying to catch up on work that had piled up in the past few weeks. The days spent dealing with the Senate committee and the EMCorp board, the negotiations with Michelle Dominique and China—and freeing his people—had put him behind with everything else.

But what had finally broken him for the day was a pair of emails he'd only reached a minute ago. One, from Dominique, suggested a particular line on the next day's coverage, while another, from the Chinese, suggested a different approach. While the emails were couched in polite terms and carefully manicured to appear appropriate if they fell into the wrong hands, he knew they weren't suggestions at all. For Ernest, there could be no clearer illustration of the prison he'd engineered for himself.

He didn't regret the choices he'd made at various points to save himself, his company and his staff. He consoled himself with the fact that, in a time of great stress, he'd done what he'd had to do. Not everyone in his position would have. But the deal with the Chinese, on the back of the one with Dominique, had placed him in an impossible bind. He felt the agreements strangling the life out of him.

He'd hoped the arrangement would last a little longer, but it wouldn't. He felt old, and knew that if there was to be a reckoning for the decisions he'd made, it may as well be now. With another sigh, he opened his eyes and reached for the phone on the desk. He dialed in a number he'd committed to memory and switched the call to loudspeaker. The phone rang and Ernest used this time to steel himself for the coming conversation.

"Hello, Ernest." Dominique's tone was impatient. "I hope this is important."

"It is. I need to renegotiate our deal."

She gave a small laugh. "Why would you need to do that?"

He rubbed his head. "I'm in a hopeless situation, but I want to honor both our agreement and another I've made. I can only do that if you're flexible."

There was a pause. "Being flexible wouldn't really be in my interests, Ernest, nor would it lead to you honoring our agreement in any way. My terms were clear. I delivered. The Senate inquiry has gone away and your company is off the hook in the United States. I expect you to continue to live up to your end of the bargain."

Any hope he'd had for a reasonable negotiation was out the window. "I had all good intentions of honoring my agreement with you, but things have changed."

She laughed again. "The Chinese? Yes, Ernest."

He was genuinely shocked. "You know? How?"

"I know you made a deal with the Chinese, that's clear. I don't know why, nor do I care."

He changed the topic. "I don't like being backed into corners and forced into impossible decisions I don't want to make."

"I know." She sounded chirpy again. "And it's precisely why I used the Senate inquiry to bait you. And now you're mine, to be blunt."

"What I'm proposing will help you retain some day-to-day control over editorial direction. It's the best I can offer."

"Not interested."

"I suggest you think again. You've got me, but I do have the means to slip your net. If I step down from the board entirely, then you're left with nothing."

She laughed. "Oh, I love the fishing analogies. Let's keep those going. Think of me as a fisherman, which I'm not, by the way. I've just caught a whale—that's you—and now it's struggling on the hook, fighting to get free. At the same time, the whale—that's you, remember—got your tail caught on *another* hook—the Chinese."

Ernest was growing tired of her, but hid his annoyance. "I don't quite understand the point."

"The point is: I've caught the big daddy, the trophy. I don't care what else happens, there's no way I'm letting go, no matter how much it wriggles. The Chinese can rip your fucking tail off, but your head and your company are mine. I'll rip your head off if I have to, but you're not getting away."

He swung back in his chair again while he thought. He ran through as many scenarios as possible, but he saw no other option than to break faith with one side. Having decided that, it became an exercise in risk assessment: while crossing Dominique would cause him pain, crossing the Chinese government in the current climate was unthinkable. He'd take the angry wolf pack over an angry dragon.

"Ernest?" She sounded annoyed. "Is that all?"

He gave a long sigh. "Yes. We're done unless you're willing to negotiate. Contact me."

"You've got little time to change your mind, Ernest. Don't throw everything away."

He was about to reply when the call cut out.

MICHELLE SWIRLED the amber liquid around in the tumbler then brought it up to her nose. She inhaled the scent of the whisky before lifting it to her lips and taking a small sip, then another. When her glass was empty, she leaned forward and placed it on the table. She smiled and leaned back, looking down the length of the table at the assembled men and women, each the leader of a Foundation cell. For all intents and purposes, this was the entire leadership of the Foundation now that Anton was gone.

"Anton is dead."

She kept a passive face as the cell leaders digested the news. A few gasped, another swore under his breath and the others just stared at her or looked around the table. She waited as the news sank in and for the most animated of them to regain their composure.

The leader of the Foundation's West Coast cell, Vanessa Dunstan, leaned forward. "How? Why weren't we told right away?"

Michelle considered her response. She knew that if there was going to be civil war among the Foundation in the aftermath of her actions, it would be led from California. Dunstan and her cell were the furthest from the Foundation's power centers of Washington and New York, both geographically and ideologically. She'd opposed some of the more extreme methods employed in recent years, and made no secret of it.

"I didn't want anything captured electronically." Michelle shrugged. "I also decided it was better to bring everyone together to sort out succession quickly and cleanly."

Dunstan rolled her eyes. "I bet you did. You still haven't answered the how."

Michelle knew that Dunstan had been close to Anton, and that intimacy had kept her adventures at least partially in check over the years. While it was unlikely that Michelle would get the same level of cooperation, she also knew that there was no sense hiding from the truth. Some of it, anyway. They could never know the real reason she'd killed him: that he'd tried to take her out, and she'd taken control as a result.

"I killed him." She looked Dunstan straight in the eye. Her

tone was even, completely matter of fact. "I discovered evidence that he was acting unilaterally to explode a nuclear device in Cleveland, and paint Islamic fundamentalists as responsible."

The room erupted. Michelle had wondered if any of them would assault her, though she had a fully armed Andrei Shadd a shout away. The usually reserved head of the Midwest cell, Mike Douglas, tapped his finger on the table, increasingly loudly, to get the attention of the room.

Once the room was silent, he spoke. "And why would he do that?"

"I don't know, but if he'd succeeded, it would have diverted the attention of the President and his administration from the war with China, and placed America's sight on the wrong target. It also would have made a mess of our efforts to get a large number of us into Congress."

Douglas nodded. "It sure fucking would have."

"We've wasted a decade and trillions fighting in meaningless deserts, more of that needs to be avoided."

A look of grave doubt appeared on Dunstan's face, her forehead creasing with stress lines. "Very well, if it's as you say, it needed to be done. I trust you have proof?"

Michelle shrugged. "Plenty—I'll make it available to you all after the meeting. I regret it, but my actions were necessary. We set it up to look like a street assault."

Dunstan nodded. None of the others spoke up. She'd won.

"Very well, if there's nothing else on that matter, we need to elect a director. There are too many balls in the air to not have someone in charge of the juggling."

There were nods up and down the table. The people gathered were used to quick-moving situations. Anton's death was forgotten.

The head of the New England cell, Bruno Cagliari, cleared his throat. "I'd like to nominate Michelle. She has the experience, contacts and the most in-depth knowledge of our current operations. Our cause will thrive or die on the success of a plan she and Anton developed. I throw New England's lot in with her."

Michelle gave Cagliari a barely perceptible nod. He'd be rewarded later. "Thanks, Bruno. I accept the nomination, but I'd also invite others to put their hand up."

She looked down the length of the table and the representatives remained silent. She had them. Apparently the weight of her claim, along with the lack of support from the others, had aborted any power play by Dunstan. She felt the rewards were finally coming her way, after so long and so much planning. When no other nomination came forward, others began to swear their cells over to her.

"The Mid-Atlantic cell is yours."

"The South East is on board with the new administration."

Michelle had a nervous moment when the leaders of the South and Midwest cells, Duke Callister and Mike Douglas, shared a wordless exchange. They were traditionalists and the staunchest conservatives, even in a room full of them, and she was not sure they'd go for a woman who'd just murdered the boss. Finally, Callister leaned in and whispered something in Douglas' ear. Michelle exhaled deeply when Douglas nodded.

Duke Callister spoke for the two of them. "If this evidence is as compelling as you say it is, Michelle, we're on side. But you'd better hope it is."

She nodded and smiled at him. "It is. I appreciate your support, Duke."

Michelle knew she was close, all she needed was the Mountain cell and Dunstan's West Coast. With the others on board—and the South in particular—she knew they didn't have the strength to resist her control. She looked at Dunstan and then at Mark Harrison, head of the Mountain cell.

Harrison looked at Dunstan, then shrugged. "Okay, but I don't like it. You've got an inch of wriggle room, Michelle."

That left Dunstan. Michelle stared at her, right down the other end of the table. "Vanessa?"

Dunstan sighed. "Okay."

Michelle was elated, but didn't show her emotion. "Okay. Next order of business is an update from the director. In short, everything is on track and we're about to see the rewards. We're unblemished by Shanghai and the war has started nicely. The next part of our plan is more of us in Congress. I'd ask that you all focus your efforts on that."

Dunstan scoffed. "I never understood this part of the plan, and how you expect the media to warm to our agenda, given their lack of enthusiasm in the past."

"Easy. Through control of EMCorp. Which I've had for the last few weeks."

She smiled, and enjoyed their reaction. They were more shocked by this news than they'd been about Anton's death. She omitted the fact that the head of EMCorp was being a particularly large pain in her behind and might slip loose. This was no time to dilute her authority or have them doubt her achievements.

She stood and held her hands out. "We've got our endgame within reach and now we've got the means to broadcast exactly what we want."

Douglas nodded and crossed his arms. Cagliari smiled. Even Vanessa Dunstan looked content as she spoke. "Well done, Michelle."

"Right, now that's covered, I think it's a good time to take a five-minute break. We'll discuss regular business after that."

She didn't wait for agreement. She left the room, aware that nobody else had moved. As soon as she was outside, they'd be gossiping about the changed environment, but she had control. Once out of earshot, she pulled her phone from her purse and dialed.

Through her friendship with Sarah McDowell, Michelle had put contingencies in place for controlling EMCorp if Ernest got out of control. Now she was ascendant in the Foundation, she couldn't risk him following through on his threats from earlier in the day. Losing EMCorp after announcing it was in hand would be a loss of prestige with her colleagues. It would also make achieving her agenda all the more difficult. Better to cut her losses. If she couldn't have him, nobody could.

"Chen? It's me. I need you on a flight to New York. I've got another job for you."

She hung up. Just as the Foundation meeting was about to reconvene, she wrote a quick text. *Sarah, let's catch up, I've got some wonderful news for you.*

14

As the war continues to escalate between the armed forces of the United States and China, Americans pause for a few hours today for the beginning of the Major League Baseball playoffs. The build-up has been subdued this year, but that's done nothing to dull the excitement of the New York Yankees fans, who are out in force to cheer on their home-town team against the visiting Red Sox. This year's coverage will include crosses to US troops serving in Taiwan, in Japan and on ships in the South China Sea, and the broadcast will include a special tribute to their service.

Michael Pompei, Chicago Tribune, *October 5*

Jack was impressed. While he'd only agreed to attend the first game of the American League Division Series out of a sense of obligation to Ernest, since he'd arrived at Yankee Stadium with Celeste they'd each had a smile on their faces. It seemed like the perfect way to finish their recovery. While the nightmares of their torture remained, some of the physical damage had healed. Jack felt almost human again.

Once a stadium staff member had spotted the lanyards they

were wearing, they'd been escorted to the cavernous EMCorp corporate suite. Jack felt like some sort of king as they walked through the double doors, even though he knew the service being heaped upon him was only because of the color of his pass.

He turned to Celeste. "Pretty impressive, isn't it?"

The suite was deep and rectangular, with floor-to-ceiling glass on one side showing off the field. On the far wall was a full-service bar. Guests had a choice of sitting at one of the dozen or so dining tables or in the leather recliners along the window with a view of the field. The room was already full, though it was over an hour until the opening pitch.

"Sure is." Celeste beamed as she eyed the bar. "It's going to be great. Want a drink?"

Jack hesitated. "You go ahead."

She smiled and left him. A few months earlier, he'd have been up for the free booze. Now, he just wanted to sit in a corner, out of the way, until the game started. He avoided the large huddles of people making small talk and ignored the glances from the other guests as he crossed the room. Those who knew him were probably curious about his wellbeing, but he didn't want to talk to anyone at the moment.

He nearly managed to find his way to a table and sit down when he was intercepted by a tall man with a broad smile and newsreader good looks, who stretched out his hand. "Warwick Jenkins. I work at the *Boston Herald*. You're Jack Emery, right? Hell of a story, you making it off that carrier."

Jack was surprised that Jenkins knew so much, given the details of their release had been tightly guarded. Jack watched the man's eyes drift to the cuts and bruises on his face. For the first time, he knew how an attractive woman felt. Jenkins' roaming eyes felt like an assault that he was powerless to stop without being rude. He didn't know Jenkins, but if he was here then he was important to Ernest.

Jack gave his best attempt at a smile and shook Jenkins' hand. "Just lucky, I guess. Lots of guys didn't make it."

"You're just modest, son."

Jack tried to change the topic. "Surprised you're not in the office, if not for the injuries, I'm sure I'd be missing the game."

"The war? We've got that covered. I don't miss a Red Sox playoff game for anything short of nuclear winter. You watch, tonight the war will be number two on the news." Jenkins laughed. "Say, I'd love you to meet my wife. We're suckers for an Australian accent. Spent some time in Sydney a few years ago."

Jack's mind was scrambling to find an excuse when Ernest appeared alongside them. It was the first time Jack had seen him since his return from China. He nearly blurted out his thanks. Though he knew the price for his release must have been high, he didn't know exactly what Ernest had had to agree to. He intended to find out and somehow repay him, but for now he needed to stay professional.

Ernest patted him on the back. "Hi, Warwick, good to see you. Jack, I'd like you to meet someone, he'll be here in a minute."

Jenkins clearly knew how to take a hint. "Mr McDowell, good to see you, and Jack, good to meet you. Let's talk soon."

Jack exhaled and smiled at Ernest as Jenkins backed away from the conversation. "Thanks for the intervention."

Ernest patted him on the shoulder. "Don't mention it. I didn't invite you here to be a social piñata. How are you, Jack?"

Jack hesitated, unsure how to answer. "I'm out of there, thanks to you, that's what counts. I wanted to say thanks."

"Don't mention it."

Jack leaned in closer. "I have a fair idea why I was tortured. What did they extract out of you to secure my release?"

Ernest's eyes narrowed and he started to say something, but hesitated. "That's not your concern, Jack. Relax and enjoy yourself. I need to find my daughter."

~

CHEN CEASED his climb up the ladder and opened the access hatch as quietly as possible. He pulled himself through, closed the hatch carefully and locked it behind him. He had plenty of time to prepare. The day had gone to plan and he was slightly ahead of schedule with the game about to start.

He walked to the far side of the space. The walls were covered in dust and grime, as well as an amusing cartoon some tradesman had made years ago, presumably of his employer. He was glad to see the case he needed was on the concrete floor. He next looked to the small ventilation hatch on one wall and saw the key to the whole plan—the height and breadth of view the steel grate provided. It was as perfect as Michelle Dominique's representative has promised.

Following the job at Anton Clark's house, he'd agreed to her request for one more piece of wet work. In his head, he'd owed her one job for saving his family and another for saving him after the Shanghai attacks. If she'd wanted to, she could have hung them out to dry. Chen was an honorable man. He paid his debts. After this, they'd be square.

The space allowed one of the most breathtaking views in the entire stadium, from a location few knew about and even fewer visited. Importantly, it also gave a clear view to some of the corporate suites. He knew all of this thanks to the briefing pack that had been provided, along with his rifle and uniform. He thought again about his disguise. An amazing beast, the cleaner, often maligned, never considered. Invisible. He'd moved his way through the stadium and to his perch without being questioned.

He moved to the case and opened it. He took in the beauty of one of the tools of his trade. It was pristine, cold and deadly, even disassembled into a half-dozen pieces. The long-barreled sniper rifle was as clean and beautiful as the day it had been manufactured. South African by design, it was light and portable, its sight able to zoom many times the magnification of the human eye. Most importantly, Chen had used it before and considered it suitable to cover the mission.

He assembled the weapon in silence and worked through all possible scenarios in his head. He mentally rehearsed the shot and how he'd escape from the scene. He could count on a few seconds of paralyzed fear that would grip the crowd and the authorities alike. If all went to plan, it should be a relatively easy job. In and out quickly.

If not, then all bets were off.

As he slid the gun onto its tripod, he didn't think for a second about the life of the man about to be snuffed out. He'd done something to irritate the wrong people, and that was it. To Chen, it was a business transaction, as normal as ordering dinner. He owed Michele Dominique one more job, and this was her chosen payment.

With the gun in place he stripped off his janitor's uniform and changed into some New York Yankees gear. All was now in place for the job to proceed. He slid up alongside the weapon, looked down the sight and touched his finger lightly on the trigger. He slowed his breathing and waited with well-practiced patience for the right time.

~

ERNEST SHOOK hands with Claire Paine and left the conversation. Paine was a political reporter he'd been trying to poach for a while, but since she'd won a Pulitzer the price had gone up. She'd declined Ernest's latest offer, so Ernest saw no point in continuing to talk to her.

He walked to the bar and asked for a whisky. As it was poured, he mused darkly about the last phone call he'd shared with Michelle Dominique. She hadn't been happy at his request to revise their deal, and it had been several days since he'd heard from her. His attempts to contact her had been fruitless.

He needed to think about something else. He scanned the room and smiled as he watched his daughter fend off the advances of the latest young suitor. Since Sarah had abruptly lost interest in the Wharton grad she'd been dating, word had reached every young, eligible bachelor on the East Coast. Even here, among friends, she was targeted.

While it would have been easy for him to march over and rain fire and brimstone down on the young, overly drunk EMCorp sales executive, he waited. He'd learned long ago that she could take care of herself, and there was no point in ruining a promising career unless it was absolutely necessary.

As her suitor leaned in to whisper something into her ear, he also placed his hand on the small of Sarah's back. The hand then began to trend downward. Ernest recognized a grope when he saw one and felt a flash of anger. Sarah was wearing a conservative gray tunic dress, but that clearly wasn't enough to dissuade those intending ill. As soon as the hand reached ground zero, Sarah took a step back and swung her small purse right into the exec's face. He didn't get his free hand up in time to defend the shot, but he did remove his other hand from her backside without delay. Sarah glowered at him and he backed away, mumbling some sort of apology.

Ernest chuckled and picked his whisky up from the bar. As he walked over to his daughter, he reflected on her fire and her focus—traits they shared. Despite this, he hadn't managed to focus her in the same direction as he had taken. While he'd been driven to succeed in business, Sarah was interested in art and theater.

"You okay?" He leaned in to kiss her on the cheek. "I hope you're not getting into too much mischief."

Her eyebrows furrowed in mock contempt. "It's your staff trying to get me into mischief. It's like they see a big dollar sign above my head or something."

He laughed. "Not quite. More likely they see a dollar sign above my head and a big green arrow pointing at me above yours. I'm an old man, after all. Won't last forever."

"Don't be stupid." She punched him softly on the arm. "Besides, you better last a few more years yet, because I sure as hell don't want your company."

He thought about saying something, but decided against it. They'd had that particular argument a few too many times. "Enjoying yourself?"

She shrugged and smiled. "Prefer Broadway."

He laughed. Truth be told, he hadn't really enjoyed the pre-game reception and the meal. His mind was on other things and he couldn't escape the crushing knowledge that a reckoning was coming. He was playing with fire, and it was only a matter of time before he got burned.

His gloom was penetrated by the mighty roar in the stadium, which seeped through the glass windows of the suite. A few of his guests shushed others as the stadium announcer gave some cheesy tribute to the American troops currently battling the Chinese in the skies above Taiwan. Once the announcer was finished, the national anthem was sung.

A short while later the game started. Ernest watched the first Yankees hitter put one into the stands. The reaction on the field seemed subdued compared to the scenes in the crowd, as grown men jumped up and spilled their eight-dollar beers and cold burgers. A few of the guests in the EMCorp skybox cheered and one Red Sox fan groaned, but most gave it little thought, continuing to chat and enjoy the hospitality.

"Wow, that was awesome." Sarah laughed.

He had a momentary pang of regret, and thought for a moment that he should have just taken his daughter to the game and jettisoned the freeloaders. The thought passed quickly. As much as he loved his daughter, it was commercial necessity that he use the box widely for events like this.

He turned to Sarah and smiled. "Plenty of time left for some more fireworks."

～

CHEN THOUGHT it would have been all too easy to pull the trigger the moment Ernest McDowell entered the crosshairs. The amateur—or immature—killer might have taken the shot, which was both simple and inviting. Even some professionals would have been hard pressed to turn down one of the easiest kills of their careers.

But those weren't the instructions.

At the crux of it, he knew that despite the veneer of legitimacy and professional standards of the special forces, retired or not, he was paid to kill people and break stuff. The same colleagues who would have taken the shot, though, were thugs; they had no restraint, no appreciation for detail or the art of their trade.

He was different. He followed specifications exactly. It was the reason he'd kept vigil on Ernest McDowell for forty minutes, not taking the first shot, but waiting for the best one. A perfect shot that not only produced the desired result, but gave the best chance for escape from the scene with minimum fuss.

He'd watched McDowell enjoy the highs and suffer the lows of the game so far alongside his daughter. McDowell seemed to pay no attention to the hangers-on who were also in the box. One innings had passed, and then another, until finally the time to strike had come.

With little emotion, Chen made sure his breathing was slow and waited. He had a perfect understanding of his weapon and his finger pressed on the trigger as much as possible without firing. He applied slow pressure until the precise moment. He was a hair's breadth away from his final squeeze when he aborted the shot.

McDowell's daughter had wrapped her arms around him for a hug. He eased off on the trigger and readjusted his aim slightly. He inhaled deeply, and then exhaled. He took the new target profile into account, inhaled again, and as he exhaled he squeezed the trigger slowly. This time it was enough to fire the weapon.

He nearly screamed. The girl had fucked it up. He could see the small spray of fine red mist through his sight and knew the shot had hit. But even as the man fell limp a moment after the round struck home, and chaos and confusion erupted in the box, he knew the shot was off: the girl had punched McDowell on the arm just as Chen had fired.

The movement had been enough to put the shot through McDowell's neck, instead of the center of his head. He knew it would probably still be enough to do the job, but it was not the perfection he sought.

JACK FROZE. His mind was screaming in protest at the scene in front of him, only vaguely aware of his glass of Coke falling to the ground. Each second felt like an eternity, and all he could seem to recognize was the clunking of the ice on the floor and the slosh of the liquid on the carpet.

His immediate instinct in that first second or two was to run, but as the others in the suite began to scream and run away from the source of the violence, he stood still. His feet felt like they were set in cement, refusing to move forward, as much as his mind refused to let him run away.

A woman's voice called out in distress: "Somebody fucking help my dad!"

Jack's feet started to move, his vision widening and life speeding up again. Past the panicked guests who were rushing right at him, he saw several people huddled around a figure on the floor. He had a sinking feeling he knew who it was and what had happened. He had to help.

He turned to Celeste. "Get out of here!"

He didn't wait for an answer as he broke into a run. His legs moved faster with each step as he ran the length of the function room. A few times he had to push his way forcefully through the crowd, and the closer he got the more chaos there was. Jack's mind had not had so much to process since China.

Ernest McDowell was on his back, writhing in pain and surrounded by blood. His daughter Sarah and a few others were crowded over him, while Peter Weston was shouting for help. When Jack reached Ernest's side he fell to his knees. Ernest was gulping for air, but when he saw Jack his eyes bulged wider than Jack thought possible.

Jack grimaced. "Ernest, just take it easy, help is nearly here."

Ernest tried to speak, but the gurgling sound that emerged from his throat sounded as if he were trying to suck all the air from the room.

"Where's the fucking help, Peter? He's going to bleed to death." Jack looked up to Sarah. "And someone get her out of here, she doesn't need to see this."

Ernest coughed and tried to speak again, but all that came out was a gargling sound. Jack didn't know much about medicine, but the very dark blood running down Ernest's neck and mouth was not a good sign. Jack's eyes widened in surprise as Celeste slid down beside him and put her hand over the wound to stem the bleeding.

"I told you to get out of here!" He stared at her. "It's not safe!"

Celeste gave him a dark look. "He saved me too, Jack."

"They're here!" Peter's voice sounded relieved. "The paramedics are here."

Jack looked up. A pair of paramedics were rushing to Ernest's side. One of them kneeled and took over from Celeste, placing a gloved hand over the wound. The other waved them all away.

"We'll take it from here, everyone. You all need to step back."

Jack started to climb to his feet and back away, but felt someone squeeze his hand. He looked down. Ernest was pressing his cell phone firmly into Jack's hand. He grabbed it and looked around. Celeste had noticed and raised an eyebrow, but nobody else seemed to see as he slipped the bloodied phone into his pocket.

Less than three minutes after his shot had struck home, Chen had finished disassembling his rifle. He walked back to the access hatch and paused only to press a button on his cell phone. He put his hand on the hatch as he heard the small charges he'd placed at four locations around the stadium detonate. The explosions weren't very large, merely designed to make a lot of noise and blow out smoke. They'd add to the gunshot and together be enough to send the crowd rushing for the exits faster than the police and venue security could handle. The confusion was his ticket out.

With one last check of his surroundings, making sure no trace was left of his presence, he opened the hatch. He looked down the ladder and saw that despite the mayhem of the past few minutes, the passage was deserted. He closed the hatch on the way down and grunted as he dropped the last few feet to the concrete below.

He put on a crumpled Yankees cap that had been in the case. He looked the part, complete with an old jersey. He walked quickly along the maze of passages that led him back to the main concourse, where he quietly joined the tidal wave of people rushing to the exits.

He saw a few police officers and security staff. They were

trying hard to wrest back control of the situation, but they had no chance. They were too late to catch him. He was no longer vulnerable to detection. He'd packed up and left the scene flawlessly, now just another scared fan.

Within five minutes, one suspect suddenly became thousands. There would be an unparalleled manhunt, but with no DNA, footage or fingerprints, the job was complete. A few might remember the Asian Yankees fan with the briefcase, but for all that they may as well have seen Elvis.

Chen allowed himself a small, barely discernible smirk. For all the money spent on security, it was still easy. The art of killing was not complex once emotion was removed, it simply required thought and planning like any other worthwhile human endeavor. The engineer doesn't build a bridge without a plan, nor should a killer pull the trigger. There had been no messy bomb killing hundreds, just a single round and a clean getaway. To Chen, it was another face filed away among many. While he was mad his shot hadn't been perfect, he hoped the result was the right one.

Even the best got it wrong sometimes.

15

There has been significant fallout from the attack on Ernest McDowell, billionaire owner of EMCorp. The Department of Homeland Security has stated it has credible evidence linking the attacks to terrorists and, as the investigation continues, the attack has caused chaos in the markets this morning. The Dow and the NASDAQ, which have both been hammered by the war with China, experienced further falls at the opening bell. EMCorp's board attempted to soothe the market by announcing caretaker arrangements, though EMCorp shares were off 14.2%.

Maree Silaski, Wall Street Journal, *October 6*

J ack was fascinated by the complex series of machines keeping Ernest alive. He'd watched them for hours, the monitors that bleeped, the screens with colored lines and an array of constantly changing numbers. Another machine—the respirator—inflated and deflated with its own rhythm, ensuring that Ernest continued to breathe.

Jack had been there from the moment Ernest exited surgery. The only others allowed into the suite were Peter

Weston, Josefa Tokaloka and Ernest's daughter, Sarah. They'd kept a constant vigil for the last day, sharing some dark jokes about the suite being big enough for all of them to move into permanently.

Nothing had changed with Ernest's condition in those hours, all Jack had noticed was the increase in the number of well-wishers sending flowers, presents and other trinkets. It had been a constant stream. While the hospital had flexed their muscles and restricted the number of visitors, they seemed powerless to stop the avalanche of gifts.

He had spent hours searching through the cell phone Ernest had handed him. He knew that the phone must have some answers, given the energy Ernest had expended handing it to him. At first, he'd tried to unlock the phone using any date or number of significance he could find on Ernest's Wikipedia page. None had worked, until he'd tried Sarah McDowell's birthday. The problem was that there was so much on the phone it would take days or weeks to dig through everything and find what Ernest wanted found. Jack wouldn't give up.

He sighed and looked away from the machines. He knew that his presence here would make no difference to Ernest's recovery, but he didn't leave. He was not a religious man, so there was no point in praying. So he waited and watched the machines keep Ernest alive. He owed it to the man who'd secured his release from China. Was this the price that had been paid? Was he the reason Ernest was lying there?

Jack heard the electric door behind him whir open. He turned to see Peter Weston entering the room with an armful of flowers and cards. Jack patted his pocket, making sure the phone was still there, then smiled sadly at Peter as he placed the gifts on a coffee table. Peter collapsed into the armchair next to Jack.

Peter looked up at him and rubbed his temples. "Still here?"

"Yeah, there's been no change."

"You can go home for a while. Nobody will think less of you."

Jack shrugged. "I would. I owe him. Sitting here is hardly a big deal."

Peter nodded and sank back into his seat. They sat in silence for several minutes. Jack considered telling Peter about the phone, but held off for now. Ernest had handed the phone to him, not to Peter, and he wondered if there was a reason. Maybe Ernest had distrusted Peter, in which case telling him about the phone would be a mistake.

Peter sighed, breaking Jack's reverie. "Cops came by the office earlier."

Jack nodded. "They came here again too. Just confirmed a few facts. I still don't really understand it though. It was the sort of attack normally aimed at a president, except Ernest didn't have the Secret Service by his side."

"Homeland Security is saying terrorists, but I'm not buying it." Peter shook his head. "He's a prominent man, with a lot of enemies. The cops won't find anything."

Jack was silent as he watched Peter closely. He had a pained look on his face, especially when he spoke of the enemies Ernest had made. Jack considered that Peter had probably been at Ernest's side when he'd made some of them. He made his decision, rummaged around in his pocket and pulled out the phone.

"It was a pro—had to have been. We do have one thing the cops don't, though." Jack held up the cell phone.

Peter's eyes widened. "Where did you get that?"

"Ernest handed it to me as the ambulance crews rushed toward him. He was so intent on me having it, I'm convinced there's something important on it."

Peter inhaled sharply. "And is there?"

Jack shrugged. "No way to tell. There's so much on it that it would take a dozen journalists a month to sift through it all."

"Well, whatever information he wanted you to have, I hope

you get to the bottom of it. Let me know if you want some help."

"I'm sure you've got other things to worry about."

Peter looked over at the still form of his boss, lying on the hospital bed. "Ernest being in a coma has caused some problems."

"What do you mean?"

"There's a few rumblings on the board. Nothing I can't handle. Just certain individuals taking the opportunity to make waves while Ernest is incapacitated."

Jack sighed. "Sounds like we've both got plenty to be getting on with. I just wonder if we'll get anywhere."

"What choice is there?"

"None. I owe Ernest too much to give up. I'll keep searching through this phone until my thumbs bleed. We'll get to the bottom of this."

Jack sighed and closed his eyes. He was tired. He hadn't slept properly since the shooting, and it was starting to catch up with him.

He woke a few hours later, looked around, and saw Peter asleep in the second armchair. After a few seconds' thought, he decided to try his luck on the voicemails. He plugged his headphones into the phone and dialed.

"*You have no new messages.*" The voice was polite and feminine. "*To hear all saved messages, please press 3.*"

Jack pressed the button.

The first message played: "*Hi Dad, just wanted to make sure...*"

Time passed slowly as the voicemail messages he listened to—or truthfully, half listened to—blended into one. He found it hard to believe that one man had so much contact with so many people. He dozed off again at one point, because he woke having dreamt of Erin. With a sigh, he pressed a button for the next message.

"*Ernest, we had a deal. Stop being a fool. You don't have a lot of time left to make the right decision.*"

"Bingo!"

MICHELLE SAT on a plastic chair in the middle of the hardwood floor of the Georgetown University basketball stadium, home of the Hoyas. She kept a pleasant smile on her face as students, faculty and some members of the public filtered into the bleachers. The usual butterflies that fluttered in her stomach before a major speech were there again, made worse by the uncertainty of the situation. She'd be fine once she was underway.

When the crowd was settled, the dean of the Graduate School of Arts and Sciences introduced her and gave a brief biography of her career to date. Michelle kept the smile throughout, but her mind was focused on the events of the last few days. She'd planned this speech carefully around her run for Congress, Ernest McDowell's death, and the fate of EMCorp. McDowell's ongoing ability to breathe was a significant problem.

She'd decided that McDowell's recalcitrance about their deal was too great a risk. With Anton dead, the Foundation cells under control, the war kicking along and the rest of her agenda ready to fly, the last thing she needed was problems from a geriatric business magnate. She'd put insurance in place for the control of EMCorp in the event of McDowell's death, so she'd ordered Chen to do the job.

Unfortunately, he'd failed.

The audience broke into enthusiastic applause. She smiled broadly, stood to approach the lectern then thanked the dean. It was all a blur until she laid her speech notes on the lectern, brushed some imaginary dirt from her dress and looked up. Then there was clarity. She gave a small wave and waited for the applause to subside, then cleared her throat.

"Good evening. As you know, if not for a fatal street assault, my late colleague Anton Clark would have been addressing you tonight. So first off I'd like to acknowledge his contribution to American public life, and the enormous void that his passing has left. He was a fountain from which torrents of intellect flowed."

There was more applause, subdued this time. If only they knew that every significant political event to strike the United States in the last few months was her responsibility—they'd storm the court and probably toss her severed head through the ring. It was a burden she carried gladly. There was nobody else who could put the country on the right path in such a manner.

"His death is one in a series of dire events that's afflicted our country, and the world, in recent months. The death of so many Americans in Shanghai, the underhanded sinking of the USS *George Washington* without a declaration of war, and—in recent days—the mysterious shooting of Ernest McDowell. Worst of all, of course, is the war."

She gazed into the crowd and was happy to see Sarah McDowell smile sadly in the front row, wiping a tear from her eye. Michelle knew that the next few lines would be the ones picked up by the television cameras. She glanced over carefully rehearsed words. It was the coming together of the remaining strands of her plan—with a few amendments, after Chen's failure.

"These events have led me to ask some important questions of myself. I've reflected on what I can do to aid our country in the most desperate crisis we've faced since we had our finger over the button, ready to deal with a nuclear force hosted by Castro. All Americans should ask the same."

She smiled straight at Sarah. While McDowell's daughter had been the central plank of Michelle's insurance policy, even with her father alive she was important. With Ernest McDowell in a coma, Sarah—beautiful and educated—became a massive lightning rod for public opinion. The public, and the EMCorp board, would fall in behind her.

"I've come up with two things. Firstly, I've ordered that much of the financial assets of the Foundation for a New America be spent purchasing a significant shareholding in EMCorp in the coming weeks. Despite the attack on Mr McDowell sending the share price tumbling, I want EMCorp to continue being a strong voice for America."

Michelle took a deep breath.

"Secondly, as I seek a mandate from the people to join Congress, I promise that if elected, I will not be joining the legislative sewer that has passed for our democracy in the last decade, for which both major parties are responsible. Instead, and with the support of as many likeminded Congressional colleagues as I can find, I will be a strong and unyielding voice for bringing strength and leadership back to America. It is time to fix the problems and bring America back to greatness."

This time the applause was thunderous. She made sure to give each of the cameras a good two-second look straight down the barrel. She held her hands up and waved the applause away, grinning from ear to ear. She waved again, then stepped away from the lectern and approached Sarah. The younger woman was beaming as they embraced. Michelle held the hug, to be sure that the cameras picked it up.

"Well done, Michelle, that was inspirational." Sarah's voice was soft enough only she could hear. "Thanks for the kind words about Dad."

Michelle pulled away slightly and nodded. "I just hope he pulls through. His absence is the last thing the country needs right now."

Michelle's timetable had been pushed forward by Ernest McDowell's double dealings, and complicated by Chen's failure. With the looming purchase of a huge shareholding by the Foundation, and Sarah's help, she was well placed to take control of the company when McDowell finally kicked the bucket. When he did, Sarah would become the star at the center of the story.

Sarah nodded. "I'm glad you're investing in the company. Though the family business isn't really my thing, it's nice to have a friend until he pulls through."

16

"Thanks, Stan. As you mentioned, things are getting bleak on the island. Despite the best efforts of the US Navy, the Chinese naval and submarine blockade has stopped most shipments of food and medical supplies to Taiwan. While the US has managed to airlift enough food onto the island to prevent mass starvation and people are able to eat at crisis shelters, there's a growing sense of desperation. This comes as the capital was rocked by another day of non-stop missile attacks, and as reports filter in of Chinese special forces troops active in the hills south of Taipei."

Royce Miller, Asia Today, *October 11*

Michelle sat back in her seat and watched as Chen's wife refilled the three delicate bone china tea cups with practiced grace. Not a single drop was spilled, and the whole process seemed effortless. When she was done, she placed the teapot back on the heat mat, stood and picked up her own cup.

"I'll leave you two to discuss your business." She smiled at Michelle. "But I want to thank you again for saving my family."

Michelle smiled as she leaned forward to pick up the tea. "No thanks are necessary."

The other woman nodded, then left the room. Michelle didn't speak until the door had closed and she was certain nobody would overhear the conversation, using the time to plan her approach.

She looked to Chen, who seemed relaxed. "Your wife moves like a ninja, or a ballet dancer, I can't decide which."

Chen gave a small laugh. "It's hell on the children. They don't ever hear her coming."

Michelle lifted the cup of tea to her mouth and took a small sip. It was a stupid move, and her tongue screamed in pain at the intrusion of the boiling liquid, far too hot for her taste. She did her best to mask any discomfort, but when she looked up at Chen, he had the slightest smile on his face. Scalded, she placed the cup carefully back on the table.

"Ernest McDowell is alive." Her voice was matter of fact. "That is unacceptable."

"So I saw on the news." He lifted his own tea and took a small sip, apparently with no discomfort. "Good for his family, but not for your organization."

"Indeed. I needed him dead."

Chen looked her straight in the eye. "It's through no fault of mine that he lives. The operation was a success. I inserted, took the shot, and got out."

Michelle couldn't believe what she was hearing. "He's alive, Chen."

"Because he shifted as I pulled the trigger. It was bad luck, and when he fell to the ground he was out of my gun sights. He's alive by the grace of his God."

Michelle sighed. She hadn't expected this to be easy. Chen had told her explicitly when she'd asked him to kill McDowell that this was the last job he'd do for her. But nor had she expected that he'd fight her so hard. She needed to convince him to finish the job, to march into McDowell's hospital room and yank a cord or two. Sarah McDowell's positive reaction to her Georgetown speech the day before had convinced Michelle that she'd have the support of McDowell's daughter once the old man was dead. Sarah would inherit his shares the moment his heart stopped beating, which for Michelle was good enough. Sarah McDowell was malleable.

She leaned forward. "I need the job finished. His continued ability to breathe will have unacceptable consequences, to say the least."

Her ideal situation had been to control EMCorp through manipulation of McDowell, but failing that, the best option was his death. In recent days she'd instructed the Foundation to prepare to buy up a great deal of EMCorp stock. She'd also put in motion efforts to blackmail, bribe or outright bully other board members onto her side. But with McDowell still conceivably in the picture, every contingency had gone to shit. Michelle had little to show for her efforts a week after she'd told the Foundation cell leaders that she was in the driver's seat.

"Ernest McDowell needs to die. I want you to finish the job. Say what you want about deities and bad luck, but you owe a debt to me, and I expect it to be made good."

She looked into Chen's eyes, and his black irises suddenly seemed like unforgiving vortexes that sucked her in and nearly extinguished the flame of her confidence. He leaned forward slightly and placed his tea cup on the table. He lifted his hand to his chin to scratch it. For the first time with this man, she felt like she was not in control.

His face was completely expressionless. "I don't see it that way. I told you I owed you two jobs: one for extracting me and one for extracting my family. You asked me to take care of Anton Clark's computer and I did. Then you asked me to shoot Ernest McDowell, and I did. I've repaid the debts."

Michelle gave a small laugh. "If I gave everyone I owed favors to the same spiel, I'd be dead in a week. I wanted you to kill him. There's a pretty big fucking difference."

Chen shrugged. "You told me to shoot him. I shot him. Death was not guaranteed. Your instructions should have been clearer. I will not be moved on this."

Michelle struggled to contain her anger. "You know as well as I do, Chen, that when you play in the big leagues, sometimes you need to work a bit harder."

"I understand, and that's why I took care of your deceased boss." His tone was calm.

"I killed him, in case you forget."

"But I removed the knife from your throat."

She hated to admit that he had a point. She'd been hoping to convince him to take one last action on her behalf, but his efforts to plant the evidence on Anton's computer and help her take over the Foundation had been invaluable. Deep down, she'd prefer to leave him and his family alone, but she didn't have that luxury.

Michelle knew there was no point pushing the issue further. He didn't seem like the sort who would change his mind once it was made up. She smiled and lifted her tea. She took another cautious sip and was glad that she wasn't scalded for her efforts. She swallowed, placed the cup carefully back on the table and stood.

"Patronage can be revoked, Chen. I hope you'll reconsider your decision. Please thank your wife for the tea."

JACK HAD one clue to unlock the mystery of Ernest's shooting—an unidentified female voice. He'd tried to call the number back, but it was disconnected. A burner phone. It seemed hopeless, but he'd made stories and a career out of less. Like a police detective, he knew he needed an overlooked fact, a new angle or a chance encounter. If he pulled the right thread, the whole mess would untangle before his eyes.

Since finding the voicemail on Ernest's phone, he'd spent

most of the last few days in his office at the *New York Standard* trying to find that thread. He could do pretty much whatever the hell he liked without reproach at the moment, because his experiences in the last few months had made others treat him with a light touch. They seemed surprised that he was at work at all.

He'd decided he could do nothing with the mystery woman's voice for now, and the hours spent trawling through Ernest's phone had otherwise proven fruitless, so he'd focused on finding some other blemish in Ernest's life that might explain the attack. He typed the date of the shooting into Wikipedia, but found nothing.

With a frustrated sigh, he swung back on his chair. He needed a break. He looked away from the computer and up at the television in the corner of his office. It was a good enough distraction as any and better than the scotch he'd sworn off. He lifted the remote from his desk and turned on the TV.

The screen flashed to life and showed a news replay of a speech given at Georgetown a few nights prior. He knew no easier way to get his mind back on the job than a few minutes of watching this sort of thing, though he had to admit the attractive speaker would keep his attention for longer than usual.

"*Firstly, I've ordered that much of the financial assets of the Foundation for a New America be spent purchasing a significant shareholding in EMCorp in the coming weeks.*"

Jack's eyes narrowed, then widened. He continued to listen as he leaned forward in his chair and dug through his pocket until he found Ernest's phone. As quickly as he could, and while the speech was still going, he pulled up the mystery woman's voicemail and played it on loudspeaker.

"*Ernest, we had a deal. Stop being a fool. You don't have a lot of time left to make the right decision.*"

He played it again, to be sure. After the second playback, he was convinced that it was the woman on the screen, announcing that her organization was buying shares in EMCorp and that she was ready to shake Congress up. A broad smile crossed his face, and he had to stop himself from cheering aloud when a box appeared on the screen.

Michelle Dominique
Director, Foundation for a New America

He typed her name into Google as he continued to look at the woman on the screen. She was beautiful, black haired, well dressed. The page delivered instantly: a profile, a website for her foundation—a treasure chest that would take him no time to unlock. He wasn't sure if she was the one who'd ordered Ernest shot, and even if she had, he had no idea why, but deep down he knew this was the thread he'd been looking for.

A coffee cup slammed—a little too loudly—on his desk. He hadn't heard anyone enter his office, but the shock was soon replaced with a smile when he spun around in his chair to see Celeste with her own coffee in hand.

"How long have you been sitting here for?" Her voice was terse as she put a hand on one hip. "You've got to sleep at some point."

"A while." He laughed. "Think I just figured it out."

"Oh?"

"Yeah, these guys." He pointed to the laptop, then up at the television. "Her. She left a nasty message on Ernest's voicemail, and she's buying a chunk of the company."

Celeste leaned over his shoulder and read what was on the screen. "Foundation for a New America. Looks like your average, run-of-the-mill conservative think tank."

"I've heard of them, vaguely. Extreme right-wingers. They hang out with the Republicans but aren't really welcome."

"All sounds promising." Celeste patted him on the shoulder. "Come on, time for lunch. Let's game plan this."

17

What this war has shown, more than any other in history, is the difference of warfare in the modern age. Smart weaponry has reduced the number of men needed to prosecute a war, but increased the drain of material and financial resources. The Chinese sank the George Washington, the US retaliated and struck at a number of Chinese air and naval bases, and now both sides are in stalemate over Taiwan. Billions of dollars' worth of military equipment is wrecked daily, and while both states have the power to deny the other the air, sea and land, neither has the strength to exert much control. The concern expressed by United Nations Secretary General Hans Voeckler is that as the frustration continues, both sides will be tempted to use nuclear weapons to end the deadlock.

Jim Teague, Jane's Defence Weekly, *October 15*

Jack held up his phone and took a few more photos of the woman. It hadn't been hard to find her, given how much of a public figure she was, and since then he'd watched her from a distance for almost a week. Michelle Dominique, Director of the Foundation for a New

America and Congressional nominee. He pushed himself off the wall he'd been leaning on and walked in an easy stride to intercept her.

After hearing her voice on the news, and matching it to the voicemail, he'd hopped a short flight from New York to Washington. He'd spent his days trailing her, and his nights digging deeper into her character. She was his sole focus. He was intent on learning more about this woman, who was somehow entwined in Ernest's shooting. Unfortunately, she was surprisingly private and he'd struggled to find much dirt.

Now he walked twenty yards behind her, careful not to get too close. Not that it mattered all that much, since she didn't seem overly aware of her surroundings. Whatever her part in all of this, he doubted she was some kind of super spy. After another block, she slowed near a bar and entered.

He had a choice to make. He could go in now and try to engineer some sort of contact, or he could wait and see what happened. He deferred to his professional judgment. There was no point in waiting any longer. An idea formed in his head, which he spent the next few minutes turning into a plan.

He crossed the road and entered the bar. It was more upmarket than he was used to. A bar ran the length of the small room and soft lighting accentuated curves and forgave blemishes. There were leather booths, which afforded privacy to those who wanted it. He had no doubt that the step up in class would be reflected in the drink prices.

Jack felt at home, or close enough. As he closed the door behind him and approached the bar, heads turned—he knew he was being sized up. In this sort of place, that analysis consisted of two things: how much he earned and how attractive he was. Lucky he was wearing the most expensive suit he owned.

He stepped closer to the bar with all the confidence he could muster and looked around. He recognized his target standing at the bar. Dominique was one of the few who hadn't turned to look at him when he'd entered. Her jet black hair flowed down the back of her dress and confidence seemed to radiate off her.

As he stood next to her, he was terrified that she'd recognize him, but he had to take the chance. He left just the right distance between them to ensure he didn't arouse her suspicions, but not enough for someone else to slip in between them. Jack rested his elbows on the bar and when the barman looked his way, he slid a fifty onto the counter.

The barman looked at the note, then up at him with a smile. "What can I get you?"

"Whisky on the rocks." Jack had no intention of drinking, but the act was necessary.

The barman frowned. "Any in particular, sir? We've got quite a few."

"Surprise me." Jack turned to Dominique. "And I'll get the lady's drink too."

Jack turned his head back to the barman and kept calm. He sensed slight movement to his left as the ice hit the bottom of the glass with a clink. He felt her gaze upon him as the top-shelf Irish whisky was poured over ice with the measured practice of a professional. He heard Dominique clear her throat as the barman put the scotch and a small bowl of nuts on the bar with a smile, then placed another whisky in front of her.

Dominique took the drink but left the nuts. "Thanks."

As she walked away, Jack exhaled heavily, glad that she hadn't recognized him. Though he wasn't exactly a household name, a lot of Washington insiders knew who he was. Newsprint clearly still gave him a fair bit of anonymity. His name was known by most, but his face wasn't. He remained perched on the bar as the barman returned with his change, but Jack waved at him to keep it.

The barman smiled and gestured his head in Dominique's direction. "Hey, thanks, buddy. Looks like you're in with a good shot."

Jack grinned. "I've got no idea what you mean."

Jack rapped his knuckles on the bar and walked to the only vacant booth, right at the back of the bar. Dominique was nowhere in sight, and his heart was threatening to leap out of his chest with its rhythmic thumping. He sat and took a few deep breaths to calm himself as he waited. Though tempted to take a sip of whisky to calm his nerves, his recent addiction was still too raw, and he left it alone.

A minute or so after he'd sat down, Dominique passed. He caught her scent: it was something floral but not overpowering, made all the more intoxicating by knowing he was close to getting her answers. Before he knew it, she'd placed her own drink on the table and was sliding up closer to him in the booth.

"Thanks for the drink." Her voice was soft but thick with suggestion.

Jack kept his voice even, despite his nerves and excitement. "No problem."

She smiled slightly. "What's your name?"

Jack knew he had her attention, but it was potentially fleeting. There were a dozen other guys in the bar who'd give her exactly what he could, probably better. He pressed his leg into hers and she responded in kind. He dug into his pocket and placed a fake business card on the table.

She picked up the card and considered it. "So, James Ewing. Farzo? What's that?"

"Social media, video conferencing, that sort of thing. It's a start-up I'm working on."

"Sounds dull." She placed the card back on the table. "I'm Michelle."

He grinned. "It is, until it outgrows Facebook. What do you do for a living, Michelle?"

"Lobbyist." She clearly didn't want to say any more. She lifted her drink to her mouth, drained it then placed the glass back on the table so firmly that the ice clinked.

"Get you another drink?" While Jack knew things might be easier with Dominique if she had booze in her, he couldn't shake the feeling that he was acting predatorily.

"Yours will do." She grabbed his drink and downed it in one go. She obviously knew how to have a good time. "Let's get out of here?"

Jack tried his best not to look stunned. He hadn't expected her to be so forward. "Um, my hotel is miles away."

This was his gambit. Getting Dominique interested, getting her into bed and escaping the next day with his story intact would be the easy part. But the entire effort hinged on whether he could get to her place, search through her things, and get a feel for who she was. Finding something useful would be a bonus. She started to stand and he hoped.

"My place is close." She shrugged. "Come on."

Jack stood and followed her to the exit. He was aware of every pair of eyes in the bar tracking him, scoring him much higher than when he'd walked in. Even though he had a purpose to all this, he had to admit he enjoyed the attention. He reconsidered his feelings from a moment ago.

Predatory or not, he had no qualms about his actions. He knew that he was about to start down the very slippery slope that had made his colleagues in Britain think that hacking phones was logical. But he didn't care. He was in control again. He felt like a lion stalking a gazelle.

He was going to enjoy this.

~

JACK STOPPED and winced as Dominique stirred next to him. He'd been about to get up and start searching, but wanted to be sure that she was sound asleep. The minutes passed and he waited, eyes wide open. He looked at the clock on the bedside table. Midnight. Plenty of time.

Besides, she'd warned him the night before that she was

intending to sleep in, so he could leave if he wanted to be up and off early. He wondered if she was as blunt with all the men she bedded, and decided it was a safe bet. She hadn't been what he'd expected. She'd been harsh, demanding, physical. He'd had to work harder to satiate her than any woman he'd been with, and they'd tried things Jack never had before. Not even with Erin.

It gave him all the more motivation to do the next part right. He needed information, and this was the last place he could think of to get it. He listened and waited. She stirred again slightly, one more time, before she started to snore softly. When he was sure she was asleep, he pulled back the covers and moved quietly into the ensuite. Once inside, he took his time and sat on the toilet far longer than needed to conduct his business. He wanted to be sure she stayed asleep.

When he left the bathroom she hadn't stirred. He dug around in the pocket of his jeans, which were on the floor next to the bed. He grabbed his keys as quietly as he could and moved toward the door. Once through it he closed it softly. He turned on the flashlight on his key ring and moved the small, bright beam of light around the apartment.

He didn't really know where to start, so he went straight to the iPad on the coffee table. He sat on the couch with it and put the flashlight between his teeth as he rolled back the lime green cover. The screen lit up, nearly as bright as the flashlight. A box asking for a code popped up. He cursed. It would have been all too easy for her to have no security on the iPad, but she wasn't that stupid. He probably had three tries to get the password right before he was locked out. He tried one random, four-digit code. The iPad buzzed, and "Wrong Passcode—Try Again" flashed in red at the top of the password box. He tried another. It buzzed again. He knew he could have one more try, but there'd be no surer way to inform her that he'd been rifling through her stuff than a locked iPad.

He sighed. While the iPad was the obvious place to find

incriminating documents and information, it was closed to him. He shut the cover and put the iPad back down on the table where he'd found it. He took the flashlight out of his mouth and waved the beam around the room again.

He spent the next twenty minutes fruitlessly searching the apartment. He searched the kitchen, living area and main bathroom, but found nothing of worth. He knew there was one room most likely to contain some information, and he'd deliberately left it to last. He opened the door to the study, which seemed to pull double duty as a study, second bedroom, clothes storage room and general junk depot. There was no computer, but there was a desk littered with documents and a safe.

He left the safe alone, having no illusions that he was MacGyver, able to open it with a paperclip. Instead, he went straight for the notepad. He grabbed a lead pencil from the stationary caddy and tried the oldest trick in the book. He scribbled the lead pencil all over the yellow paper, and writing appeared.

Chen–608-558-2015.

A phone number. An Asian name. It might be nothing, or it could be a lead. He tore off the sheet of paper, crushed it into a ball and placed the pencil back in the caddy. He'd be able to look up the number easily enough later. He searched through the pile of documents on the desk but found nothing of use, though there was a boarding pass stub for Shanghai.

He left the study and made his way back to the bedroom. On his way through he looked longingly at the iPad, sorely tempted to try again, but he left it. He returned to the bedroom and put the keys and the screwed-up piece of paper into his jeans. He climbed back into the bed. Leaving now would just make her suspicious. Next to him, Dominique stirred, rolled over and placed an arm over his midsection.

"Thanks for last night." Her voice was heavy with sleep. "I really enjoyed it."

"No problem."

His mind buzzed with the possibilities of what he'd found. He knew it could end up being nothing, or it could be the key to unlocking the whole puzzle. He had a number, and knew she'd been in Shanghai. He'd have to call in a favor to get the number traced to an address, but that wouldn't be hugely difficult. He'd leave first thing in the morning and start down the path that had just opened for him. He hoped it led somewhere.

He felt energized. It was enough for now.

18

There has been a major development in the war between the United States and China today, as Japan announced it would be committing air and naval assets to the conflict. The Japanese Government has justified the move by stating the forces would be used in self-defense only. Japanese Prime Minister Hiroshi Matsui stressed that the Japanese forces were tasked solely to protect Japanese shipping lanes through the South China Sea. Japan has lost three merchant ships in the conflict so far and the deployment of the highly capable Japanese military will free up US assets currently spent defending convoys.

Kris Brady, New York Standard, *October 16*

Michelle woke for the second time. She'd enjoyed the sleep in, and was particularly glad that Ewing had left without much fuss. It made for a nice change, as did the quality of the sex. She stretched like a cat, relishing the fact that she had the bed to herself. She had loose plans to sleep for a bit longer, followed by coffee and then a jog. Her plans were interrupted in their infancy by her cell phone, which buzzed on the nightstand.

She considered leaving it, but then sighed and hit the answer button. "What?"

"It's Andrei Shadd."

"What the fuck, Andrei? It's my day off, and it's too early."

There was a pause on the other end. "Sorry, Michelle, but I think your iPad has been stolen, and I thought you'd want to know."

She frowned. "No, it hasn't. I used it yesterday."

"I can't explain it then. The security guys recorded someone trying to unlock it. Whoever it was got nothing, but the guys have remotely wiped it."

"It's in my apartment. Unless Spiderman broke in while I was sleeping, there was no need to wipe it. Not fucking impressed, Andrei."

The phone line was quiet.

She stretched her legs out again under the covers. Her body ached—a good ache. "I want whatever you wiped restored by the time I'm out of the shower."

"Doesn't work like that. It's all gone, and the last backup was over a month ago. You should really plug it in more often, Michelle. The manufacturer recommends once—"

"Fuck off, Andrei. Send me the details of whoever broke into it, I need to know who to hate on for a couple of days."

She hung up and threw the phone on top of the covers. She stretched out again and winced as a sharp pain stabbed her in the back, and wondered again what some of those positions had been last night. She'd have to remember them. She was just dozing off again when her mind screamed and her eyes shot open.

She'd been half asleep during the phone call, so had failed to connect the dots. It hit her like a brick. She rushed out of bed, tripped in the covers and fell to the floor. With a curse, she got up and ran to the living room. Her iPad was where she'd left it, on the coffee table, undisturbed. Her fears had been unfounded.

"Fucking idiots."

Ewing had probably just wanted to check his Facebook account. He hadn't seemed like the brightest spark, so she severely doubted that he was an international super spy, as Andrei seemed to think. She was about to call him back and abuse him some more, just so she'd feel better, when her phone beeped.

The message was from Andrei, and contained the information she'd wanted—a log of activity that confirmed someone had tried to unlock the iPad at a ridiculously early hour. She'd thought he might have done it once the sun had come up, or just before he'd left, but the odd timing aroused her suspicions.

"Fuck."

She did a quick scan of the room, but couldn't see anything obvious missing. If she'd been robbed, the diamond earrings she'd left on the kitchen bench as they'd undressed would be gone. So would the iPad, for that matter. She rushed to the only place in the apartment she cared about, because it contained information that could ruin her.

Her safe was in plain sight in the study, but she'd been assured it was the hardest to crack in the world, short of those found in banks. It was intact and seemingly undisturbed, though some of the papers on her desk had been rifled through. But none of those mattered.

She knew she was being stupid, but she put in the code to the safe, waited until it beeped then entered the second code. It beeped again and she opened it quickly. Her body flooded with relief when she saw that the single manila folder was still there, along with a decent amount of cash, a handgun, some USB sticks and her duplicate ID.

She closed the safe and sank to the floor. She exhaled heavily and spent a few moments trying to regain her composure. Whatever he'd been looking for, the things that could destroy her life and her work were safe. She cursed at her carelessness. She'd underestimated the possibility that one of her casual pickups could mean her harm.

She called Andrei back. "You were right."

She had a hunch he was smiling on the other end. "Oh?"

"I had a guy here last night. My iPad and my safe look like they're okay, and I doubt he got much else, but I can't be sure. I want you to find out what you can."

"Got a name?"

"James Ewing. Probably fake though." She ground her teeth. "I think I got played."

"Leave it with me." He paused. "That all?"

She thought for a few seconds. Michelle didn't think she'd been compromised, but that didn't remove the horrible feeling in her stomach. She had enough to worry about without free agents ruining her plans. She'd considered another, different problem for days, but this seemed to be the perfect time to make a decision.

"Andrei?" Her voice was laced with anger. "I want Chen Shubian taken care of. Family too. Clean and final."

"I'll get the local cell onto it."

She lowered the phone from her ear and ended the call. Chen had failed her, and then declined her request to finish the job. She'd wanted to give him the benefit of the doubt, given his previous service, but he was someone who knew too much and offered her too little. The decision was made.

She sighed and shook her head. "I've become Anton."

CHEN'S EYES shot open and his mind was immediately alert to the high-pitched squeal from just outside his bedroom. He held his breath and listened again for the sound—a loose floorboard that his wife had implored him to fix half-a-dozen times. Chen had been reluctant, though, as the sound of the floorboard being stepped on, even by the lightest person, had inadvertently become a good alarm against sneaky children out of bed in the night.

There was no further sound.

Chen smiled, despite his annoyance at being woken up. Ongoing silence meant that the children were frozen in place, aware that Dad was about to come and march them off to bed with a swift spank for their troubles. He swung his feet out of the bed and sat up. The full moon had cast a shadowy hue over the whole room, and he envied his wife still sleeping soundly beside him.

He was about to stand when he heard the creak again.

"Shhh!"

Chen's plans changed in an instant. That wasn't his children outside the door, imploring someone to silence. He swung back into bed and rolled over to his wife. Resting on his side, he put one hand over her mouth and shook her head gently but with intent. In the light of the moon he could see her eyes open, as alert as Chen had been upon waking. She had learned long ago to sleep very lightly.

When he knew she was not going to speak, he removed his hand from her mouth and tapped her on the chin: once, twice, three times. She knew the signal. Her eyes widened a little, but she nodded and immediately started to rise. They could do this in the complete darkness, but the moonlight made it easier. As she slid out of bed and onto the floor, Chen knew that she'd do what needed to be done.

He knew he was almost out of time. As quickly as he could, he rolled back to his side of the bed and opened the drawer on his side table. He pulled out his favorite pistol—the Heckler and Koch USP Tactical. In complete silence, he checked the gun was loaded, pressed the safety off and lay back in bed. He pointed the gun at the door and waited as he heard his wife slide under the bed. It was the safest place she could be.

He aimed, and was surprised that whoever was invading his household chose to open his door slowly and quietly, rather than burst in to get the jump on him. Chen didn't move as the door opened fully and a large, balaclava-clad man entered the room cautiously. It was nearly too easy. Chen squeezed the trigger once, then again, then one final time.

One of the rounds hit the man in the head, and he fell to the ground with a thud. Chen was already moving. He slid out of bed and aimed the gun at the wall. Whoever was on the other side had obviously seen the first man fall. He had partly contained the threat, now he needed to seize the initiative.

Chen felt sorry for them. He knew their playbook better than they did. Chen knelt, using his bed as some degree of cover, and fired four rounds into the wall, low enough to hit anyone standing outside but high enough that the bullets would whiz over the head of any children in the vicinity. His children.

The drywall gave way to the bullets like a bar of soap to a razor blade. Chen heard a cry of shock, and knew he'd hit something. One neutralized, another wounded. If they were following standard doctrine, there would be a team of four spread among his house, chasing their objectives. Two more. His children were still in grave danger.

He left his wife to hold the room, knowing that she'd give anybody who entered a dose of buckshot from the Remington 12-gauge she was cradling. He moved swiftly to the door of the bedroom and stepped around the corner. The wounded man he'd shot through the wall was whimpering, with several bullet wounds. Though he was no longer a threat, Chen put a round into his skull to be sure.

He reloaded and moved further into the hallway, which was lit by a single bulb. Chen turned the corner, low, and ducked lower still when he heard the impact of a bullet in the wall behind him. At least his attackers were using silenced weapons, so the police and the neighbors would stay away. Less fortunate was the sight of the third balaclava-clad man holding his daughter hostage. He saw confusion and fear in her eyes.

"Let her go." Chen raised his pistol. "Let her go, now."

"We're here for you, not the k—."

Chen didn't let him finish. He fired, glad there was enough light for perfect aim. The attacker's head jerked back slightly as Chen put a round through the man's open mouth. A fine mist of blood and brain matter evacuated from the back of his head and Chen was already moving up the hallway toward his daughter.

She started to cry as he reached her, and squealed as Chen put another round in her attacker's head. He put his arm around her, lifted her and carried her to the master bedroom, where he called out to his wife before entering, lest she fill him with shot. Once inside the bedroom, he let his daughter run to his wife and turned around again.

His senses burned, trying to locate the fourth attacker. There were always four.

Chen heard the back door slam. The fourth attacker must have lost his nerve and started to run. He threw the pistol onto the floor. Having to shoot inside had been bad enough, but he knew he couldn't fire off a few shots in the backyard of a quiet Wisconsin street without drawing police attention. Even with a silenced pistol, it was too risky.

He ran for the back door, thankful that the house was small. He burst through the door and it swung back hard on its frame with a loud bang. As he ran across the yard, Chen saw his prey was at the fence but struggling to climb over. He closed the distance quickly and pulled the man back.

The attacker cried out in surprise and landed heavily on top of Chen's wife's favorite flower pots. Chen picked up a large, pointed piece of broken ceramic pot. He pulled the man by the collar, just as his pistol was rising in Chen's direction. Chen drove the point of the shard into the man's face with all the force his adrenalin and training allowed.

It was enough. The man went limp as the clay pierced his skull and slid into his brain. Just to be sure, Chen rammed the piece into the man's face again, then once more, creating a series of bloody craters. Done, he dragged the man's dead weight back into the house, leaving a bloody smear.

Once he was inside and the door was shut, he shouted up the hall: "We need to go!"

When he reached the master bedroom, he watched the scene with a combination of awe and admiration. His wife had already gathered the children. They were frantic but as disciplined as always. She'd also gathered the single getaway bag they kept for emergencies and had car keys in her hand.

"Go to the car, it's safe now."

As they left the room, he went to the other side of the bedroom. In less than a minute he'd gathered the second getaway bag he kept for himself. It had a fresh pistol, cash, fake documents and everything else he needed to get them away. If his hunch was right about his attackers, he'd have to get far away indeed.

As he heard the sound of the electric garage door grind its way open and looked at the room one last time, he felt a pang of regret. They'd only had a brief time here, but it had been enjoyable. His wife had made friends with the neighbors, he'd started work and the children had settled in at school. Their cover had been perfect.

That meant there could only be one attacker: the Foundation.

He regretted having to leave, but in Chen's world, nothing was forever.

19

Local police currently have made no arrest for the quadruple murder in Spring Green, Wisconsin. In a statement today, the Sauk County Police Department revealed that the dead men were involved in a home invasion gone wrong. They've appealed for the occupant of the house to hand himself in, stating it is highly likely he was defending himself and has little or nothing to fear. Channel 4 News spoke to neighbors in the street, who described the residents of the house as a quiet Asian couple and their young children. The neighbors added that they were baffled by the deadly episode.

Frank Tait, Channel 4 News, *October 21*

Jack sat in his car across the road from the house. When he'd traced the number from Dominique's notepad, it had proven interesting enough to be worth a trip. He hadn't expected to arrive and find it surrounded by police tape and a smattering of media. Any hope he'd had of interviewing the person who lived here and somehow finding answers to Ernest's shooting now seemed lost.

He watched as Celeste walked away from one of the neighboring houses, shaking her head. She'd flown into

Madison, Wisconsin, a day after him, and they'd made their own way to the town of Spring Green—population 1500. Since then, they'd joined the rest of the local media, and some national media, outside the house. Thankfully, the rest of the media had gone now. Most had left a few days ago, three days into the stakeout, and the last of them had gone the previous night. A small town couldn't hold the attention of the major city papers and networks for long, especially when the locals had no answers. They'd rely on subsidiary networks to cover any follow-up.

Jack was just glad he could finally get down to the real reason he was here—getting answers about the mysterious Chen. The murders just piqued his interest even more, given the sheer impossibility of one normal man taking out four armed intruders. That made Chen special.

Celeste reached the car, opened the door and got in. "Neighbors aren't talking, Jack. Just general gossip."

He found it hard to believe there was no clue about the character of a man who'd killed four home invaders. "No idea who he was?"

She grabbed his Big Gulp and took a long pull. "Not that they're sharing. Some real weirdos live here."

"They just don't like us city folk." He gave up on his best attempt at a redneck accent. "Plus they've probably had their fill of journos asking questions."

She laughed. "Doesn't change the fact that we might be too late."

"Let's go look." Jack already had the car door open.

Celeste followed him across the street. "What about the cops?"

Jack smiled as he looked around. With no neighbors in sight, he ducked under the police tape and tried the front door. It was securely locked, a rarity for this part of the country. He searched underneath the welcome mat, inside the dying pot plants and in the letterbox for a spare key, but came up empty.

Celeste kicked the door in frustration. "So much for stereotypes. A house in the quietest street in America and no spare key? Ram it, Jack. That works in the movies."

Jack rapped his knuckles on the door. It sounded solid, not that Jack knew a lot about wood. "It'll just give me a sore shoulder. Not so keen on that. Let's try around the back."

She laughed but walked with him. "Coward, I had you pegged as an action hero, Jack."

He snorted but didn't reply. They walked through the latched wooden gate and down the side of the house. Once they reached the backyard, Celeste walked over to investigate the fence and the shattered plants while Jack tried the door.

"There's been a struggle here! There's blood and a whole lot of broken flower pots."

He didn't respond, too engrossed in the door. Unlike the front, the back of the house had a screen door with no lock, which Jack opened with no trouble. Unfortunately, the back did have the same heavy wooden door he'd found at the front. With one notable exception—the lock was broken. He tried the handle and it opened.

He laughed and called out to Celeste, "Looks like the cops didn't want to wait around for the locksmith. Thanks, Sauk County PD."

Celeste came up beside him, shaking her head. "See, you're an action hero. Or at least the luckiest guy on the planet."

Jack was about to make a joke in reply when he pushed the door open. The joke disappeared, replaced by a sharp inhale as he took in the scene before him. There were bloodstains on the carpet and a large, crimson streak on the wall halfway down the corridor. The scene was worse than he'd anticipated.

Concrete floor. Blood. Fists and feet pounding him. Metal instruments. His bowels contributing to the miasma.

Celeste put her hand on his shoulder. "This place is creepy, Jack."

Jack shook his head, trying to clear away the flashbacks from China. "Yeah."

Celeste pushed past him. "Some evil shit happened here."

She was right. Jack had hoped that it wasn't him breaking into Dominique's house that had brought the hammer down on this place. But whoever this Chen guy was, he looked like he could handle himself. He was more convinced than ever that Chen was involved in Ernest's shooting.

He flicked on a light switch. "Let's see what we can find. The cops will have scoured the place clean, but it's worth a shot."

Celeste nodded and went to search one of the bedrooms. "You never know. They weren't thorough enough to lock the back door, so they might have missed something."

He went to the master bedroom and called quietly, "Ten minutes, then we're out of here."

Jack searched the room without result. While there was more blood and signs of a gunfight, he found nothing useful. The possessions of the house's occupants were still here, too. They'd probably left in a great hurry. Jack wished he knew where they'd gone.

"Going down to the basement, Jack!" Celeste called.

Jack was impressed. Celeste had already searched the kitchen and living room and made her way to the basement. Jack was creeped out and wanted to leave, but he went to join her. He walked down the stairs but stopped halfway. Something felt wrong. The light flicked on and he saw a large man pointing a pistol at Celeste.

"Stop right there." The man's voice was Eastern European. "Who're you?"

This was leading to no place Jack wanted to go. "We're journalists."

"Unlucky ones." Their captor waved his pistol at him. "Back up the stairs, please."

Jack had the distinct impression that the hulking foreigner wouldn't ask again. He walked up the steps from the basement, with Celeste and their captor behind. He gave some thought to running, but didn't think he could outrun a bullet. The man led them to the front door, which had a button on the back of the door knob to unlock it.

They were taken out to the front of the house. Jack looked back, and saw that their captor had put his gun discreetly inside his large jacket and was pointing at a large black SUV parked a few houses up the street. Jack approached it as slowly as he legitimately could. His mind raced. He knew that inside that car was death for both him and Celeste.

They edged closer, and Jack was about to do something desperate when a police cruiser turned the corner at the top of the street and drove toward them. Jack stopped and waited for either the cop car to pull alongside or to get a bullet in his back. The shot didn't come, but as the cop car rolled alongside, the cop looked straight at Jack.

The car braked and stopped. Jack would never know the officer's name, but he'd have to make sure never to slag off the fine men and women of the Sauk County Police Department ever again. He knew a lifeline when he saw one. He turned quickly to grab Celeste's hand and started to walk toward their car.

He snuck a glance at their captor, who looked back at them impassively as Jack led Celeste away from the SUV and back toward his own car. The man made no move to intercept them as he started the car, and Jack wasn't sticking around. He drove up the street, away from the house.

Jack looked in his rear-vision mirror and saw the cop car driving away. "We're safe now."

"That was too fucking close for my liking." Celeste was shaking and staring straight ahead, but was holding up a USB stick. "I found this."

He turned his head. "What is it?"

"A USB stick."

He shrugged. "Let's worry about it later. I want to get miles from this place."

~

CHEN CLOSED THE CUBICLE DOOR, turned the latch and then pushed on the back a few times to be certain it was locked.

He placed his bag on the floor, sat on the toilet seat and cradled his head in his hands. He took in a deep breath and let it out in a long, slow sigh. His heart was racing, but he knew this was the best way to calm down. He needed to regain his composure before he took any action, and kept reminding himself that he had time and was safe.

He'd flown from Wisconsin to Los Angeles, and was now in Hawaii on his way to Taiwan. His family was already in the air. He was panicking because he'd left his insurance policy—the USB that contained Anton Clark's file dump—at home in Wisconsin.

He'd spent a frantic few minutes in the terminal searching through his bag, but hadn't found the envelope. He'd cursed all of the gods and deities that he knew, from Allah to Zeus, unable to believe that he'd been stupid enough to lose it. He'd thought back and determined that it must have fallen out of his bag during the rushed departure.

If someone else found it, his identity and the safety of his family would be at risk. And with four dead bodies in full combat gear, he was sure that a diligent police search would find it. He just had to hope that the local police weren't smart enough to crack the encryption and recognize its importance.

As it was, he couldn't worry about the USB for now. He had little choice. He had to access the Darknet for the first time since he was contacted by Dominique, to finalize the arrangements for his return to Taiwan. There was one computer in the airport that had the Darknet browser he needed, but before he could use it he needed a credit card so he could pay for the internet kiosk time without being traced. He could have used cash, but he wanted the user log to point to someone else entirely.

Chen didn't move an inch as he waited, seated on the toilet, just breathed deeply and tried to slow his heart. After about ten minutes, he heard the bathroom door open with a squeal. As the door closed, he could hear the staccato beat of business shoes on the tiles. Chen sat in silence as the new arrival entered the cubicle next to his and closed the door bolt with a snap.

Importantly, once the door was locked, Chen heard a scraping sound as the man in the cubicle next door hung his jacket on the hook on the back of the door. Chen waited another few moments, until he heard the man's belt buckle rattle against the tiles and the beginning of his business.

Standing up from the toilet, Chen picked up his bag and unlatched the door of his cubicle. He stepped out and looked around, sure that nobody else was in the bathroom except his neighbor but wanting to double check. Satisfied they were alone, he stepped in front of the other occupied cubicle, swiftly reached over and stole the jacket.

He was already walking toward the exit when the man started shouting in German. Chen didn't understand what he was saying and ignored him as he searched through the pockets, hoping for some luck. He found the man's wallet in the inside pocket. He rummaged through it just as he heard the cubicle door unlock. He grabbed a few credit cards from the wallet, and as the cubicle door opened, threw the jacket and wallet behind him. He pulled open the door to the washroom and the man to pick up the contents of his wallet.

The door closed behind him and Chen was safe, just another Asian traveler. He walked the length of Terminal 5, past coffee shops and newsstands. He reached into his pocket and pulled out a business card. On the front were details of a dry cleaner, but it was the back that interested him: hastily scribbled instructions on how to find the one computer in

Honolulu International Airport with the necessary browser to access the Darknet. He'd scrawled the instructions in the last frantic minutes before leaving Wisconsin.

He inserted the stolen credit card into the payment terminal and the computer lit up. He accessed the Darknet and started to make arrangements for his return to Taiwan. Though the island was under daily attack, it was still safer for him than the United States would be for a while.

He was on the move again. He also had somewhere to go.

20
_____

The inquiry of the UK Parliament into the conduct of EMCorp tabled its findings yesterday. The report recommended that EMCorp be forcibly divested from some of its UK interests and that Mr McDowell surrender his position on the board of the UK operation, should he regain consciousness. Though a severe blow to the company, the recommended measures are considerably more lenient than most analysts had expected, perhaps reflecting sympathy for the attempt on Mr McDowell's life. Prime Minister David Kennedy is expected to make a statement about the report today, and in particular about how the government will proceed.

Paul O'Brien, Financial Times, *October 22*

J ack sat in his pajamas. The heat of the laptop on his thighs had warmed things up downstairs a little too much for his liking. Next to him, Celeste was similarly clothed, but without the laptop threatening to burn a hole in her privates. He looked over, she smiled at him and gestured with her head at the screen. The message was clear—get on with it.

Jack was still uneasy about the events from the previous day.

It had taken all his self-control not to crack open the motel minibar and neck a few beers to ease his nerves. He sensed that Celeste felt the same, but was conscious of encouraging his continued sobriety: she'd opened the fridge, looked longingly at the booze, then settled on a juice.

He sighed and leaned back on the sofa. Neither of them had slept the previous night, too wound up from the events at the house. Now, in the early hours of the morning, he resumed searching through the documents on the USB. The run-in with the Eastern European man was all the confirmation he needed that they were on the right track. They'd speculated on what could be on the USB during the drive back to the motel. They'd expected secret plans to bring down the government or the names and locations of dozens of master criminals. They'd come up with all sorts of wacky ideas, but the reality had been more disappointing than that.

He looked back at the screen and clicked on the next set of documents. It was a record of receipts with dates, items from a shopping list and a receipt code next to each—a series of letters and numbers. Another document was a budget, listing some fairly random items and a cost. Another was a copy of a receipt for a child's toy.

Celeste sighed. "This is all useless."

Jack had to concede she was right. He was interested in none of them. "Yeah, none of this makes nearly getting kidnapped worth it."

Celeste laughed. "A shopping list doesn't cut it. I'm buying a gun tomorrow, by the way."

Jack snorted and looked up at her. "I'm not sure that's the best idea."

"A big one." She smiled, but he wasn't sure if she was serious or not. "A shiny one."

"Actually, it's a stupid idea."

She frowned. "I don't care, there's no way I'm ever going to feel like that again."

Jack sighed. "You know, research shows that pulling a gun in a situation like that makes it more likely that you'll end up dead?"

"Don't care. What've I told you about facts?"

Jack laughed and turned back to the computer to scroll through the file names. He came to an .exe file and stopped. While he'd spent most of his life in peaceful, ignorant coexistence with technology, he knew that an .exe file made shit happen. He clicked the file and gasped at the same time as Celeste. They both leaned forward as a black box appeared on the screen, asking for a password.

Celeste punched his arm. "What've you done? Is that a virus or something?"

"Don't think so, it does something, though. Shame we don't know the password."

Jack tried a few obvious combinations, but had no luck. Thankfully, the program didn't appear to restrict the number of password tries; he knew he'd need a fair bit of luck to crack it. He was not looking forward to the flight between Wisconsin and New York, but at least it would give him something to do.

Celeste yawned. "I'm sleepy. What about one of the tech guys at the *Standard*? Or paying someone to do it?"

Jack looked at his watch. It was very late. Or, more accurately, very early. "Maybe, but I'd like to try to work it out first. There could be all sorts of funky stuff behind this password, or it could be completely innocuous. I'd rather we find out what we've got before we hand it over."

She raised an eyebrow. "I get the feeling it's something big."

"Me too." He handed the machine to her. "Keep trying?"

She nodded as he got to his feet, walked to the bathroom and closed the door. As he did his business, his mind wandered through the collection of documents on the USB—the budget, the grocery list, the receipt codes—it all felt like hundreds of pages of complete, meaningless gibberish.

As he was finishing up, he spotted the newspaper that

Celeste had left on the floor. He read the date and something clicked. He flushed, washed his hands and rushed out of the bathroom. Celeste was mashing away at the keys and looking disinterested, trying to crack the password but having no more success than he'd had.

He flopped back on the sofa. "Hey, pull up that weird shopping list."

She turned and looked at him. "Pomegranates? Baked custard tarts? What about it?"

"It had dates, even into the future. And items next to the dates. But how can you have a receipt code for something you're buying in future? They're passwords."

He took the computer and looked at the shopping list, found the date and the particular shopping item for the day, then copied the receipt code. He opened the .exe file and the password box popped up again. Jack looked at Celeste and shrugged, then pasted in the code. The password box disappeared and a document browser appeared.

"Holy shit." Jack's eyes widened. "Seems like a lot of effort to hide some porn."

Celeste laughed. "Must be more to it than that. Open one of them."

Jack let out a hoot and clicked a random file. When it opened, another box appeared asking for another password. "Fucking hell, there's multiple layers of encryption. There's a meta password, then every file has individual protection. This is going to be a nightmare."

Celeste stared at him. "What?"

"It means we need some help with this." Jack sighed and ejected the USB. "We need to get it cracked, but it'll take some smart tech heads to do it."

~

MICHELLE SMILED as she pointed the remote at the television

and hit the mute button. The talking head who'd been summing up the war between China and Taiwan was silenced immediately, though the picture continued to shift between the studio and highlights of the war coverage.

Michelle had realized days ago that she was addicted to footage of the war. It had a potent placebo effect, letting her see how much China was bleeding as well as the growing strength of the US and its allies in the region. That didn't mean she needed to love the reporters, most of whom annoyed her with their spoon-fed analysis.

The war was proceeding as well as she could have hoped. While China had bombed the crap out of Taiwan, they'd failed to mount a successful invasion. The US Navy and Air Force were duking it out with their Chinese counterparts, and both were more than capable of sea and air denial, but not of superiority.

This worked for Michelle. She was relying on a protracted US engagement that avoided the deployment of ground troops or nuclear weapons. At least until after the midterm election. After that, if the US won the day and China retreated from its claims over Taiwan, so much the better.

She was certain, deep down, that as long as the US didn't suffer a disastrous loss, things would be okay. The right Congress would be elected, full of Michelle and her colleagues. The right messages would be broadcast to Americans. The US would prosper. The decay that had set in would be reversed.

The country could look to the future in the knowledge that its power was unchallenged.

Her power would be similarly unchallenged.

Events closer to home weren't progressing as well. After the news that the hit team she'd sent after Chen were dead, she'd received a call from Andrei Shadd. He'd had a pair of snoops bailed up in Chen's house—more than likely it had included Michelle's mystery lover—but they'd gotten away. Her favorite vase hadn't survived the news.

She sighed, picked up her phone and dialed. She waited through the series of strange sounds that signified an encrypted line, then the line started to ring.

"Hello, Peter's Dry Cleaning." Erik Shadd played the role well. "Make sure you ask me about our five shirts for five dollars special. How can I help you today?"

"It's an encrypted line, Erik." Michelle had little patience, even as far as the Shadd brothers' cover was concerned. "I need you to come to my office and escort me tonight."

Erik didn't hesitate. "Where to?"

"An event for the campaign."

"No problem."

Michelle leaned back in her chair and took a deep breath. Her plans would unravel if she didn't get matters closer to home under control. Chen had slipped the net, had a head start and was probably halfway to Asia. In addition, the mystery man was turning into a major annoyance, popping up in inconvenient places. That was more manageable.

"And Erik?" She picked up the remote and turned the television off. "I need every asset looking for that man. If he sticks his head above the parapet, I want it shot off."

"I'll take care of it and see you tonight."

The line went dead.

Michelle stood and walked to the large bay windows. The view of the Mall was commanding, and she never got tired of it. As she locked her hands together and stretched them over her head, she heard several vertebrae in her back pop. She'd been working too much.

She looked at the Capitol building, off in the distance. The good judgment of the American people willing, she and other Foundation candidates would take their place in the Congress within a few months. Once there, she'd join a small group already in Congress and loyal to the Foundation. Others still would be bribed or blackmailed.

She'd have a great number of votes. She'd have power.

She walked to her desk, picked up the phone again and dialed.

"Hi, Michelle." Sarah McDowell clearly recognized the number.

"Hi, Sarah, how're things?"

"Bad. Dad isn't any better, the suitors won't fuck off, and I still have no interest in the company, no matter how much the board and my dad's advisors tell me I need to."

Michelle rolled her eyes. "Sorry, Sarah, I'm trying."

Sarah hesitated on the other end of the line. "I didn't mean to criticize you! You've been fantastic through the whole thing. It's all the other rent seekers that I hate."

She had her, Michelle realized then. She'd cultivated the relationship with Sarah McDowell to the point where she was now the girl's trusted friend and sounding board, particularly on matters concerning the company.

"It's going to get worse before it gets better, Sarah. The UK Parliamentary inquiry handed down its findings today. I'd expect a bit of blowback once the PM speaks."

Sarah sighed loudly but didn't answer. Michelle smiled and readied herself for an hour or so of gossip.

Some things were out of hand, but others were well under control.

JACK CURSED as he stepped into the full-body scanner, the only way past security and into the passenger terminal at Charlotte Douglas International Airport. He'd had his fill of airports lately, yet he had little choice but to wait as some security guard looked at an X-ray of his junk. After a moment, the TSA official waved him through. He scowled at Celeste, who'd already passed security and was waiting for him.

"Every fucking time. It's like I've got a tattoo on my head saying terrorist or something."

She smiled. "Get over it, we're through and we know your friend is here, so let's go have a chat to him."

"Right, come on then. Hickens won't wait for us if we're late."

After a bit of a sleep at the motel in Wisconsin, he'd called Peter and asked for help cracking the USB. Peter had called him back an hour or so later, with flights already booked for them to Washington via North Carolina, where he'd told them to meet up with a special friend at the airport. A special friend Jack hadn't seen in over a year—Simon Hickens.

As they walked in silence through the terminal, past sleeping travelers and ads for Swiss watches and expensive clothing, he hoped Hickens might help them. He was one of the smartest tech guys in the world, and EMCorp had used him exhaustively over the years. He'd been caught up in some of the UK mess, but managed to stay out of the worst of the trouble. Most of all, Jack trusted him completely.

"Jack fucking Emery!"

Jack knew the voice instantly and turned around. Hickens had placed his bag on the ground and opened his arms wide.

Jack closed the gap between them and wrapped the smaller man in a bear hug. "How are you, Simon? Good to see you."

Simon Hickens was the best hacker Jack knew, and the most difficult to work with. Despite having known him for a long while, he still had a lot of trouble understanding the surly thirty-something from Chelsea.

Hickens patted Jack on the back firmly, then backed out of the hug. "Good to see you too. Been too long. I was really sorry to hear about Erin, mate."

Jack felt a stab of pain in his heart. "Thanks. She rated you a lot, Simon."

Hickens laughed. "You're a liar. She hated my guts."

Jack shrugged. "Good to see you're still on the job, anyway."

"On the job? Not since this shit back home. Not a pound in

it for an honest gent like myself. I'm having to spend more time in the States to find work. And who's this, then?"

Jack felt a little possessive as he watched Hickens look Celeste up and down. His gaze lingered on all of Celeste's curves, and she went red in response. Jack didn't take it personally, since he'd seen Hickens do the same to plenty of other women over the past few decades.

"Eyes up here, Simon. She's still got access to your HR department."

Hickens looked at Jack and seemed offended. "But she's packing heat, mate!"

Jack laughed and Celeste walked closer to them.

Hickens held out his hand to her. "Simon Hickens, at your service."

Celeste rolled her eyes as she shook his hand, and made a particular note of his ring finger. "Celeste Adams. How is it you don't have a wife? You're such a charmer."

"Standards. You see, the average woman just can't hope to live up to this." He gestured up and down. "I'm like the Chelsea FC of single guys. A challenger might come along, get some luck or buy themselves into contention, but everyone knows who'll last."

Jack laughed and Celeste rolled her eyes again. If there was one thing Hickens was known for in addition to his skills with a computer, it was his big talk with the ladies.

Hickens grinned. "Now, your average woman, she's peaked at about twenty-eight, thirty tops. After that, it's all downhill. Give it another couple of years and you'll be all jiggle-jiggle yourself, love, and for a discerning sort like myself, that's just not cricket.

"Your average bloke, on the other hand, doesn't really hit his prime until later. Simple economics, and knowledge that the curls get the girls." Hickens ran a hand through his hair.

Celeste smiled. "You know, you're proof that at least some

humans are just an overly complex transport method for an asshole."

"Thanks, love. And don't stress too badly, you're fine. Enjoy it while it lasts."

Celeste rolled her eyes, and Jack could see she was amused. He changed the subject. "We've got something that needs your particular set of skills, Simon."

Jack knew that if anyone could crack open the security on the USB and find what was inside, it was Hickens. Jack was certain the USB was the key to everything, and hoped that something with so much security might have some information he could use.

Hickens frowned and his features became serious. "Yeah, Peter mentioned it is encrypted to hell and back. I can do it, but it'll take time. I'm willing to help as long as it isn't going to be something that stokes this fucking war."

"I don't know about that, but it has everything to do with Ernest McDowell's shooting."

"Suits me. Don't understand the line the company has been taking lately, especially since he got shot. It's like we want half of Asia to be killing each other. If we can get to the bottom of his shooting, it might bring some fucking sanity back."

Jack held out the USB. "Here it is."

"Shouldn't be too hard to figure out." Hickens plucked the USB from Jack's hand, then nodded at Celeste. "And hey, miss, if you change your mind, your old mate here will be more than happy to provide room and board."

21

As the midterm election campaign heats up, analysts are wondering just what effect the war with China will have on the balance of Congress. The White House freely admits that the President has had little time to campaign on behalf of Democratic candidates, and sources say that President Kurzon is banking on the goodwill and confidence of the electorate to stem the predicted landslide toward the Republicans. The wild cards for the GOP are the candidates aligned to the ultra-right Foundation for a New America, who have made no secret of their distaste for both the Democrats and the majority of Republicans in recent years. In a number of Congressional districts, hard-right, Foundation-aligned candidates have overthrown moderate Republicans. There remains talk in Washington about the potential for GOP leadership to cut ties with these fringe-dwellers.

Hannah Naylor, The Soapbox, *October 23*

Michelle hummed as she drove along the Columbia Pike, returning to her office from a campaign event. Her latest polling numbers were excellent and her staff were convinced that she'd easily take her seat in

Congress at the midterms. Though she had to keep up the effort of the campaign, the strong numbers let her focus energy on other problems.

She took a left, glanced for a moment at a pair of pedestrians on the sidewalk and almost rear-ended the car in front of her. She slammed on the brakes but never took her eyes off the men, even as she pulled the car over and drove it onto the sidewalk. A ticket was the last of her concerns.

She unbuckled her seatbelt and got out of the car as quickly as she could. The pair were seemingly oblivious to her interest and kept to their slow walk. She didn't even take the time to lock the car as she hurried after them at a brisk but casual walk.

One of the men was a consul at the Chinese embassy—Consul Li Guo—while the other was the man she'd slept with who'd tried to crack her iPad. Their pairing could be entirely coincidental, but she doubted it. The more she thought about it, the worse the range of possibilities seemed. She needed to know who'd breached her trust and attempted to learn her secrets, and why he was talking to the Chinese.

She pulled her cell phone out of her pocket and dialed Erik Shadd. "Erik, I'm near the Pentagon. I've found the bastard who tricked me."

"Need some help? I'm pretty close if you need me."

She kept her eyes locked on to the two men. "No, I'll sort him out myself. But he's with a consul from the Chinese embassy. Take care of that for me?"

"Which one?"

"Consul Li. Do what you need to do. I'm going after my friend personally."

Michelle clenched her teeth. Ever since the mystery man had ransacked her apartment and tried to discover her secrets, she'd felt less in control than she usually liked. He had found his way to Chen, and there was some chance that he had started to piece together the puzzle: Shanghai, the war, McDowell, the election. He had to go.

"You sure that's a good idea?" There was a note of concern in Erik's voice. "Are you armed?"

"Yeah." Michelle felt instinctively for her concealed pistol. "I've got some unfinished business I want to discuss with him."

"Okay, be careful though. We don't know the guy's story."

"That's what I want to discuss."

JACK HAD HAD to catch up fast. He hadn't seen Li Guo in a few years, but they were close from Jack's time in Afghanistan, where Li had been a Chinese consul in Kabul—and a key source. Somehow Jack had missed that Li had been posted to the States at some point. Probably not surprising considering his recent issues.

Li had surprised him at a coffee shop, and it hadn't taken long for them to reacquaint. As they'd walked back to the Mall, they'd shared a laugh and discussed Li's work at the Chinese embassy. But the more they spoke, the more it became obvious that their chance meeting wasn't so random—Li had sought Jack out.

He stopped. "Li, what can I do for you?"

Li turned and looked into Jack's eyes for a moment. "I need your help, my friend."

Jack laughed. "Short on resources these days, but I'll do what I can. I owe you."

Li looked around, as if their every move was being watched and their every word monitored. "What I'm about to tell you is highly confidential, but it needs to be heard."

Jack frowned. "Sounds ominous."

Li nodded. "You were tortured by my government because of editorial concessions made by Ernest McDowell to the Foundation for a New America."

Jack stared at him, his mouth open. While he had suspected that Ernest had made a deal with the Chinese, and that

Dominique and the Foundation had their claws right into him too, he had no idea that it was to such an extent that it worried the Chinese. It all made sense— and made Dominique more important than ever.

Li placed a hand on his shoulder. "Are you okay? I understand what I'm telling you is difficult to hear."

Jack shook his head. "Just a lot to process. Let me guess, Ernest made a deal with China to free us and then got himself stuck. Why tell me?"

Li smiled sadly. "The war."

"It's not going that badly for China, is it?"

"Not on the face of it. But while the missiles fly, our navy and airforce battle it out and the army sits on the southern coast, China is smoldering. The US Air Force has been relentless and my people are rising. They're frightened. They want freedom, not an island. The Party has kept it quiet, but it gets more difficult by the day."

Jack was shocked as the penny dropped. "So you want to stay in the United States?"

Li smiled. "Who says you're not an investigative journalist any more, my friend? The whole thing is smoke and mirrors, and the Party may well fall. I don't want to be on the wrong side of history. I can give you information about the initial deal between McDowell and the Foundation and the subsequent deal with China."

Jack smiled. "What's in it for you? And me?"

"The profile it gets me will help me stay safe. As for you, another Pulitzer?"

"And getting EMCorp out of hostile hands?" Jack thought for a moment. "Let's do it right now, then."

Li shook his head. "I need a day to conclude a few other matters. We'll do the interview tomorrow. I'll call you with the location an hour before."

Jack frowned. He never liked to delay big interviews like this, especially with a source as important as Li. If the slightest whisper of Li's intentions made it into the wrong ears, Jack doubted he'd ever get the chance to do the interview. He considered pressing the matter, but knew better. Li wouldn't budge.

"No problem, Li. Look forward to helping you on this."

~

MICHELLE HAD FOLLOWED them for a quarter of an hour and now watched the men talking from fifty yards away. She'd snapped some poor-quality pictures on her cell phone and sent a few to Erik. Impatient, she'd decided to go in for a closer look, but just as she started to move, the two men parted ways. She had no doubt who she should follow.

She sent a quick text to Erik, telling him that the targets had separated. She closed the distance to her target. He continued to walk with no great urgency and at one point pulled out his cell phone to make a call. She was determined to decipher his piece in the puzzle, but it was important to be patient. If she made a mistake and he got away, she might never get another chance to deal with him on her terms. Michelle edged closer, hoping to catch him unawares and subdue him with the threat of her pistol.

Michelle was about thirty feet away when he slid his phone back into his pocket. She groaned as he started to turn, knowing she'd made a mistake. She'd moved too close, sucked in by the chance to discover his secrets. There was nowhere for her to hide. She froze as his eyes locked on her, then widened in surprise before narrowing in apparent recognition. She held her breath and didn't move, waiting for whatever he might do next. He took the predictable option, turning around and walking briskly away from her.

She ground her teeth and followed him. Now he'd seen her, it was even more important that he not be allowed to get away.

This was her one chance, and she'd be damned if she was going to let it slip.

～

JACK LOOKED STRAIGHT AHEAD and walked as fast as he could without breaking into a slow jog. He knew that if he panicked and ran, she'd be on him like a gazelle.

He'd never expected to see Michelle Dominique again, unless it was on his terms and preferably with her in prison orange and separated by a large slab of Perspex. But she'd found him, whether by dumb luck or a cunning plan—or more likely his own stupidity in returning to Washington so casually. Now he had to get away.

He struggled to control his breathing and he could feel his palms starting to sweat. He hoped that she hadn't spotted Li, or else the break he'd received less than an hour ago could be for nothing and he'd be back to square one.

His mind was racing, trying to think of a place close by where he might be safe. He could stay in the open, but she'd just need to keep sight of him and call in her goons. He could talk to any of the police officers nearby, but that would lead to all sorts of awkward questions about why he was so fearful of a slightly built woman.

He looked left and right, and his eyes settled on the National Museum of American History. It was as good a choice as any. At this time of day it would be teeming with tourists and school children, and if he could lose her in some of the more popular sections he could be at Dulles Airport and on a plane to anywhere by the end of the day.

～

MICHELLE CURSED as he entered the museum. She'd hoped he might make a run for it down some back streets, giving her a chance to strike. But clearly he was smart enough to stay in plain sight until he'd lost her, to give himself the safety of the crowd and from any weapon she might have. Like her pistol.

She saw the museum's metal detectors up ahead and, without breaking stride, dug the small weapon out of her pocket, wiped away any prints with her blouse and dropped it into a trash can. It gave a metallic clang as it hit the bottom of the empty can, but she wasn't concerned. The safety was on and the weapon couldn't be traced to her.

She entered the museum through the white automatic doors. There was no line, and she walked through the lobby and passed through the security scanner. She smiled at the guard as she collected her things and started her search. There was no sign of her target.

As she continued to search for him, she was rapidly downgrading her plans. While she'd wanted to find out who he was and then kill him, now she just hoped to learn who he was. She slowed only once, in the cafeteria, to pick up a steak knife that someone had left unattended on a table. With no other weapon to hand, it would have to suffice.

She moved as quickly as she could, contorting her body to squeeze past the crowds of school children marauding through the museum. She was getting frustrated, until she rounded a corner and caught a glimpse of him before he disappeared from sight again.

She moved faster, past countless treasures of the United States, and watched him duck into the 9/11 audiovisual room. He clearly thought he'd lost her and would be able to lay low in the theater for a short while before leaving. She had other ideas.

She entered and spotted him near the front, facing the screen. He was the only person in the room. If she hadn't seen him enter she was certain she'd have missed him. She smiled at the small stroke of luck, approached him and took a seat to his right.

"You've a very difficult man to track down." She kept her voice low and even. "Don't do anything stupid."

When he saw her he tried to get to his feet. Michelle dug the knife into his ribs just deep enough to stall his movements. She heard him take a sharp breath, and then he slowly sat back down again. She could tell he was frightened as he turned and faced her with a nervous smile.

"Look." His voice trembled. "If this is about the other day, I'm sorry, alright? I got spooked."

"Shut up and give me your wallet." Michelle kept the knife against his ribs.

He complied and she opened the wallet. There was just enough light in the room for her to see the name on his license —Jack Emery.

She stared at the name. An alarm in her head was ringing, but she was struggling to figure out why. She kept the knife pressed against him as she thought. Suddenly, she recognized the name, and a lot of different pieces of a difficult mental puzzle fell into place. It was both reassuring and frightening to finally know who he was.

She gave a small laugh. "Well, looks like I can cross fucking a Pulitzer Prize winner off the bucket list, and I didn't even know. How impolite."

He didn't speak until she dug the knife into his ribs a little harder. "Sorry to keep you in the dark, but so goes the lifestyle of the rich and the famous."

"You're becoming a pain in my ass, I'm just not quite sure why. Surely you've got better things to do than harass my organization?" She looked into his eyes.

He glared back with a look of hatred that surprised her. "Because you seem to have a whole lot of coincidental involvement in a whole lot of things that have gone wrong in my life lately, that's why. I can't prove anything, yet. But I'm certain you were involved in the shooting of Ernest McDowell, and probably the war in China."

She laughed, but her mind was racing. She wasn't sure how he'd caught her scent originally, but he was the sort of problem she didn't need. A journalist of his talent wouldn't relent until he found a chink in her armor. With McDowell still alive and Chen out of hand, this was one thing she could tidy up easily.

"I'm involved in a whole lot more than that, Mr Emery, and there's a good reason." With her spare hand she pointed to the screen, showing a video of the Twin Towers collapsing. "That's the moment America got kicked in the nuts, Mr Emery, and we never really got up off the mat."

He shrugged. "What are you going to do?"

"I'm afraid you're a loose end I'm going to have to tie up." She swiftly brought the knife to his throat. "I find this place fitting."

She thought he might struggle, but he waited, clearly aware of how easy it would be to cut his throat. She pressed harder and was about to strike when she heard a giggle. Her head snapped around and she saw two schoolgirls peeking through the curtain and into the theater room.

"They're kissing." The girls giggled again. "They saw us!"

"Hi girls, come on in." Michelle smiled as she lowered the knife, then brought her mouth to Emery's ear. "You're a very lucky man. I'm coming for you."

He didn't move an inch, even as a whole class of elementary schools students filled the room. She threw the knife onto the carpeted floor, stood and walked out of the theater.

Her cell phone was already in her hand.

22

The prospects of peace between the United States and the People's Republic of China may have taken a turn for the worse with the death of Chinese Ambassador to the US, Mr Du Xiaoming, in a motor vehicle accident. Regarded as a voice of restraint in PRC–US relations, the ambassador was a long-serving diplomat with significant achievements in the US and elsewhere. The circumstances of his death are being treated as suspicious. One other embassy staff member, Consul Li Guo, also perished in the accident. Comment is being sought from the State Department.

Jan Fraser, DC News Central, *October 24*

An ambulance screeched its brakes near the emergency entrance. The driver killed the lights and hospital staff rushed the unfortunate passenger inside. Michelle had been parked near the entrance of New York Presbyterian Hospital for over an hour. While she'd killed some time watching the ambulances drop off their cargo, she was getting impatient. She looked again at the cell phone that was sitting in its cradle on the dashboard, waiting for the call that would change her fortunes.

Finally, it rang and she smiled and answered. "Hello, Andrei. Took your damn time."

Andrei Shadd grunted. "I've got confirmation from our source at the Stock Exchange. Sarah McDowell has nominated you as proxy for all of her share holdings."

"Enough?" Her heart threatened to leap out of her chest. "Will it be enough?"

He didn't hesitate. "The eggheads say so."

"Okay. Get our man ready to purchase EMCorp shares as soon as the news strikes." She thought for a second, to be sure she'd covered everything. "And security?"

"Taken care of."

"Good enough for me." She hung up and took a deep breath to calm her nerves.

Now that she'd been nominated proxy for Sarah, it was time to act. Little did Ernest's daughter know that she was about to get a whole lot more shares. Michelle also had to trust that Andrei was ready to purchase bucketloads of EMCorp shares once they hit rock bottom. She smiled as she opened the car door, climbed out and crossed the car park, careful not to look too eager. Once she'd passed through the electric doors of the hospital, she found herself in a lobby even busier than the emergency bay. The place buzzed as people rushed around, visiting sick friends and family.

The staff were calmer, walking around in their uniforms with confidence, some clutching takeaway coffee cups. She looked down at her pant suit and brushed some imaginary lint off her jacket, then made sure the wig and glasses she was wearing were firmly in place. Combined with the heavy makeup she wore, she was unrecognizable. She followed the signs to intensive care. A disinterested-looking ward clerk held court at the reception desk, flicking through a magazine. She looked up as Michelle approached.

"Can I help you?"

Michelle smiled, pulled her identification out of her handbag and held it up for the clerk. "Jane Michelham, I'm with the Bureau. I'm here to check in on Mr McDowell."

The clerk stiffened, stared at the fake FBI identification badge then up at Michelle. "Okay. Are you on the visitor's list?"

"Should be." Michelle dropped the ID back in her bag. "My field office was supposed to call you."

The clerk gazed at Michelle for a few moments too long for her comfort before turning to her computer screen, but she eventually nodded. "Here it is."

Michelle smiled and did her best not to betray her relief. Andrei had assured her that she had been put on the list of authorized visitors, and the fictional Agent Michelham would have no trouble gaining entry to McDowell's intensive care suite. Now she hoped that the implied authority of an FBI agent would keep the clerk's questions to a minimum.

"Great. Can I go through?"

"Sure. Let me check you off. Are there any problems that we should be aware of with Mr McDowell's security?"

"No, nothing to worry about. This is just routine. I'll only be a few minutes."

"Okay, Agent Michelham." The clerk nodded and handed Michelle a keycard. "There's nothing much going on up there, but go through. It's room 402. The card will let you in."

Michelle nodded and masked her relief at not being recognized by the clerk. Though she didn't have a huge public profile outside of Washington, she had made more television appearances lately. As she walked to McDowell's room, she kept her head down, hidden from the security cameras. Andrei had briefed her on their locations. It wouldn't do to be careless.

She followed the signs to the right room. She could see through the window of the suite that McDowell's body was receiving significant technological assistance to stay alive. She thought again of Chen's failure and her anger spiked. But so too did her resolve to do this herself, rather than risk someone else making another mistake. She scanned the keycard and walked into the room. As she moved closer to the bed, she wondered if she'd been naive to trust McDowell. He was always a chance to get a better offer.

She approached the bed and touched him gently on the arm. "Oh, Ernest, we could have been so good together."

She reached into her handbag and pulled out a small case. Inside was a syringe already filled with a poison that had been organized for her. It was potent enough to do the job, but slow-acting, so it would take hours to stop Ernest's heart. By that time, she'd be a long way from the hospital. Best of all, it was undetectable. All she needed to do was inject it into one of the IV drips connected to him. The syringe gave a little squirt when she tested it, being careful not to let any of the mist touch her.

Michelle glanced at McDowell, ready to inject the syringe into an IV. His eyes opened.

She froze in place, all thoughts of the syringe leaving her mind as a million possible scenarios jostled for attention. He had the look of a caged animal, clearly confused about where he was. He was unable to move, under the influence of some pretty strong drugs, but there was no mistaking that his eyes were locked onto hers. Michelle took a deep breath and jabbed the syringe into the IV. She was morbidly curious about how the poison would work, but couldn't afford to stick around.

"Nothing personal." She pressed her thumb on the plunger. "I didn't think it would be as easy as they said it would be, Ernest."

There was no response. He gave no indication that his body had just been invaded by poison. His eyes continued their unblinking stare.

Without further delay, she removed the syringe from the IV and, careful not to let it prick her, put it back inside the protective case. She slid the case into her bag and allowed herself a nervous laugh. She knew that at this moment the poison was coursing through Ernest's system, and would soon start to shut down his body.

She needed to get away and be ready to console Sarah when the inevitable call came, even as the Foundation scooped up a motherlode of EMCorp shares once news of McDowell's death hit.

Things were looking up.

~

JACK SIGHED as he put down his cell phone. He sat up in bed, turned on the lamp and ran a hand through his hair. He glanced at the clock and wasn't impressed. He had been asleep for a few hours since he'd arrived back in New York and checked in to a shitty motel, but it was still well before midnight.

He'd have gone back to the Wellington Hotel, but didn't want to risk it given Dominique now knew who he was. He was afraid. Worse, he'd had to tell Celeste and Peter to go to a motel, unsure of how much Dominique knew. He'd also called Li to warn him, but clearly he'd been too late on that front. The news had come in a few hours later.

Now Ernest was dead too. He had no doubt that Dominique was involved, given how many pies she had her fingers in lately, but it still came as a shock. In hindsight, perhaps it shouldn't have. She'd shown herself so willing to go to nearly any length to consolidate her control that murder hardly seemed out of the question.

He picked the phone back up and called Celeste. She answered after a few moments.

"Jack? Everything okay?"

He sighed. "Sorry to wake you. I just heard from work. Ernest is dead, Celeste. "

"Fucking hell." Her voice was throaty and she was clearly

struggling to wake up. "So now Ernest is gone, along with your lead at the embassy. I'm sorry, Jack."

Jack sighed again. In truth, he was more shocked by the death of Li. He'd slowly become used to the idea of Ernest not waking up, but Li had been the key to everything. Though he'd filled Celeste and Peter in on the threat from Dominique, he'd provided only basic details about the conversation with Li. With both dead, he spilled it all.

"Li was shaping up as a great source, linking Dominique to EMCorp and the war. He also told me that Ernest cut a deal with the Chinese to get us released. Looks like he was caught between the two of them and killed. But it's over, Celeste. We had them, now it's over. Li was the only real link. And now Dominique is free to do whatever she likes."

"She is." Celeste went silent for a moment. "Unless we get something off the USB. But I spoke to Hickens earlier. He's having some trouble. He's untangled some of the encryption but some of the information has been destroyed."

Jack frowned and laid back on the bed, keeping the phone to his ear. "Meanwhile, we're all in danger. You, me, Peter. None of us might survive this."

"I'm sure we'll be fine. With Ernest and the embassy staff dead the threat of anyone finding out about their control is now neutralized. She'll just forget about it."

Jack doubted it. "Stop kidding yourself. These people don't leave loose ends."

"Then I'll harass Hickens even harder to get me the contents of that USB and we'll go after Dominique. There's nothing else to be done."

"No. I want you and Peter to stay out of it. I'm going to take care of her."

She scoffed. "So you want me to hide while you act like some lone gunman? You need to let me help you, Jack. You need to let *others* help you."

"No, I don't."

He hung up and instantly regretted it. He knew that Celeste was right and that he should let her help him, but he wasn't prepared to risk her getting involved any deeper. They were in danger and it was his fault. Once more any good in his life, lovingly built, was crushed under the weight of circumstance.

He should have left it alone, let the police and the authorities deal with Ernest's shooting and moved on with his life. But he'd thrived on the game since finding the voicemail on Ernest's cell phone and had been playing with fire ever since. He'd pushed too hard and let Michelle Dominique force his move. He'd gambled and lost.

He pushed himself up from the bed and walked to the minibar. He opened the door and stared inside. He ignored the soft drink, instead eyeing off the bottles of beer waiting to be opened. They glistened and held the prospect of mental relaxation, at least for a night. For Jack, that was good enough.

As he cracked the first beer and slumped into the room's single armchair, he sighed deeply and tried to clear his thoughts. He wanted the world to go away, to leave him alone and for the carnage around him to stop. It was a forlorn hope, because as soon as one thought exited his head, it was replaced by a newer, darker one. He took a long swig of the beer and thought of the maelstrom of death and violence that had surrounded his life in recent months. Erin, Celeste, Ernest, the war in China, Li—his torture. In one way or another, it was all linked to one person, pursuing one agenda.

As he worked through the supply of beer, Jack wondered if it was worth fighting for anything anymore. He considered drinking until he couldn't lift a bottle, comforted by the thought of dark oblivion. He was not afraid of death, because he had nothing left to lose. He'd been on borrowed time since his release. Time granted to him by Ernest McDowell.

Long after he'd finished the final beer and moved on to the small bottles of hard liquor, he decided that it was time for redemption. He decided, whatever the cost and however much the odds were stacked against him, he'd go down swinging. He decided it was all or nothing. Everyone lost sometimes. And some people lost big. But he also knew that the difference was how well you fought back and recovered.

If he was sure of one thing, it was that he could get rid of Michelle Dominique from the world's throat.

ACT III

23

"Thanks, Kim. As you mentioned, there's been a great deal of activity at the New York Presbyterian Hospital overnight, following the death of Ernest McDowell in his sleep yesterday. McDowell had been in a coma following his shooting. His death leaves considerable question marks over the control of EMCorp, with the company's share price taking another huge hit following the magnate's death. McDowell is survived by his daughter, Sarah. Back to you in the studio."

Dan Wilkins, CNN, *October 25*

J ack hated the phone. He hated its incessant buzz, face down on top of the wooden dresser. It had reverberated like a hammer drill against his skull several times now. When it had stopped, he'd fallen asleep again in seconds, but before long the pain would start over, punctuating the first hangover of an unreformed alcoholic. This one hurt more than most.

He'd tried a pillow over his head, then tried throwing the pillow at the phone, before, in desperation, he tried to will the phone into spontaneous combustion. None of these ideas had worked. Now, as he lay face down on the mattress, the springs of the cheap bedding cutting into his cheek, the phone started to buzz again. He pressed his face into the mattress and let out a shout of rage.

That didn't work either.

He stood uneasily and kept a grip on the furniture as he made his way to the dresser. He answered the phone, tried to talk and realized his throat was as dry as the Gobi Desert. He must have sounded like some sort of terrifying alien menace to whoever was on the other end.

"Jack? It's Peter." His tone was all business, without a hint of appreciation for the pain Jack was in. "Any sign of Dominique or her people?"

"Hello." Jack's attempt to force a word failed. He swallowed several times and tried to get some moisture into his throat, then tried again. He didn't appreciate the chuckle on the other end of the line.

"You sound like shit, Jack."

"Feel like it too." His stomach roared. "What do you want?"

"Just checking in. You're clearly alive, if a bit worse for wear."

Jack couldn't argue with that. He'd worked his way through the minibar with a vengeance, then called reception for a restock. The staff member who'd brought the fresh booze to his room could barely conceal her disdain as she spied the empty bottles. Jack had worked his way through most of the fresh stock as well.

But, for all that, he was alive. Deep down he wondered if they'd find him at the hotel anyway. If they did, it would make his experience in the Chinese prison seem like a Caribbean cruise. While the Chinese had tortured him, they'd deliberately kept him alive. Dominique had no reason to.

Blood everywhere. Cold, hard concrete. Fear for Celeste Adams. Confusion. Pain. Lots of pain. And shit. In his pants and on the floor.

"Jack?" Peter's voice cut through Jack's flashback.

"I'll live. How're you going?"

There was a long pause on the other end of the line. "Honestly? Don't think it has sunk in yet. I've worked for him for years. He was closer than family. It'll take a while."

"Sorry, mate." Jack didn't really know what to say to console Peter.

"Thanks. Got some good news for you, Jack. Hickens has been trying to call you. He couldn't get through and so he called me instead. He's cracked it."

Jack sat down on the edge of the bed, shook his head and tried to clear away some of the fog. "The USB? You'd better not be teasing."

"Kidding you about the key to all of this? I'm not. He's filled me in. We've cracked the USB. He lost a heap of information in the process, but he said what he opened was a treasure chest. It all points to this Chen guy, but there's stuff about it all: Dominique, the Foundation, the attacks in Shanghai, the war, their run for Congress. Everything."

"Fucking hell. Peter, we might just have a fighting chance." Jack couldn't hide his excitement. He smiled; now he could do what he'd pledged to last night, the one thing that had the potential to return him from the precipice of self-destruction: send a swift kick right to the head of the person responsible for all of this, Michelle Dominique.

"More than a fighting chance." Peter laughed softly. "This deals us back into the game, and we're sitting on a great big stack of chips."

Jack didn't say anything right away. He considered what came next. He'd known that when he'd handed over the USB, it had been a long shot to produce a dividend even if Hickens could break it. Now, it seemed like he had. And unless Ernest's former assistant was exaggerating—something he wasn't known for—it changed everything.

"Will it be enough?"

"Maybe." Peter didn't hesitate. "But there's a catch. We've

got fragments. We're going to need to talk to Chen to bolt all of this information together into a story that will make people listen. Clean yourself up, you've got a flight to catch."

"Where to?"

There was a pause. "That's the interesting thing. Taiwan. Hickens found a clue on the Darknet that Chen has fled there, but we've got nothing more concrete than that. It's not a great lead, but you've got to find him. I'll email you."

Peter hung up and Jack grunted and threw the phone on the bed. His head suddenly felt quite a bit better, but it would be improved by a few more hours' rest. He lay down again but doubted sleep would come. There was too much to think about, too much to do.

He was just dozing off when the phone rang again. This time, he reached for it as quickly as he could. He thought it must be Peter again, but he smiled when he saw the caller identification. He hadn't expected her to call. He took a deep breath, exhaled and then answered the phone.

"Hi."

"Jack? It's me." Celeste sounded cautious. She'd clearly cooled down since their last conversation. He was glad that she was talking to him. "Enjoy your drink?"

"Yep."

"Where are you? Peter told me you had a sore head."

"I'm at a motel. Come over and we'll go from there."

"Go where? There's nowhere we can run from these people."

Jack was relieved she recognized the danger. "There might be one place. I'm not sure any of them have heard of Yeppoon, Australia, let alone been there. We're going to fly home—to my home—and that will give us time to think and consider our next move."

She didn't talk for a minute, and despite the situation, he smiled at the look he knew she'd be making: there would be a frown in the ridge between her eyes, and her forehead would be wrinkled with worry.

"Okay, Jack. Okay. I'm out of ideas so I'm happy to go with yours. I'll be over there within the hour."

He hung up and took another long breath and let it out through gritted teeth. He hated lying to Celeste, but had no choice. If he was going on a wild-goose chase to find Chen in Taiwan, then he had to do it alone. And to do that, he had to know she was safe. He stood, still unsteady, and looked around the room. He had an hour to make himself respectable, get packed and ready to fly. All the while he had to try to stay upright and keep the contents of his stomach from exiting his body.

No sweat. For Jack, this was living.

MICHELLE HATED MEETINGS, but was looking forward to this one. She could have attended the extraordinary general meeting of the EMCorp board and significant shareholders via video link from Washington, but she gained particular satisfaction from slaying her enemies in person. Metaphorically, at least. She was not going to give this one up.

Seated around the table were the usual members of the EMCorp board, along with the top twenty significant private and institutional shareholders. The most prominent of these was Sarah McDowell, but Michelle also had a seat at the table, following the Foundation's purchase of a large amount of stock. The board had called them all together to determine control of the company moving forward. They'd resolved to sort the matter quickly.

She looked down the table to Sandra Cheng. She looked like she was about to drop dead on the spot, with heavy eyes and limp hair. After her divorce, she'd gained a board seat. Now

Ernest was dead. It looked like the news had hit Sandra particularly hard. Michelle nearly sympathized with the stress the woman must be under—the death of her ex-husband and the fact that Ernest's daughter had chosen to confide in Michelle rather than her stepmother. Sarah, for her part, just looked sad.

As if on cue, Peter Weston cleared his throat. "Good afternoon, ladies and gentlemen. We've got a lot to get through. Moving right into it—"

Michelle interrupted. "Excuse me, Peter, before we kick off, I'd like to ask that the meeting minutes record condolences to the family and friends of Ernest McDowell."

Weston could hardly hide his scowl. "Very well."

She smiled. "Ernest was a visionary. He's a terrible loss for all of us. Sarah and Sandra, let me offer my personal condolences for your loss."

Michelle looked down the table and saw several nods and sad smiles. Sarah gave her a warm smile. Sandra didn't even manage that, offering nothing but a half-hearted nod.

Weston waited for the small amount of chatter to die down and then continued. "First item of business: the ongoing leadership of the company."

Sandra leaned forward. "I hope you'll all be willing to support my bid for chairmanship, given the trauma we've all gone through."

Michelle chuckled as several outraged board members barked their disapproval. One she didn't know spoke. "Sandra, you're grieving. There's no need to be silly."

Sandra was unrepentant. She raised her hands, palms facing outward, to block any attempt at rebuttal and further flare ups of the argument. "My family and I hold enough of this company to retain the chairmanship. Ernest may be gone, but it's important that we keep things in the family."

Michelle cleared her throat. "Excuse me if I'm being too forward, but I do wonder what particular family you're referring to? The man who divorced you or the stepdaughter who hates you?"

As Sandra blustered, Weston spoke up. "Ernest's will specified that his entire portfolio go to his daughter. There's no correlation between Sarah's holding and your own, Sandra. I've invited her to this meeting to make her views known."

Anthony Tanner, a Foundation-aligned board member, spoke up. "Indeed, given the size of her holding, we should hear from her."

Michelle smiled. Tanner had been easy to buy off: a large amount of money and a small number of revealing photographs outside the Ruby Slipper. He was another piece of the EMCorp puzzle in her pocket, and also an effective mouthpiece in her current fight to gain total control. Michelle sat back as Sandra started to protest.

Tanner shook his head again. "You have the floor, Sarah."

Sarah looked nervous and unsure as she looked down the table. "Okay."

Sandra tried to steal the march. "Sarah, tell them that you want me to be chairwoman. It's ridiculous to consider any other possibility."

Michelle was fascinated by the interplay between the two as Sarah narrowed her eyes at Sandra.

"That's not what I want." Sarah's voice was haunting. "I'm combining the weight of my shareholding with Michelle's stock. I trust her to look after the best interests of my father's company."

Michelle felt a wave of relief wash over her. After having Ernest in her hand, then losing him, this was sweet vindication. McDowell had been a loose cannon, a man of such immense power and ego who had proved difficult to control. She wouldn't make the same mistake twice. She'd ensure her appointed chairman was completely loyal.

She smiled, aware the others were looking at her. "I thank you for the show of faith, Sarah. I'm sorry, Sandra."

Sandra bristled but kept her mouth shut, and Peter Weston leaned forward as though about to talk, a look of concern on his face.

He didn't get the chance, as Tanner forestalled any reply. "Right, who will it be, Ms Dominique?"

"Thanks, Anthony." Michelle nodded to Peter Weston and gestured toward the door.

Weston looked confused, but moved as instructed. Michelle waited as the doors to the boardroom were opened to admit a tall, well-dressed man—Michelle's answer to controlling EMCorp. She was not actually interested in the daily workings of the company, just in ensuring it was on message. Her flunkies would sort that out, so she could focus on her bigger problems: Chen, Jack Emery and the approaching election.

As the newcomer walked to the head of the table, Michelle kept talking. "I'd like to introduce Gavin Marles. He joins the board and assumes the chairmanship with a wealth of experience. He has the full support of Sarah McDowell, myself and several other significant shareholders. I hope you'll join me in endorsing his board appointment and chairmanship unanimously."

Michelle didn't add that Marles was also as pliable as they came and in utter lockstep with her agenda. As she looked up and down the table, there were no dissenting voices. She was impressed that the board members could read the situation. Even Sandra, who sat with her arms folded and a sour look on her face.

Marles smiled. "Good morning, all. It's a pleasure to be here. I intend to hit the ground running, with a review of all of our operations. I'm concerned that at times in recent months our focus erred slightly. I intend to rectify that."

Michelle smiled. Marles might be a patsy, but he was a capable one. Most importantly, he was her patsy. He'd ensure the war was covered properly. Just as importantly, he'd throw a wave of support behind the bid for Congress by the Foundation candidates.

"Now, with the chairmanship settled, I'd like to get onto the guts of the meeting." Marles paused. "Peter, could I ask that the shareholders be excused?"

Weston nodded, a sad look on his face. "I'll send minutes of this meeting to everyone in attendance. You have the company's thanks for taking the time today. There'll be light refreshments served in the executive dining room that you're all welcome to enjoy."

Michelle smiled and stood without a word. She walked toward the door and met Sarah McDowell. She placed a hand on the young woman's back and guided her through. Sarah turned her head and smiled, but kept quiet. The meeting had gone as they'd planned.

"I'll catch you in the dining room?" Michelle kept her voice low.

"Okay, see you there." Sarah nodded and kept walking.

As Sarah walked away, Michelle smiled. Things were traveling nicely. The war against China was kicking along, and there had been a positive increase in US economic figures. Most importantly, public sentiment had swung back in a conservative direction which gave Michelle and the other Foundation-aligned Congressional candidates a good chance to win a decent number of seats.

Once that happened, the fun would begin. Power. And rebirth.

As she started down the hall toward the dining room, she checked her cell phone. It had a message that needed her attention. It was confirmation that Jack Emery had boarded a flight at JFK Airport to Hawaii and on to Taiwan. There was only one plausible scenario—he had tracked down Chen and was on his way to find him. She frowned, less happy with the progress made in dealing with those two problems.

She knew that the end game was coming, and that if those

two were allowed to meet, then there was a real chance that everything she'd fought for would be lost. She needed to terminate both of them, but knew that Emery was a far easier proposition than Chen. It was fortuitous that they'd both be in the same country at the same time. Or at least that's what her gut was saying. If Emery was going to Taiwan then Chen must be there.

She sent a simple message: *Send assets to Taiwan. Follow Emery until he leads us to Chen. Then sort it out.*

With luck, Emery and Chen would be dead in a gutter within a few days.

24

The Chairman of the Joint Chiefs of Staff addressed media in Washington today, providing a comprehensive update on the progress of the conflict against China. Admiral Matt Glennon detailed the NATO and other allied assets that had arrived in theater, spearheaded by the French aircraft carrier Charles De Gaulle. The flotilla of forty-eight ships from nineteen countries will join the Japanese Navy's efforts to protect sea lanes in the ocean around the conflict. While their involvement in the conflict will be limited to defense of merchant shipping, the presence of such an international coalition is an important public relations win for the United States, further isolating China among the international community.

Lee Jordan, New York Standard, *October 27*

Jack knew that the Happy Kitchen and Bar wasn't everyone's cup of tea, but it suited him just fine at the moment. He'd left Celeste safe in Hawaii and boarded a flight to Taiwan. She hadn't taken it well, once she'd realized they weren't going to Australia, nor was she following him to Taiwan. At first she'd raised her eyebrows slightly, as if waiting for him to reveal it was a gag. But her expression had quickly changed to a frown. He'd told her that he was traveling to Taipei to finish this business.

She'd protested and refused to stay behind. He'd desperately wanted to concede and let her come, but he hadn't. He'd reviewed some of the information on the USB, and it was awesome. He just had to track down Chen and get the last lot of evidence they'd need to end the serpent-like grip of Dominique and the Foundation for a New America on EMCorp. He knew it was dangerous and he couldn't do what needed to be done if he was worrying about Celeste. She'd backed down only after he'd laid on a fairly heavy guilt trip on her about needing to know she was safe, and that he'd already lost too many people who were important to him. The end result was the same, though: she was safe in Oahu and he could get on with what needed to be done.

He sighed and got back to work. He'd spent countless hours trawling through the information on the USB that Hickens had managed to unlock, and it was scary shit. There were pieces linking the Foundation to everything, but Chen was the only glue that could bind all the bits together. Jack had no idea where Chen was, but Hickens had found a tiny fragment on the Darknet to show that Chen had returned to Taiwan after he'd been forced to flee America. It was also the logical place to go.

The only interruption to his trawl had been an email from EMCorp Human Resources, telling him he'd been fired at the request of the board. Jack couldn't explain it, and hadn't spent much time thinking about it, but he somehow knew Dominique was involved. He'd determined to worry about his employment situation once Chen and Dominique were dealt with. They were his priority at the moment, and the first step was finding Chen.

Jack heard raised voices and looked up at the bar. He hadn't noticed the entry of the four well-dressed Chinese men who were now harassing the barman. Jack did his best to keep cool, but the barman's occasional nervous glance toward him was enough to tell him the gig was up. He closed the browser window and hit the shutdown icon on the desktop. As the machine whirred and then went silent, he pulled the USB free from the slot.

He looked up as the group of new arrivals approached his booth, reaching behind where he was sitting to slide the USB between two cushions. It was a tight fit, but as they came to a stop before his table, he was confident that the device was hidden.

Jack smiled at the men as they crowded around the table. After another moment, one of them slid into the booth opposite Jack. One of the others stood facing him, while two more faced outwards. Jack glanced over to the bar and noticed that the barman had made himself scarce. He wouldn't be surprised if there were another couple of goons standing outside, directing pedestrians away from the bar. One way or another, it was clear that this meeting was on their terms and wasn't to be interrupted.

"Hello, Mr Emery. I'm sorry for this display, but it's quite necessary to ensure my safety—and yours." The man who'd sat opposite him spoke in decent English.

Jack scoffed. "I'm struggling to see the imminent threat to your person, quite honestly. Afraid I might put a fork through your eye?"

The other man laughed. "A fair point. My name is Wen and I represent Michelle Dominique. You're on a fool's errand that has placed you in grave danger."

Jack made an effort to keep his facial expression neutral. "I know this area is a bit seedy, but I'm only after a beer and a night with a warm body."

Wen laughed and waved his hand dismissively, clearly not buying Jack's version of events. "To ensure your safety, I require you to tell me where Chen is. We know you've traced him here. Once this information is provided, my colleagues and I will escort you to the airport. You may then go anywhere you want with our blessing."

Jack laughed. The Foundation were getting desperate. Though they'd traced him here, the fact that they were talking to him rather than putting a bullet in him showed they had less idea where Chen was than he did. If the Foundation knew where Chen was, they'd have no use for Jack. Their entry into the situation made it a three-way game of hide and seek. He hadn't expected finding Chen to be easy, but this made things significantly more difficult. He had to find Chen before they did.

"Sorry, mate, even if I knew what you were talking about, a good journalist doesn't reveal his sources." Jack started to stand when one of the Foundation men took a few steps toward him, reached out and pushed him forcefully back into his seat.

Wen's expression darkened. "Mr Emery, you'll give us any information you have about the whereabouts of Chen sooner or later. But the longer you delay, the greater the potential threat to your health."

Jack could have taken issue, but he had no doubt about the sincerity of their threat. "Look, you'll need to find another tree to bark up. I don't have any idea what you're talking about. So I'll pass, if it's all the same to you."

Wen's eyes narrowed menacingly. "Give me what I want, Mr Emery."

Jack sat in silence. The information on the USB and finding Chen were the only ways to bring McDowell's shooting and the subversion of EMCorp to the fore. If he surrendered it then he'd lose the key to justice for McDowell, and the company's influence would continue to be used to push an agenda.

After a few moments, Wen shrugged, stood and gestured for his men to leave ahead of him. Once they were out of earshot Wen put both hands on the table and leaned in close to Jack's face. Jack didn't flinch, even though he could smell the tobacco on Wen's breath and see the anger etched on his face.

"We will meet again, you and me. And when we do, I'll shit in your mouth and have my men force it closed until you choke on it."

Jack didn't get the chance to respond, as Wen turned on his heels and left. It was bad enough that Dominique knew about him, but now her men were on his heels, waiting to pounce the moment he found Chen. His life was in greater danger by the day.

He needed to find Chen. Soon.

$\sim$

CHEN HAD SEEN his share of blood, but it had never seemed as important as this.

He stood with his mouth open and slack. His feet were planted like the roots of the mightiest tree, and refused to move despite signals from his mind. His entire consciousness worked furiously to process the sight of the thin ribbons of crimson that were interrupted only in a few places by small puddles. His training had abandoned him and he could focus on nothing else for several long moments.

He'd traveled the short distance from his hideaway in central Taipei to the luxury apartment his wife and children were living in. Chen had taken all necessary precautions: he'd checked that he hadn't been followed and discreetly entered the car park of the apartment building. He'd made his way cheerfully through the door and expected to be mobbed by his children and a relieved wife. It was to be their reunion.

He had been met with silence.

He'd first rushed to the master bedroom and found no sign of anyone. He'd shouted out and rushed to the next room in the apartment—the bathroom. There, near the entrance, he'd seen the blood. He'd looked inside the room and frozen. He knew, deep down, that he'd find a heavy toll at the end of the trail. The real mystery was how steep the price would be. Wife or children? Wife and children? Chen feared the answer.

He shook his head, reached into his pocket and pulled out a small flick knife—the only weapon he had on hand. Carrying a gun around in Taipei was far too risky at the moment. He doubted that whoever was responsible was within a hundred miles, but hoped there would be a hostile foe in the house to help him expunge his sorrow by plunging a blade into their throat.

He followed the trail of blood. As he did, the speed of his heartbeat increased and he struggled to keep his breathing even, despite his training. He knew the pattern of the blood—thin streaks along the carpet—meant someone had been moving quickly. But in some places there was a larger stain of blood, as well as handprints and streaks on the wall. Most concerning were the bloody footprints, bigger than any feet in his family.

The trail snaked up the stairs, to the top level of the apartment. Chen gripped the knife tightly as he followed, knowing that anyone waiting in the expansive living area at the top of the stairs would have a free shot at his head once he reached the top. He moved cautiously and listened for any sound, but he could hear none. Whoever had done this was long gone, or very good.

He peered over the lip of the stairs and felt his heart break. He gripped the knife tightly as the first tear rolled down his cheek. He climbed the last few stairs and rushed into the middle of the living room. On the large rug, with the debris of the living room splayed around her, his wife lay still and abused. Chen inhaled deeply, then let his training take over.

Though he found it difficult, it was important that he secure the room before moving to his wife's side. He scanned the area, knowing that there was only one possible hiding place from his current vantage point: the kitchen. He crossed the room, the small knife ready, but there was nobody there. Apart from his wife, the apartment was empty. That included his children. Whoever had killed her had most likely taken them.

He moved to his wife's side. Her face was barely recognizable. Her eyes were closed, but even if they weren't he doubted it would make any difference. Purple and puckered, her eyelids didn't reveal any hint of the black pearls he remembered. Her lips were cracked and cut. Her hair was matted and clumped together with her own blood. She had a nasty gash on her head, but what had killed her was a cut throat.

Defying logic and moving like an automaton, he fell to his knees beside her and felt for a pulse. There was none. He listened for sounds of breathing. She was silent. He scooped her into his arms and rocked her gently, his sobs coming in ragged and heavy fits. Her body was a dead weight, her clothes ripped and displaced. She'd been beaten nearly to death and then killed.

He rocked her back and forth, his tears falling to her broken body. He wasn't sure how long passed, with him simply holding her body and weeping, but slowly his senses returned and his vision broadened. It was only then that he looked up at the wall and saw a white piece of paper pinned there by a knife.

He placed her body gently back on the rug and stood. He walked slowly to the wall, not really wanting to read the message but hoping it might provide him with a hint of her fate. He pulled the knife from the wall and dropped to the floor, then opened the sheet of paper.

This is the interest charge on debts unpaid. No further payment is due unless you divulge anything about Shanghai. In such case, your children are your next best asset. They'll be kept safe and well for the next few months, while your loyalty is tested.

Chen screwed the note into a ball as he thought of his daughter and son. He threw it with as much force as he could muster, but it hit the wall and fell to the floor with nearly complete, unsatisfying silence. He picked it up and put it in his pocket. He ran a hand through his hair and moved back to his wife's side.

He'd taken every precaution after leaving the United States. He'd used the Darknet to reach out and secure safe passage and lodging in Taipei for him and his family. They'd traveled and been accommodated separately, and he'd thought it would be enough. Obviously someone had made a mistake. The Foundation had found his family. Now his children needed him.

He was thinking a bit clearer. He'd report this to the local police anonymously. His wife had no identification, her fingerprints weren't on file and his children were gone. She'd be a random, dead female in the middle of a country at war. He regretted enormously that she wouldn't have a proper funeral, nor would he attend, but it was the only way. He had to think of his children.

And vengeance.

～

"GOOD MORNING, Mrs Hamilton, good morning, Ms Dominique."

Michelle stepped forward and smiled as the few dozen bright-eyed fourth graders chanted the greeting. As they stared back and forth between the school principal and her, Michelle lifted her hand and gave another wave, then moved aside as the principal gained the attention of the class.

The principal spoke. "We're very lucky to have a very special guest with us today, children. My friend Ms Dominique is running for Congress in two days."

The children continued to stare, clearly unmoved by Michelle's pending triumph. She knew that the media hacks would get enough to edit up a thirty-second video, so she relaxed and let the event take its course. She just had to nail the sound bites, flash a smile, avoid any problems and they'd do the rest.

Ms Hamilton continued. "Is there anything you'd like to ask Ms Dominique, children?"

Hands shot into the air, and Michelle made sure she flashed a wide smile.

The principal pointed at one doe-eyed girl, who looked down at the table as she spoke. "Why do you want to be a Congress?"

Michelle smiled warmly at the gaffe. She split her glances between the camera and the child as she answered. "Because, young lady, I want to make sure you grow up in an America that is exceptional, that leads the world in knowledge and innovation and is a beacon of freedom and prosperity."

The girl smiled nervously, and after a brief moment of silence the principal asked another child for their question.

A boy's hand shot into the air. "Why are we fighting China? My mom says it's bad to fight."

Michelle frowned, then walked over to where the boy was sitting. She kneeled down, and put her hands on his shoulders. "Unfortunately, sometimes countries do things that are wrong. China has attacked a place called Taiwan, like a giant bully. Have any of you ever been bullied?"

Michelle waited for the nods and then continued. "Well, like when a bully bothers you, you hope that there'll be someone to help you and look after you. Maybe your teachers or your parents. Now, our country, America, has had to stand up to the bully and look after our Taiwanese friends."

Michelle flashed another smile. She loved children and their simple questions. They let her ram home any point she wanted without any backtalk or danger of going off message. She'd used the tactic liberally during her campaign, so it was fitting that her final public event would be at a school.

She took the boy's hand in hers. "Unfortunately, it shouldn't have become this bad. For many years, we've watched the bully get stronger, while we've become weaker. One of the things I want to do, if I'm allowed into Congress, is make sure bullies are never able to push us around again. I want America strong. Wouldn't that be nice?"

Ms Hamilton stepped forward with the smile. "Well, thank you, children, we'll keep moving along and let you get back to your class."

After a short tour of the rest of the school, Ms Hamilton farewelled Michelle at the front steps. Michelle was careful walking down them, lest the last televised moment of her campaign be her falling down stairs. The polls were showing a comfortable win for her and for many of the other Foundation candidates, as long as they avoided mistakes.

As she reached the final step, the two members of her security detail—also Foundation loyalists—stepped forward to intercept a man who was pushing through the crowd toward her. She backed away, but as he reached the front of the crowd he lifted his arm and threw something at her.

She cowered as the plastic cup sailed through the air and her security tackled him to the ground. She couldn't avoid a substance that smelled like urine splashing all over her.

The man shouted uncontrollably, even as he was wrestled into submission. "Do not vote for this woman, she's worse than Bush, she's a neo-con who will bring war to America and plunder our public services! Do the right thing, America, stand strong!"

"Alex, Grant." Michelle stood proud as her guards turned to look at her. "Let him go."

The two guards looked confused, but nowhere near as confused as the protestor, who gave her a quizzical look. Her words were even enough to stop his ranting. Michelle tried to mask her disgust as she stood tall, aware that the cameras were still rolling.

She gave the man the steeliest look she could muster. "While I don't condone your assault, I agree with your call for a strong America. I may not agree with your views, but I'll defend to my very last breath your right to hold those views. Our founding fathers would have expected nothing less."

Without another word, she resumed her walk to her car, which was waiting with its back door open.

The campaign had just been won.

25

"There you have it, explosive footage that has emerged from China, despite the media blackout. While much is unclear, we do know that a large protest in Beijing's Tiananmen Square has been violently put down by elements of the People's Liberation Army. This is the latest of several such videos, showing at least a degree of dissent and an undercurrent of dissatisfaction inside China at the moment. We spoke to an analyst from Jane's Defence and Security earlier, who speculated that the protests are being sparked by the stalemate of the war, the damage caused by US strikes to energy and infrastructure, shortages of fuel and food, and the continuing harsh curfews."

Len Oakes, ABC Newsflash, *October 29*

J ack glanced at yet another table of baubles and miscellaneous shiny junk as he followed the flow of the crowd through the busy Taipei market. At least he had a good disguise: a pair of Levis and a New York Yankees cap. America and US citizens were fairly popular in Taiwan at the moment, given that the United States Armed Forces were the only thing separating the Chinese dragon from the Taiwanese lamb.

As he paused to look at a stall that sold second-hand books, his cell phone rang. He pulled it out of his pocket, and sighed at the caller ID. Celeste was still mad at him, but at least she was talking to him. She was safe in Hawaii, but he didn't want to talk to her right now. He let the call go to voicemail.

He continued to walk through the market, which was riotously busy considering the constant threat of Chinese rocket attack. Someone bumped into his shoulder. Jack turned his head and recoiled. The stranger who'd bumped into him was perhaps the ugliest man he'd ever seen. Though the man was well dressed in jeans and a collared shirt, he had burns and a shocking scar down the entire left side of his face.

"Out of the way, Yankee."

"Sorry, mate." Jack took a step back and overplayed his Australian accent, hoping the man would go away. He didn't need the attention right now. "My bad."

The man stepped closer and pushed his face closer to Jack. "You should come and see my shop, buy lots of things and atone for your assault."

"No, thanks." Jack turned and started to walk away.

The Taiwanese gentleman didn't give up, and started to walk after Jack. Before he knew it, he had a large, barrel-chested Pacific Islander in front of him, and the ugly, yammering salesman behind him.

Jack turned. "Look, I don't want any trouble, I'm just not interested in whatever you're selling."

"I was talking to you. You should listen to what I have to say or my boy will make you listen. Nobody walks away from me."

Jack turned back to the man mountain, just in time to hear bone crack. The Islander howled in pain and crumpled and the Chinese man who'd inflicted the damage aimed another vicious kick at the Islander's leg. The pain must have been immense, and the man screamed in agony. Jack stepped out of the way of the man's two hundred and eighty-pound bulk as he fell.

As onlookers screamed and ran, the Chinese man who'd delivered the kick spoke to the ugly man in decent English: "Walk away and don't do anything stupid."

Jack swallowed hard, knowing that was nearly the universal signal for someone to do something stupid. He took another step back as the man reached for a small knife in his boot. Jack's Chinese savior stepped forward, easily deflected the quick thrust of the blade, and caught the man in a wrist lock. Jack heard something snap, and the Chinese man gave his victim a punch to the throat for good measure.

Jack breathed a sigh of relief, the immediate threat gone. He stepped toward his Chinese benefactor and held out his hand. "Thanks a whole lot for that. I'm not quite sure what their problem was."

"You've been looking for Chen?" The man's whispered tone was harsh. "You've found me, but we need to get away from here. They're amateurs, but others are closing in. The next bunch might not be so sloppy."

Jack's eyes widened. He reached into his pocket and pulled out the knife he'd been carrying for exactly this eventuality. He hadn't expected Chen to find him, but Jack's approach was unchanged. He flipped open the knife and held it out. His hand was shaking.

Chen sighed. "Didn't you just see the futility of that? You have a strange way of thanking someone who just saved your life."

Jack ignored him as he held the knife out. "You're Chen Shubian."

Jack was disappointed by how calm the Chinese man seemed. "I am."

"Your bomb killed my wife."

Chen shrugged. "Did it? Unfortunate."

"That's it?"

"It was not deliberate. She could have just as easily been hit by a bus, or been stabbed and mugged. But I'd suggest neither of us have time for your vengeance at this moment. The Foundation want me dead, and my own wife is dead thanks to them, so we've something in common."

Jack didn't lower the knife. He hadn't expected to find Chen on quite these terms, and clearly someone had told the two idiots to attack him, yet he was still torn between a desire to rip Chen's throat out and the need for his evidence that only Chen could give him.

Chen sighed again. "Look, the only reason you're alive is because they think you can lead them to me. You're more useful next to me, and probably safer too. So if it's all the same to you, I'd like to get out of here."

After a second, Jack nodded, pocketed the knife and followed Chen at a brisk walk through the market. A few people looked sideways at them, and Jack worried that with every corner they turned, the next street was going to be filled with armed thugs.

They were near the edge of the market when, as Jack had feared, they were surrounded on all sides by large men armed with a mix of bats and blades. At once he wondered where the rest of the crowd had gone, and how many foes Chen could take down while he ran.

One of their assailants stepped forward. "Hello, Chen. Michelle Dominique sends her regards. Hand over your friend, give yourself up and your children will be spared."

Chen laughed. "Spared what? The rape and murder of their mother? Being abducted? It's too late for that."

Jack looked sideways at Chen. But before events could proceed further, there were shouts and an ear-splitting whine. The ground shook with tremendous force and Jack was knocked off his feet. He landed hard and could taste dust and dirt, mixed with blood. He must have bitten his tongue. He rolled over onto his back and did a quick stocktake. He could see no injury. He was unhurt but dazed.

He rose to his feet involuntarily, as Chen grabbed him by the arm and pulled him up. Together they ran past screaming shoppers and away from the flames and rising plumes of smoke. The Chinese missile could have landed right on top of Jack's head, and he was glad to have a little luck for once. In all of the confusion, they lost their pursuers. He was thankful when they reached the edge of the market without further incident.

Jack stopped, trying to catch his breath when Chen turned to face him. "Now what do you want? It better be good, because you carried the vipers to my doorstep."

"How did you find me?"

"You're not as subtle as you think. Word of a Westerner asking questions about me made its way to my ear. It wasn't hard to find you. Now, what do you want?"

"I want to talk to you about Michelle Dominique and the Foundation, then kill you."

Chen laughed darkly. "I like honesty. You may hate me and want me dead, but there is one thing we both want. I can give you the rest of the information you need, and you can use it in a way I can't. Now if you're going to stab me, do it, because the noose tightens around our necks."

"How do you know what evidence I've got?"

"If you know who I am, then I know you're the one who found my USB. The fact you're here shows that you need me, and now I need you too. I'll help you."

"Okay. But why are you willing to give this to me?"

"Dominique has my children. I owe her."

⁓

CHEN CRACKED the egg shell firmly and carefully let the insides spill into the frying pan. The egg gave a satisfying sizzle as it hit the hot oil beside the steak, and he repeated the act three more times. Chen hummed a nameless tune as he waited the few minutes until the food was done. He removed the pan from the heat and divided the meal evenly between two plates. He carried the plates over to the small dining table in the kitchen.

"You sure know how to impress on a first date." Emery's tone was dry.

"The war rationing makes these steaks worth more than diamonds."

They ate in silence except for the clink of ice in their water glasses. Within a few minutes the two of them had cleared their plates. Chen stood, gathered the dishes and placed them on the kitchen counter. When he returned, he sat and looked calmly at Emery. The journalist had kept his cards fairly close to his chest, but Chen could sense a fierce intellect and a burning anger.

"Okay. You've eaten. Now it's time to open your mouth with something that impresses me."

Emery's gaze didn't waver, and if he was intimidated, Chen couldn't tell. "As I said earlier, I know you're responsible for the deaths in Shanghai, including my wife, and for the attack on Ernest McDowell. While that burns me to the core, I also know you're probably the only one left alive who can give me what I need on Michelle Dominique."

He didn't mind that the journalist knew all of this. He was here because Chen had let him in. The major threat to him remained the Foundation. The threat was twofold: they had his children and were also hunting him. Assisting Emery expose Dominique could help with that, though he didn't need to tell Emery that.

He'd spent the last two days trying to locate his children, using every network he had at his disposal. He'd had no luck. It was quite possible that they were still in Taiwan, under guard, but it was just as likely that they'd been squirreled away by the Foundation and flown to America. The trail was cold.

Without any information about where his children were, he'd needed a different approach. He'd been alerted to the journalist getting too close for comfort, and had decided to bring matters to a head. If he could use Emery to flush out Dominique, or cause her some damage, she might reach out and negotiate the release of his children.

Chen shrugged. "Why do you care so much about all of this?"

"Vengeance, justice, repaying a debt." Emery balled his fists and placed them on the table. "Because she's behind a whole lot of bad shit that's gone on lately. I know you killed my wife and others, including Ernest McDowell, but there's more at stake. You were the weapon, not the wielder; the tool, not the tradesman. Dominique is the threat."

Chen nodded. He understood the pervasiveness of a personal crusade as well as any man. "Fine. My wife was murdered and she has my children. We want the same thing— to expose Dominique and to cripple her organization. But I don't need you for that."

"You do, actually. It has taken a lot for me to swallow my distaste for you, but now we're linked whether you like it or not. I need you to finish painting the picture, you need me because I have the networks and profile to expose her using the information."

Chen leaned back in his chair and folded his arms. The next move was his. The Foundation could—and had—hurt him, and still had his children. He wanted the same thing as Emery. While Emery had some information, Chen had it all and more—movements, transactions, records of contact, plus his confessions. Enough to destroy Dominique. If Chen was the ammunition, the man sitting in front of him was the gun that could fire it. Chen stared at Emery and nodded slowly.

"Okay." Emery leaned forward on his elbows. "I want

information. All of it. Every scrap of paper, every single name, date, time, equipment manifest, motive."

"Go and get your notepad and tape recorder. Let's get to work."

26

"America wakes this morning to the first midterm elections held during a significant war in over forty years. Despite an apparent shift in the strategic balance of the war in recent days toward the United States, most analysts and polls are predicting the Republican Party will sweep the field in a show of deep dissatisfaction at the Kurzon Administration's handling of the war. An interesting kink in the elections is the emerging scandal, which first appeared yesterday in an online blog post by Pulitzer Prize–winning journalist Jack Emery, implicating a number of hardline Republican candidates in corrupt and treasonous behavior."

Charlie Rattan, MSNBC News Hour, *November 1*

As he sat on the set of a CNN studio in Los Angeles waiting for his slot, Jack was frustrated by the constant attention of the makeup and hair stylists. He was trying to think, but the primping and preening of the two women made it difficult. He didn't believe it mattered what he looked like, and if he was writing this for the *Standard*, it definitely wouldn't. But he'd lost that avenue, so had to cooperate with the norms of television.

He'd spent a few days picking Chen's brain, along with getting access to the entire treasure trove of information on Chen's USB. Though Hickens had salvaged some information, Chen still had an original copy and everything on it. On the flight from Taiwan to Los Angeles, Jack had compiled everything into a workable story: the Foundation's role in the Shanghai attacks and the war, the control of EMCorp, the shooting of Ernest McDowell, their continued subversion of large parts of US society, and a huge effort to control a large slice of US Congress.

He'd traveled with one eye open, half expecting Dominique's goons to ambush him at the airport, on the plane or once he'd landed. But nobody had challenged him and Celeste had met him at the airport in Los Angeles, having flown in from Hawaii. From their hotel room they'd crafted the stories, listing no names and making no claims that couldn't be proven with certainty in court. He'd left himself plenty of room to maneuver. He'd put the lot into a blog post, and beamed it out through his Twitter feed, timed to ensure it hit the daily news cycle. It had been a bombshell.

In the hours that followed, what had begun as a trickle of calls, texts and emails became a torrent, then a tsunami. Half of them were concerned friends, Peter and Josefa included, while the rest were offers for interviews or publication. He'd smiled at the response to his blog post. It was nice to know he still had the touch. It had actually been Celeste who had organized the spot on CNN's *Insight* program.

"Thanks. Mr Emery." The makeup girl stepped back with a pearly white smile and finally left Jack to his own devices. "Andrea will be with you shortly."

Jack nodded. "Thanks."

He turned his head and looked straight at Celeste, who was standing just behind the cameras. She smiled and gave him the thumbs up. They'd rehearsed the interview for most of the morning, but Jack had no doubt that Andrea Serrenko would be a far tougher gig. She had an impressive reputation, but if there was one way to get his message against Dominique and the Foundation white hot, nailing this interview was it.

He was about to say something to Celeste when Serrenko appeared and approached the set. She was an impressive woman, over six feet tall and higher still in heels, with fiery red hair and a personality to match. She sat in the seat opposite him, placed her notes on the counter and made sure her water glass was full.

Only then did she look up at Jack. "Good evening, Mr Emery, thanks for coming in. How're things today?"

"Jack, please." He held out his hand. "Could be worse, I could be in the crosshairs of more than one very dangerous organization."

Serrenko laughed and shook his hand. "Well, Jack, for the sake of my audience, I'm glad you're in the sights of at least one of them. It's a hell of a story."

Jack smiled. "You don't know the half of it."

As they exchanged further small talk, an assistant approached and fitted a lapel mike to each of them. Jack was a veteran of the process, having done a few interviews over the years. While each network and studio had its quirks, for the most part it was the same. Finally, a producer spoke from behind the safety of the camera and told them there was one minute until the show.

Jack watched one of the many monitors around the studio as the program's splash graphic played. When it was finished, the shot panned around the studio before landing squarely on Serrenko and himself, seated on either side of the desk. Serrenko smiled straight down the camera as the intro music faded. Jack stayed still as she read her opening.

"Good evening. Welcome to *Insight*, I'm Andrea Serrenko." She turned to look into another camera as the shot shifted. "Tonight we have Jack Emery, former political editor for the *New York Standard* and Pulitzer Prize–winning journalist, in the studio. On the same day as the midterm elections, his blog post this morning about the corruption in and subversion of American politics threatens to rock the system to its core. Thank you for joining me, Mr Emery."

Jack took a deep breath, leaned forward and smiled. "Please, call me Jack. Great to be with you."

Serrenko gave a well-rehearsed smile. "Okay, Jack. The first thing I wanted to cover is why a journalist of your caliber is out of work at the moment. This all feels a bit too convenient."

Jack swallowed. He hadn't expected this to be easy. He still hadn't reached the bottom of his firing, but from a conversation with Peter, it was pretty clearly linked to Michelle Dominique's board push. He smiled. "Well, I'm open to offers, if you're hiring."

His attempt at humor fell on deaf ears, as Serrenko raised an eyebrow.

"Look, it's a tough industry, now more than ever. My views didn't match the direction of the paper, so they fired me. But this story is authentic, I've done the hard work. It stacks up."

That was something Jack was sure about. Between the contents of the USB and the information he'd gained from Chen, he had a slam-dunk story against Dominique and the Foundation. He was certain it was enough to bring her down. And once she was eliminated, he hoped her whole rancid organization would decay and collapse.

Serrenko nodded. "Okay then, can you summarize for our viewers what your contention is? Particularly for those who haven't yet read your blog."

Jack bit his lip. This was it. "Okay. In short, there's a politically cancerous think tank operating in Washington to undermine American democracy."

Serrenko laughed in a way that felt dismissive. "Aren't all think tanks doing that though, Jack? You're going to need more than that."

"Oh, of course, Andrea. But I've got clear evidence linking

this group to the attacks in Shanghai, China—"

Serrenko interrupted. "You're saying an American organization *attacked China?*"

Jack nodded. "Not directly, but without them there would have been no attacks. They provided the funds and helped the mastermind—Chen Shubian—with the logistics."

"You have proof? Even more than what was on your blog today?" For the first time, Jack thought he might have her interested.

"Sure do—an interview with Chen Shubian. Along with documents and records that support his allegations."

"Wait a minute." Serrenko was incredulous. "You've *met* the main bomber? Wasn't your wife killed in Shanghai?"

"Yes, I have, and yes, she was. I had to put aside my personal grievances for the good of the story. So this organization has a highly complex cell structure that takes its orders from Washington. If one cell is compromised, it looks like a small group of nut jobs, but I've been able to blow the lid off the whole organization.

"Just recently, they've had involvement in Shanghai, the war, the shooting of Ernest McDowell and the subversion of his company. And this is the tip of the iceberg. They're now trying to get their members into Congress. If I had the resources, I'd have found more. I trust the FBI will have an easy time of it. I'd be more than happy to help."

Serrenko clearly knew a bombshell when she heard one, and when something was being held back. Her eyes narrowed. "Give me the name of the organization, Jack."

Jack stared straight down the camera. He had prepared most for this next part. He could have easily have dropped the Foundation for a New America and Michelle Dominique in the deep end by naming them on his blog, but he'd needed the protection of being a national celebrity with a story that people wanted to hear.

"Michelle Dominique and the Foundation for a New

America." Jack looked down at his cell phone. "And, according to the newsfeed, your next member of Congress."

∿

MICHELLE SQUINTED but kept a smile on her face as the camera flashes rolled like a wave across her vision. She smiled again, then walked to the lectern. Her mind wasn't in the whole victory event, really, but she had to go through the motions. Jack Emery's blog post and subsequent interview on *Insight* had changed the focus of the day—from triumph at being elected to damage control. She had to do this then get to work.

She rushed through her speech, batting off the same lines that had been home runs with the voters and seen her elected with a massive margin. She paused for applause at the right times, smiled for the cameras and the crowd at the right times, and gave the speech only enough mental energy required to avoid blunders. She thanked her supporters, and congratulated the other Foundation-aligned candidates who'd won.

Most importantly, she denied the allegations Jack Emery had made and explained he was a bitter ex-employee with a drinking problem. The crowd had cheered her and booed him, but she knew that the room was full of her supporters. She'd have a much tougher time with the general public. Not to mention the FBI. She waved and walked backstage.

Waiting for her in the green room were Erik and Andrei Shadd. They stood impassively off to the side, in the exact same spots from which they'd delivered the news about Emery's interview, just before she took the stage for her speech. She walked over to the side table and poured herself a drink, then threw the pitcher across the room. It exploded in a spray of glass and painted the white wall with grapefruit juice. She didn't care. She was tempted to set the whole building on fire. She'd never felt anger like this.

"All this information!" She picked up her iPad and threw it

across the room.

"All this power!" She moved to the window and ripped the curtains down.

"For what!" She kicked over a vase, which smashed with a satisfying spray of glass.

Andrei moved closer. "It's not that bad. You have a number of options."

She stared at him, tempted to punch his lights out, but after a few moments she exhaled deeply and sat on the arm of the sofa. "We need to turn this around or the FBI is going to come knocking. If that happens, it's only a matter of time before you're both being gang-banged at Rikers, and I'm giving some lady a little something to stay alive."

Andrei shrugged. "There were always bound to be setbacks. It's not possible to run an organization as ambitious and as large as ours without the odd problem. Look at all the messes Anton cleaned up over the years."

"This is more dangerous than anything he ever dealt with. We're named, gentlemen. That changes everything. In addition to the Feds, the other cells will be gunning for me too."

She thought for a moment. She was a student of politics, but equally adept at history. When things got desperate, it was the individual or the country that could be the most ruthless that generally won the day. An idea popped into her head. She mulled it over, then decided. It was her only option.

"We're going to take a leaf out of Stalin's book." She raised her head to look at the brothers, who winced at the reference to Uncle Joe. "Scorched earth."

Andrei frowned in thought, then smiled. "Let them have most of it, but protect the core."

Michelle smiled. The more she thought about it, the more it made sense. "Precisely."

The Foundation had a huge amount of influence in all sorts of areas. While it would hurt to give up some of her power and her people, by doing so she might have a fighting chance to stay alive and keep the core of the organization—and its influence—intact. The rest was expendable. It was the only way to survive. To recover. To succeed.

Michelle stood. "We need to inoculate our core. We need to totally cut off our central organs from the rest of the body. That's your job. Expose them, kill them. Whatever."

"Easier said than done, Michelle." Erik shook his head. "I doubt large parts of the organization will take kindly to being hung out to dry."

"I don't care. Do it. Today. I'll take care of protecting the important stuff."

Andrei's eyes narrowed. "How?"

Michelle smiled. "I've had something up our sleeve in case we needed it."

She picked up the phone and dialed her assistant. "Mallory, I'll need the Heisman file ready when I get back to the office. It's urgent, okay?"

She hung up without waiting for a response. Both of the brothers had confused looks on their faces, but it was Andrei who spoke first. "The Heisman file?"

Michelle smiled. "A dirt file on the President so large it will bring him down."

"Isn't using something like that a bit...final?"

"Yeah, it's like dropping the bomb on Hiroshima, but we don't have a choice. I'll meet with him and keep the government and the Bureau off our case. If we can use our leverage over Kurzon to keep the FBI off our backs long enough, we can feed most of the organization to the wolves, but protect the most important parts. We *can* recover."

The brothers nodded.

"Andrei, you take care of Emery. Erik, you handle the Foundation liquidation. When I drop this file on Kurzon's desk, he'll be eating out of our hands like a lamb and we'll be able to protect ourselves. And if he doesn't cooperate, we'll make it public and be yesterday's news."

27

The results are in and Congress looks to be taking a decidedly hawkish tone, after an electoral bloodbath left Democratic hopes shattered. While Republicans carried the day in general, perhaps the most surprising development was the election of so many extreme right-wing candidates to Congress. Though nominally linked to the GOP, there is huge concern within Republican ranks about the new arrivals, and talks already of a potential schism between moderates and the new extreme arm of the party. At any rate, the new-look Congress promises to bring a new vigor to the war against China, with analysts predicting an even stronger push to end the conflict decisively. It may be a moot point, however, given American gains in recent days and the apparent slackening of Chinese assaults on Taiwan. Whether because of tactics, exhaustion, attrition or troubles at home, sources tell the New York Standard that the sum total of attacks has fallen by thirty percent in recent days.

Phil Eaton, New York Standard, *November 2*

J ack smiled wearily at the flight attendant as he walked past her. "Thanks."

"Our pleasure, sir." The woman was far too perky for someone who flew for a living. "Thanks for flying with United."

Jack nodded then turned to Celeste. "Let's go."

She nodded. "Man, I can't wait for a shower and sleep."

He laughed but said nothing. He hefted his backpack over his shoulder and walked through the door of the aircraft and onto the sky bridge. It had been over two days since he'd slept properly, jetting from Taiwan, to Hawaii, to LA, to Washington. The entire time, he'd been getting word out about his story, which had gone all the more nuclear since his interview with Serrenko and Dominique's election win.

He wrapped an arm around Celeste as they walked. "I really appreciate your support through all this."

She leaned in and kissed him on the cheek. "My pleasure. But I don't think it's going to get any easier any time soon."

"I know." Once he stepped out of the artificial environment of the airport, things were going to get crazy.

He exhaled deeply and stepped into the terminal. As he looked around, he felt Celeste grab his arm and squeeze tight. He looked at her and her eyes were wide, locked on a group of men standing on the other side of the terminal. He looked at them and recognized only one of the four but still felt a spike of fear. Recognizing one was enough. It was the same man who'd bailed him and Celeste up at Chen's house in Wisconsin.

This wasn't good. He'd thought that in the wake of his release of the information, his public profile would be enough to prevent Dominique from moving against him. He'd been wrong.

Celeste seemed on the verge of complete panic. "Holy fuck, Jack. They're here. *He's here.*"

Jack grabbed Celeste's arm and they turned and started to

walk toward the baggage claim. In his peripheral vision he could see the Foundation goons fall into an easy stroll behind him. Jack picked up his pace, pulled out his cell phone and dialed Peter Weston. He held the phone to his ear and increased the speed of his walking. The phone rang, time after time, but there was no answer.

He looked back. The men were getting closer. While he doubted they'd try anything at Dulles International Airport, with all the security in the world watching them, he had no doubt that as soon as he and Celeste left the building and got a fair distance away, they'd strike. He had to prevent that. He could approach the police, but they'd do nothing if there was no clear threat. There was only one way they'd pay attention.

He turned to Celeste as they kept walking. "As soon as we round this corner, stop and cry out for help. As loud as you can."

"Why?" She looked at him as they turned a corner, then shrugged. "HELP! HELP ME!"

Jack kept walking as Celeste stopped in her tracks. He waited a few moments before looking back. She had gathered a small crowd of airport staff and concerned travelers. Most importantly, the gentlemen trailing them had kept moving. He was their primary target, and they weren't interested in making a scene with a woman who was already shouting for help. Celeste was safe. Now he had to figure out something for himself.

He walked, mind racing for ideas but coming up blank. He looked down at his cell phone, thinking of who else to call, when he became vaguely aware of someone else getting in his way. He put the phone down and stopped walking, looking up at the pair of strangers with a mix of curiosity and dread. After all he'd been through, from the carrier to his torture to finding Chen, this was how it was going to end.

One of the suited man took a slight step forward. "Jack Emery?"

Jack cursed himself for not anticipating that the Foundation would send two teams—one to flush him out and one to scoop him up. Despite that, he saw no reason to make it easy for them. Whatever noise and fuss he could make as they dealt with him, he'd make. He turned around. The four men who'd initially pursued him had stopped dead in their tracks and were now doing their best to look completely disinterested.

"Are you Jack Emery? I won't ask again."

Jack relaxed slightly, turned back around and summed up the new arrival. Dark suit, dark sunglasses, a buddy dressed in exactly the same way. He nearly laughed. "Yeah?"

The other man was expressionless as he produced ID. "I'm Agent Brenner, FBI. This is Agent Vaughn. Looks like you could use a friend or two right now."

Jack looked back again. "Yeah, you could say that."

Brenner was impassive as he put a hand gently on Jack's back. "Come with us."

"Can you look after my colleague, Celeste Adams? She's back there near gate 6A."

Brenner turned to Vaughn. "Go get her and meet us at the café."

"Thanks." Jack smiled with relief as Vaughn peeled off and headed in the direction of Celeste. It had been far too close a call for his liking. He looked back at his pursuers. The one he recognized from Wisconsin seemed pissed.

He walked with Brenner in silence through the arrivals hall. He didn't really know what was in store, but the FBI would no doubt be better company than the Foundation. His interview with Serrenko had clearly had an impact, both on Dominique and on the Federal Government, now he just had to hope he had enough ammunition to keep the authorities interested.

After a few minutes, Brenner stopped next to one of the cafés in the airport. "Mr Emery, the director will see you in here. I'll keep the bad guys away."

"Thanks. And Celeste?"

"Sorted. I suggest you don't keep Director McGhinnist waiting."

Jack entered the cafeteria and stood next to the only occupied table. Seated there was a large African-American man, who looked as if he could crack Jack open like a walnut. Jack had done his research and knew that Bill McGhinnist, ex-Navy Seal, Director of the FBI, probably could. McGhinnist calmly took one last sip of his coffee, put the cup down then stood to face Jack.

"Good morning, Director McGhinnist." Jack held out his hand. "I'm Jack Emery."

"Bill will do, Mr Emery." McGhinnist shook his hand. "Thanks for agreeing to meet."

Jack laughed. "Your agents made a pretty compelling offer. And please, call me Jack."

"Glad they could save you a headache or two. I thought a little show of force might be helpful." McGhinnist laughed and sat down. "I won't even charge you for it, if your information is as good as you claim. Take a seat, Jack."

Jack did as he was told. "It is."

"You have made a lot of people nervous and you've hardly set about making friends in all of this. But I was intrigued by your blog and your interview. So I'm giving you the benefit of the doubt. You better not be wasting my time, Jack. It's a busy time for everyone."

Jack could tell that McGhinnist had a lot on his plate, no doubt because of the war. He'd also be nervous at the thought of Jack's information, which shed new light on the causes of the war and left many prominent Americans with question marks over their head, including a few brand-new members of Congress. Jack was going to have to show off his garter belt before the big dance if he had any hope of enlisting the Bureau's help.

"I've got a lot of evidence linking the Foundation and Michelle Dominique to prominent politicians, business interests, the media—you name it. It's more than lobbying and the odd long lunch. We're talking about endemic political corruption, insider trading, money laundering, perjury, fraud, blackmail, murder—and a whole lot more. They're a bunch of nasty fuckers."

Jack swallowed hard. "I've also got evidence linking them to the attacks on Shanghai and to the war with China. A Taiwanese national named Chen Shubian worked with Dominique and organized the attacks using a secure server the Foundation established. He was funded by a series of front companies that I've linked to the Foundation, plus Dominique was in Shanghai in the days before and immediately after the attacks."

McGhinnist frowned. "And there's more, I trust?"

Jack smiled. "Sure is. She's taken control of EMCorp and now Foundation-aligned candidates have been elected en masse into Congress. They're taking control, Bill."

Jack could clearly see the director tense, but he knew the man was interested. "Your allegations affect some very influential people, Mr Emery. Not to mention the war."

"Jack, remember? I've got the evidence to back it all up, both from Chen's confession and Anton Clark's computer files. Look, I know better than most the power of that organization and its people, but it changes nothing."

"Oh, it changes everything, Jack. Michelle Dominique has a large power base in Washington. I'm not sure you realize what you're asking me to do, Jack, to declare war on the entire Washington elite at the same time as we're at war with China."

Jack could see the man was torn. "That's about the sum of it, yeah."

McGhinnist sighed. "The war is going well, but we've lost a couple of carriers, countless air force birds and half of Taiwan has been flattened. The world is now a very different place. The last thing I want is to start a forest fire in Washington."

"I know. But you're my only hope."

He looked up at McGhinnist, who was silent. He'd given him everything except Ernest's links to the Foundation. He didn't quite know what he'd do if McGhinnist declined to help. He'd have to walk outside and into the arms of the Foundation thugs, having succeeded in releasing the story but failing to protect himself and those he cared about. Plus, it would likely save the Foundation from complete destruction.

His vengeance would be incomplete.

Jack dug into his pocket and pulled out the USB containing the evidence. He placed it on the table. "There are strings attached to the information. Some of it incriminates Ernest McDowell, and I want that particular part of it forgotten about. Also, Chen Shubian needs immunity. It was the price of his evidence."

McGhinnist looked down at the USB, then up at Jack with a smile. "You're a cheeky bastard, but I like that. I couldn't care less about a dead old man, so that's fine. As for Shubian, he blew up half of China, not Los Angeles or Chicago, so what do I care? You've got a deal."

Jack nodded. "The password is Erin."

McGhinnist exhaled, longer and louder than any man Jack had ever heard. "Okay, Jack. I just hope you know what you're getting us into. This is going to hurt, but I'll set up a task force and lead it personally. We'll wrap this network up in a matter of days."

Jack stood. "You have my number, if you need anything at all, or if the information isn't clear to your analysts, I'd be happy to help."

"Okay. In the meantime, I'll put you and your friend up at a hotel and put my guys on protection duty." McGhinnist stood as well, patted Jack's back then paused. "Tell me one thing, though. How did you begin to link all of this to Dominique and the Foundation?"

Jack paused, then decided it was best not to lie to the man.

"Um...would you believe that I slept with her and ransacked her apartment?"

'Damn!" McGhinnist laughed, clearly impressed. "I've admired her from afar for years! I'm going to ignore the felony just to hear that story at a later date."

~

MICHELLE STEELED HERSELF, but kept her smile pristine. "Mr President."

President Kurzon didn't stand, but gestured her to a seat. "Congratulations on your election, Michelle. How was your flight?"

"Fine, Mr President." Michelle sat. "Thanks for agreeing to see me."

She'd flown the short distance from Washington to Maryland, then been driven to Camp David. She hadn't wanted to leave the capital with the FBI threatening to roll up on the Foundation's doorstep at any moment, but it was the only way to rein in the situation.

"You didn't give me much choice, given what you claim to possess. So what can I do for you? I've got a two o'clock with the Australian ambassador." Kurzon's tone was cold.

Michelle sat. "The Bureau is about to start arresting or harassing half of my people on charges that are trash. I want you to make it stop so we can get on with our business."

Kurzon waved his hand. "A nasty situation. I don't know the specifics, but it sounds like some of your people have been freelancing, to say nothing of yourself."

"The problem is a bit bigger than that."

"How so? Bill McGhinnist wouldn't be pursuing this if he didn't have reason. Just keep your hands clean and you'll be fine." Kurzon started to stand. "Is that all?"

Michelle remained where she was. "No."

Kurzon sat back down. "Right, let me have it."

Michelle reached into her handbag and pulled out her iPad. She unlocked it and hit play on the video that was ready to go. She turned the screen to Kurzon. She didn't have to watch it again to know what he was seeing: himself having sex with a young woman. She tried to hide her smile as he realized what this meant for his presidency.

"She really doesn't look sixteen, does she?"

Kurzon watched the whole thing. He had the look of a frightened child in his eyes. "Where did you get this?"

"That doesn't matter."

He sighed. "Fucking hell."

She was a bit surprised that he didn't deny his involvement or try to talk her out of releasing it. They both knew that this would end his presidency, ruin his legacy and probably send him to jail. She was relying on it. Only direct intervention by Kurzon would make the various arms of the Federal Government go away.

She prompted him. "This can go away, if you do what I ask."

He laughed darkly. "You think I can get McGhinnist and the others to call off an investigation against you and your colleagues? It doesn't work that way. Besides, what's stopping the journalist from releasing it all publicly? He's already named you, after all."

"I can deal with Jack Emery." Michelle lowered her voice menacingly. "I just want you to play your role."

For several minutes, Kurzon seemed to think through the ramifications of the situation, for himself, his family, the Foundation, the country. With a single stroke of a pen he could protect both of them. She was sure he'd make the right decision. She was surprised when he shook his head and sighed again. She waited patiently.

"Michelle, for a moment or two I considered your deal. But I'm afraid that, no matter the cost to my professional life, I will not work, collaborate or otherwise be involved in anything you're peddling."

"You're mad." She was shocked, but wouldn't show it. "May I ask why?"

"Because I spoke to McGhinnist prior to this meeting, and discovered that your organization was probably responsible for the death of my friend, that's why. Ernest was no saint, but he deserved a hell of a lot better than a bullet in the neck. I'll try my luck with the press, Ms Dominique."

"They'll crucify you, Mr President. Your administration will be destroyed."

Kurzon smiled. "Great thing, democracy. I'm a lame duck after the midterms anyway, and there's always someone else willing to step up. I'll already be regarded as the President who took America to war with China, but I'll be happy if history remembers me as the man who also stood up to the greatest ever threat to American freedom and stopped them getting away with terrible crimes and stacking Congress."

Michelle didn't reply. She turned the iPad back around and placed it in her lap. She sent an email she'd already prepared. It gave her no pleasure and got her no closer to solving the issue of Jack Emery and his evidence, but she had to follow through. The Foundation was only as powerful as the punishment backing up its threats. Not even the President was immune. She'd have to deal with Emery another way.

"It's done, Mr President." She stood. "I hope you don't live to regret your decision."

"Miss, I kindly regret I can't shove my telephone down your throat. Get out."

28

"Addressing the nation, the President looked tired and beaten. He did his best to downplay the contents of the video and the allegations against him, revealed by the New York Standard, but had no answer for the damning nature of the vision. Kurzon has vowed to fight the allegations and any impeachment. At the same time, he commented on the allegations against Michelle Dominique and the Foundation for a New America, stating that while the investigation and arrests were ongoing, there was clear evidence showing that the organization was responsible for the attacks in Shanghai. As allegations continue to fly in Washington, following the release of the new information, the President has made a public and unconditional offer of a ceasefire with the People's Republic of China. Kurzon stressed the recent success of United States forces and noted that America had no desire to fight with China for years to come, especially given the Foundation's likely involvement in starting it. He stated that if China could accept the independence of Taiwan, peace could be had within hours. Considering their losses, and the ongoing domestic difficulties that Chinese authorities are facing in trying to maintain order, it is quite possible a deal could be on the cards."

Vanessa McKenzie, PBS News Hour, *November 3*

J ack breathed as deeply as he could, trying to calm his nerves. He twirled his pen and tapped his foot on the floor. There was nothing else to do. The television news had wall-to-wall coverage of the war and the scandal facing President Kurzon, and he was under strict orders not to use his phone. All the while, he couldn't help but think he'd made a mistake and that this would all end badly.

While the President's Suite of the Washington Marriott was a nice enough place to wait, he could think of a million other places he'd prefer to be. Earlier in the day, McGhinnist had called him with mixed news. He'd told Jack that the Bureau was rolling up Foundation for a New America cells all over the country, but still hadn't manage to locate Michelle Dominique since she'd left Camp David. Jack had convinced himself that Dominique had slipped the net, leaving him to walk the Earth as a hunted man. McGhinnist had said, when they'd first met, that the tendrils of her power base extended deeper than anyone could fathom. There was no way for him to stand up to that. So he had been forced to wait for a second day in the hotel, relying on McGhinnist, and with nobody but Celeste, Agent Brenner and Agent Vaughn for company.

His eyes were on the table when the door to the suite unlocked with a clunk. Jack looked up as it opened and he smiled with relief when Agent Brenner walked into the room, fresh from completing a security check of the hotel. Agent Vaughn had stayed in the room, silent, but he freaked Jack out a bit.

Jack held out his hands up with his palms facing outward. "Don't shoot."

Brenner raised an eyebrow. "Everything okay, Mr Emery?"

As Vaughn walked over to the window and pulled back the curtain, taking a peek outside, Jack felt like telling Brenner that, no, everything was not okay. In truth, he felt minutes away from needing a change of underwear, and that his faith in the competency of the FBI and its agents was being sorely tested. But he held his tongue and nodded. He felt exposed, and wanted the FBI to get on with arresting Dominique.

"Don't worry, there's more than a handful of decent shots between the lobby and you." Brenner clearly sensed he was uneasy. "Unless she brings an army, you're fine."

Jack smiled. "I know, I just feel a bit vulnerable. I'll be the happiest man on the planet when Dominique is in cuffs. Hell, I'll buy you guys a beer downstairs."

Brenner shrugged. "Just part of the job. You're the one who's put yourself on the line, can't say I understand why though."

"She killed my wife, started a war, ordered my boss murdered and tried to stab me in a museum. If that's not enough for you, she's also trying to stack Congress."

"Good enough, I suppose." Brenner laughed. "Quite amazing how deep this all goes, though. It's some serious shit you've uncorked."

Jack couldn't disagree. "Given the choice, I'd have preferred to be left out of it all. But once I pulled the first thread, her whole dress unraveled, and I couldn't walk away."

"Why not?" Brenner scoffed. "To use your analogy, just because a woman is undressed in front of you, doesn't mean you need to sleep with her."

Jack laughed, and the dark cloud hanging over his mood lifted. "I can't resist the lure of a beautiful woman."

Brenner opened his mouth to reply, but Jack heard nothing but a boom. Before his mind could process what was happening, Brenner's blood showered over him. Jack froze, until he heard a second boom, as Vaughn fired another shot into Brenner's skull. Jack dived to the floor and climbed under the table. Vaughn appeared to be in no hurry, slowly walking past Brenner's lifeless body toward him. The agent seemed as calm as the man in Chen's basement, but Jack had no police cruiser to save him this time.

Jack had nowhere to go as Vaughn bent down and peered at him. "Mr Emery, you've caused a whole lot of problems for a whole lot of people."

Jack's fear had gone, replaced by sheer and utter disbelief—and rage. "After all of this, *you're* the one who's going to get me? Just fucking do it."

Jack watched as the barrel of the pistol inched up. A wave of thoughts rushed through his mind, but he couldn't pin down any particular one as he waited for the inevitable. He wondered if he'd hear the shot or feel anything before it was over. Then his eyes widened as he saw a pair of legs run toward Vaughn.

Celeste. In his fear and anger, he'd forgotten about her.

She leaped and landed on Vaughn and the gun fired. Jack crawled as fast as he could from under the table. He was too late. Vaughn collapsed to the ground, a panting Celeste sitting on him and a steak knife protruding from his skull. Jack threw the gun away from Vaughn then struggled over to Celeste and hugged her.

Jack grabbed Vaughn's gun, then the cell phone in his pocket rang. "Hello?"

"McGhinnist speaking, we've found her, Jack. We're moving in at any moment."

"Good. One of your agents just tried to shoot me."

There was a pause. "Which one?"

"Vaughn."

"Fucking hell. He must have been one of Dominique's moles."

"Yep. And Brenner is dead."

There was another slight pause. "I'll get some more people up to you. Until then, take his gun and trust my other agents to keep you safe."

"Already taken care of the gun part." Jack was happy to have a weapon in his hands. "Where is she?"

"Dominique? An apartment in Baltimore. Off the grid."

"So this is it?" Jack held his breath, not willing to believe it just yet.

"Yep, we've got the place surrounded. There's a couple of large-looking dudes with her though. But we'll get her. Just wanted you to know."

Jack smiled and sighed with relief. "What about the rest of them? Doesn't seem like that particular snake will be killed by just chopping off the head."

"We've already beat it over the head a few times with a shovel. Their funds are frozen and we're rolling up their network. There'll be plenty of mop up, but this will just about finish it. We'll slice the organization into a million pieces and bring as many as we can rustle up into custody. I'll see you soon."

The line went dead. Jack gestured at Celeste to get Brenner's weapon. They resumed their hug as a pair of agents opened the door and entered. They had weapons raised and scanned the room, but could clearly see the damage was done. He spent the next few minutes explaining the ambush, and to their credit they let him keep the weapon.

It was over.

~

MICHELLE LIFTED the glass to her mouth and took a long pull of the whisky. She savored the burn of the liquid as it coursed down her throat and into the pit of her stomach. It temporarily replaced the empty feeling she'd had for the whole day, once she'd started to get reports of Foundation cells being assaulted by the FBI. The news was worse than she could have imagined.

Some of her people had been arrested, some killed. Losses were heavy and the Foundation was shattered. Scorched earth hadn't worked and there wasn't much left to save. She'd hoped to make a deal with Kurzon to prevent the complete collapse of the organization, but it hadn't happened. Her only consolation was that she was still breathing.

She pulled the glass away from her mouth and considered the last of the beautifully colored liquid, cut with just a splash of water. She threw it back with one flick of her wrist. She felt a momentary pang of regret. It was a shame to leave such a fine bottle here. Like the rest of the stuff in the secret apartment she kept in Baltimore, it'd make some FBI agent a very happy man.

She put the glass down on the table. "Time to go, boys."

She looked up to Andrei, who stood by the door. She stood as he started to turn the handle, but he didn't get the chance to open the door. There was the sound of cracking timber, and she took a step back as the door swung inward.

"They're here!" Erik's shout was barely audible over the explosion near the door. "Get down, Michelle!"

Michelle was surprised but reacted instantly. She started into a run for the other side of the room. Erik, who'd been standing by the window, already had his weapon out and had upturned her oak dining table for cover. He shouted something in Czech to his brother as she grabbed the hand he held out for her. She jumped over the table and joined him behind the impromptu shelter.

Several federal agents had already entered the room. She didn't need to see the lettering emblazoned on their vests to know they were FBI. She doubted they were pushovers, either. If Bill McGhinnist had enough balls to storm her hideout in Baltimore, he'd have sent his best crew, armed with the best gear and with backup on call. She ducked back behind the table.

"Federal agents! Give it up!"

They got their answer when the first shot boomed. Andrei was only able to get a single shot off before he was gunned down by a volley of return fire. That left Erik as the one thing standing between her and the agents. As she heard the chattering rumble of Erik's TeC-9 SMG, she reached over and pulled the M9 Beretta from the back of his pants, figuring he wouldn't need it while he was firing the machine pistol.

She looked over the table and extended her arm as shots boomed through the small apartment. She squeezed the trigger on the pistol several times and smiled with satisfaction as one of the agents fell, clutching his chest. He probably had a vest on, but it was enough to sting and take him out of the fight. She ducked back down.

Her situation was dire. She'd miscalculated the speed at which the FBI could get to her apartment. She'd wanted to clear out a few things and share one last drink with Erik and Andrei, but now they were here. Her choices were fight it out and die, surrender and go to prison, or try to escape. She didn't like any option.

But if she was to live, there was no going back for the Foundation, despite the success of her plan. She was a free agent, but she was determined to try. That meant getting far away from here, probably to the south, where she could regroup and consider her options.

As if Erik was reading her mind, she felt a pat on her backside. She looked at him and noticed tears in his eyes. The brothers had been close. He jerked his head toward the window. Her eyes widened, but he nodded. She knew him well enough not to protest his stupid chivalry, let alone when under fire. She nodded then raised her head over the table, squeezing off a few more shots. Without further thought she dropped and scurried toward the window. She heard bullets whiz over her head, but the shooters seemed more interested in silencing the return fire of Erik than in her.

From the sound of it, he was still firing as she reached the window. She looked back briefly as he loaded a fresh magazine, his last, then nodded and started to stand. Michelle got to her feet as Erik reached his full height and sprayed the far side of the room with his weapon.

The window had been destroyed by the gunfight and she

was halfway through when Erik's fire stopped. A lesser team might have ducked against such a terrifying volley of fire, but this Bureau squad was better. They easily gunned him down. She grunted as she cut her hand on a jagged piece of glass, but didn't stop. She hurried down one level of the fire escape. Looking down, she saw an agent at ground level aiming his weapon at her. A pair of bullets ricocheted off the steel railings. She moved quickly, raising her weapon and firing off a few shots, but from this range it was useless.

When she spotted additional agents running to support the lone gunman, she decided she couldn't continue this way. With a grunt she hurled herself through the window to another apartment. The glass shattered around her and she landed heavily on the floor, but after the quickest check, she decided she was still intact.

She scrambled to her feet, glad that the apartment appeared to be empty. She raised the gun and moved quickly, half expecting a squad of agents to burst inside. Thoughts of escape and taking her vengeance on Jack Emery was all that kept her going, room by room. She reached the door to the apartment and opened it.

The corridor was empty. She pulled out her cell phone and dialed a number she knew by heart as she ran down the hall. "This is Dominique, change of plans, bring the car around and be ready to move it. We're under fire."

She reached the elevator and mashed the button. When it arrived, she rode it to the lobby and waited for the door to open, gun raised. Her mind was blank as she evaluated the threat—two Federal agents. She raised her weapon and fired at one. The agent went down as the other raised his weapon. They fired at about the same time.

The agent fell, but Michelle felt something impact her arm. She looked down as she ran for the exit. There was blood and an entry wound in her forearm, but she'd have to worry about it later. There was no sign of more agents as she ran outside. She'd finally caught a break.

She spotted the car and waved furiously at it. As it pulled up, she opened the door and dived in, the car never stopping. The driver gunned the engine as she took her seat and buckled in. She was safe, but if she was going to make good her escape, the driver would need to die at the end of the drive. She pressed her hand against her wound.

She rested back in the seat and after a few blocks she started to feel safe. The car pulled up at a red light. She heard the glass on the car window shatter before she was deafened by a large bang and blinded by a million shining lights. Her head was spinning as she closed her eyes and brought her hands up to her ears.

Her breathing quickened and her heart raced, even as her hearing started to return. She heard a gunshot, which meant her driver was dead. Then the door of the car open as she fumbled for her seatbelt and any chance at survival. Still too disoriented to move efficiently, she squealed as she sensed someone slide into the back seat beside her.

"I surrender." She could barely hear her own voice over the ringing in her ears. "If the Bureau wants me that badly, they've got me. Just don't shoot."

"It's not the FBI."

Fear gripped the pit of her stomach. While she still couldn't see as a result of the flashbang grenade, she knew the voice. "Chen."

His hand grabbed her by the throat. She squealed again.

"Where are my children? That is your only chance." There was malice in his voice.

She started to hyperventilate as her vision returned enough to see him. He wore a balaclava and there was no remorse in his eyes. Her mind scrambled for the answer he sought. The Foundation—or what was left of it—had his children, but she couldn't think of where.

Then it came to her. "Pennsylvania. They're in Philly. The address is in my phone. Leave me alone and you'll be with them in a few hours. But I need a deal."

"Give me the address and I'll determine what deal you get."

She had no choice. "The code to the phone is three one five six. The address is in the notes."

She felt pressure under her chin. Something poking into it.

This time she didn't hear the bang.

CHEN STEPPED BACK and crouched down. A second later, the small charge on the door handle hissed and flared white hot. The lock was breached. Chen looked around one last time and pulled the door open. It swung back on its hinges with only the slightest whine. He moved inside swiftly but silently, his pistol raised and alert for any sound or movement. He closed the door and was alone in the dark.

Using the information from Dominique's phone, he'd tracked his children to this address in Philadelphia. While he was elated to be so close to them, he was also mindful to keep his thoughts on the job. His children were still missing and in danger, and the FBI and the Foundation were engaged in a dangerous cat-and-mouse game all across America. They could arrive at any second. That would be complicated.

The first room in the office was dark, lit only by green emergency lighting. He could make out a reception area and front desk, but the room was remarkably sparse for any sort of active business. He didn't give the area another thought as he moved cautiously to the only other door in the room, which he assumed led to the main office area. He put his hand on the door handle and turned it slowly. When it was half turned, he waited for any sound, but there was only silence. He opened the door and stepped through.

He was faced with a long hallway with offices at evenly

spaced intervals. At the end of the hall, slightly offset, was another room with no door. He moved quickly but as quietly as a snake toward it, checking each office for threats before moving on. Finally, he reached the doorless room at the end of the hallway.

He felt his breath catch in his throat when he saw his daughter, blindfolded, sitting at a steel table in what must be the lunchroom. A few more steps and he saw his son. They were both blindfolded, with ankles shackled to the table leg and uneaten sandwiches in front of them.

He raised his pistol an inch higher, but eased his finger away from the trigger. Despite his training, his emotions were on edge. He moved silently to the doorway, but kept to the side and out of sight. Finally, he saw the guard he knew had to be there. He doubted the overweight, middle-aged slob was among the Foundation's elite.

Chen moved quickly, his head clear of all thoughts except the threat to his children. He took four large steps between the door and the sleeping man, who was dozing with his chin on his chest and a newspaper in front of him. Chen placed the pistol against the man's head and squeezed the trigger as easily as turning off his television.

The pistol gave the slightest kick in response, which is more than the man in the chair offered. A fine spray of blood escaped from the other side of his head and only then did the children sense that someone else was in the room. They both raised their heads, and turned them from side to side, as if they expected their blindfolds to fall away.

When he saw his daughter grab her little brother's hand, Chen's heart nearly broke.

"Who's there?" His daughter spoke only broken English. "Please don't hurt us."

Chen crouched down to his knees and whispered, in case other threats were close by. "It's your father. Stay calm, climb under the table and uncover your eyes."

His children settled instantly. He stayed in position while they climbed under the table and removed their blindfolds, though he couldn't do anything about their shackles for the time being. Once they were in position, Chen removed the dead man's pistol from its holster and took out the clip.

There was one door left, on the opposite side to where he'd entered the break room. He moved toward the door and stood to the side. He put his hand on the door handle, but didn't get the chance to turn it fully, because a high-caliber pistol barked, blowing two large holes in the door. If he'd been standing in front of it, he'd be dead.

Chen's mind screamed with options: either advance through the door, fire back or find another way into the room.

A voice called out from the other side of the door, "I know who you are. Take the kids, leave me alive and we all walk away. The key is on the hook."

Chen processed what felt like thousands of small bits of information in a single second. He'd completed a hostile entry under fire a number of times, and it held no fear for him, but he'd never done it with two frightened children—his children —half-a-dozen feet away from him.

While every fiber of his being wanted to terminate the man on the other side of the door, he thought about the feeling he'd had when his father had been killed by the Chinese. He looked to his children, who stared up at him with wide eyes from under the table. The decision was an easy one.

He ground his teeth and took a step back. "You have a deal."

It was time to go home.

EPILOGUE

The Chairwoman of the Pulitzer Prize Board, Elizabeth Harley, smiled as she read off the autocue. "And for Best Commentary, the award goes to Jack Emery, for his incisive blogs and columns on the spread of corruption by the Foundation for a New America. Please welcome him up to the stage."

Jack smiled as he stood. He buttoned his jacket and brushed down the front of his suit, making sure no loose breadcrumbs would ruin the shot of him collecting the award. That would be perfect, end the threat of the Foundation, only to come undone at the hands of a nefarious cobb loaf. He started his walk to the stage.

Harley continued. "Jack's stories led to hundreds of arrests across the United States by the FBI, and Interpol is still executing dozens of arrest warrants overseas. Among the arrests were many prominent Americans. Most importantly, his work exposed the link between the Foundation and the war with China, and their attempts to stack Congress."

As he walked toward the stage Celeste smiled up at him,

Peter and Josefa patted him on the back and some of the others
he knew at his table and in the room offered words of
encouragement as he passed. In many ways, this was the end of
the craziest year of his life.

Jack reached the stage and walked up the handful of stairs
and into the open arms of Harley, who hugged him politely and
then shared a peck on the cheek. Jack broke the embrace and
walked to the lectern. He searched his pocket for his notes and
then thought better of it; he knew what he wanted to say.

He smiled, then leaned in close to the microphone on the
lectern. "It's a pleasure to accept this award and be recognized
by the prize board for the second time in my career."

More polite applause broke out from the room, and Jack
was forced to wait while it dissipated. "I believe the stories I
wrote about the Foundation were the most important of my
career, because of the threat they posed to our freedom.

"Unfortunately, the story won't bring back some good
people. Erin Emery, Ernest McDowell, Admiral Carl
McCulloch, and lots of others. I'd like to dedicate this prize to
their memory."

He backed away for a second, and felt a tear welling up in
his eye. He smiled awkwardly and Harley placed a reassuring
hand on his back. "Just take your time, Jack. The stage is yours
for as long as you want it."

'Thanks." He stepped forward to the lectern again. "The last
thing I want to say is that, more than anything, the last few
months have shown me that we need to be vigilant. The people
in this room are the last line."

Jack nodded and held up his hand, as long and sincere
applause broke out around the room. The short speech felt
entirely appropriate, and was about all Jack could give. He'd
said more in private to those who were closest to him. It would
do. He left the stage with a smile and returned to his seat.

"Nice job." Celeste leaned in to kiss him on the cheek as he
sat. "Nice words."

'Thanks." He looked at the trophy: a solid glass paperweight, engraved with his name. "Something else to gather dust on the shelf."

She laughed. "Such a burden to be a success."

"You'll have to win one next year and start catching up. I think I'll be stuck on two for a bit."

The others at his table—Josefa, Peter Weston, Sarah McDowell, Simon Hickens—all laughed at that thought. While the crushing tentacles of Michelle Dominique's control over EMCorp had receded, there was still a lot of damage for the new management of the company to fix.

Peter Weston had taken control of the board at the behest of Sarah McDowell, and had set about purging the company of Marles and the others who'd made their way in during the period of Foundation rule. The editors had control of content again and things were slowly getting back to normal.

"Want your job back now your price has just doubled, Jack?" Peter laughed. "I might get in trouble from the boss, but she did put me in charge."

Jack looked at Sarah, who flushed red and looked down at her wine glass. "Pretty sure you're doing better than the last person I chose, Peter."

Jack had to feel for her. While none of it was her fault, she'd put the woman who had murdered her father in charge of his company. Though Sarah had been expertly buttered up, it wouldn't be the finest hour when she got around to her memoirs in sixty years or so.

After Dominique's body had been found, the FBI had continued to scoop up the Foundation's entire network, the newly elected members of Congress among them. China, smarting from its losses and barely holding on to control, had accepted US overtures of peace after an apology from President Kurzon. The peace was holding.

Jack raised his glass of Coke. "A toast, everyone? To Ernest, Erin and all the others lost."

The others raised their glass into the air. Josefa broke the silence that followed. "You've got a job waiting for you at the *Standard* if you want one, Jack."

"No thanks, Jo. I'm starting something new."

STEVE P. VINCENT'S MAILING LIST

Sign-up to Steve's mailing list for news, new releases and special offers. It's never spammy and you can unsubscribe at any time.

Just visit: bit.ly/2swOcaI

ACKNOWLEDGMENTS

This book wouldn't have happened without the love and support of my wife, Vanessa Pratt. She's my love, my inspiration and a star. She shines plenty of light on me. I also need to mention Bear Gills II, our other family member, who stared at me agog while I wrote most of the book.

Deep thanks to manuscript tradespeople: Gerard Burg, PD Martin, Dr Kirstie Barry, Christopher Nelson, Andrew McLaughlin, Raya Klinbail, Andi Kenrick and the 2012 WV alumni. Your friendship is wonderful and your help is a bonus.

The Momentum crew are great. My thanks to Joel Naoum, who steered the ship, Tara Goedjen and Kylie Mason, who made it a lot sleeker, XOU Creative, who gave it a shiny paint job, and Mark Harding and Patrick Lenton, who showed it off. I hope you're all proud of the book and I look forward to working with you all again.

Haylee Nash at Pan Macmillan has been the Yoda to my Luke, there for all of the stupid questions (of which there were many) and to teach me the way of the force. You're wonderful and I hope to also work with you again soon.

I'm lucky to have a loving and supportive family. Love to

Lyn, Paul, Darryn, Fiona, Warwick and little Victoria. I've also got the best in-laws in town – Stephen, Maree, Ashley and Lyndon. Firmly in the family column also belong James, Kylie, Andrew, Kristy, Megan, Dr James, Tenisha and Simon.

Slightly indulgent dip of my lid to Jane Milton, who has my deepest thanks, to Lesley Morath, the first person to tell me I could be a writer, and to the army of extended family, friends and colleagues who have supported and encouraged me along the way.

A final nod to you, the reader. It means a lot that you choose to spend your spare time with Jack.

ABOUT THE AUTHOR

Steve P. Vincent lives with his wife in Melbourne, Australia, where he's forced to write on the couch in front of an obnoxiously large television.

When he's not writing, Steve enjoys beer, whisky, sports and dreaming up ever more elaborate conspiracy theories to write about. Oh, and travel.

Steve has a degree in Political Science and History, with a thesis on global terrorism. He's received instruction from the FBI and the Australian Army.

You can contact Steve at all the usual places:

stevepvincent.com

steve@stevepvincent.com

CPSIA information can be obtained
at www.ICGtesting.com
Printed in the USA
BVHW03s0835010418
512163BV00001B/180/P